The Best Thing About Dying

By

Micah Dyer

One could argue nothing is done alone. My heartfelt thanks to Margo Ducharme for talking out the ideas as they came in and for her design expertise. Thank you to William Dyer and Jill Yager for their assistance in the editing and proofreading.

Dedicated to my children, Emmett and Luna,
the best thing about living.

"You could leave life right now. Let that determine what you do and say and think."
-Marcus Aurelius

1

For the first time it spilled out of the room. He kissed her in the parking lot, breaking one of their rules. It was unlikely he noticed her discomfort. If he had noticed, she couldn't tell. Certainly not by the goofy smile he wore on his face when he turned and walked away. The whole thing happened in less than twenty seconds but it was so jarring it left her feeling unsettled for the entire drive back to work.

She shut the door to her office, sat behind her desk, and sank down in her chair. Pulsing waves of heat pricked at her skin. She couldn't focus. Static noise filled her head. The newly familiar empty feeling returned but it was joined by another feeling, a certain type of pain she recognized from somewhere in her past, but from where she couldn't remember. There was a quick knock at the door. It opened. She straightened up. A stack of folders were dropped on her desk. A deadline was mentioned. The door closed and she did something that surprised herself. Instead of boxing up her feelings and going right to work, she sat quietly. And in that quiet is when it happened. A voice from somewhere within caught her attention. A reflexive urge to silence this voice took control, so she forcibly dove into her work, and began leafing through one of the folders.

However, the voice continued. It wasn't loud, or demanding, or harsh. Instead it was soft, loving and welcoming. But it was persistent and kept repeating itself, like a mantra. Gently. Again and again. Until finally she listened, *keep going like this and the pain will only grow,* it said. She set the folder down and closed her eyes. The voice, she realized, sounded like her own, like she was speaking to herself as a loving, compassionate parent would. The voice told her the affair could no longer be compartmentalized. *Yes,* she accepted, *I know this now.* It told her that the affair wasn't just confined to a hotel room or to one part of her brain. It was everywhere in her life and everywhere inside of her. *Yes, I have always known this,* she admitted. Then she said whispered aloud, "but I don't know what to do. Please, help me."

***

The doors to the medical center slid open and everything outside looked different than it had on the way in. On the way in the world had been unremarkable but now that very same world was exceptional. From a square of dirt cut out of the cement sidewalk grew the most beautiful tree which stretched into the clear blue sky above. The very sky Elliot stood transfixed by would never again exist because the sky is never the same, it is always changing, everything is always changing, from molecules to galaxies. Of course he knew this principle but never before had contemplating its magnificence been so exhilarating. It wasn't just thoughts about the sky that was charging him up with inspiration, it was every single thing in existence. For the first time in his life he became aware of a subtle vibration within himself which extended outward connecting him to an infinite energy. Still looking up at the sky he laughed out loud. An elderly man pushing his walker shot a wary glance in his direction. With a friendly wave Elliot continued on to his car. *What is happening to me?* Elliot happily wondered.

The parking stub was lost. It wasn't anywhere in the car or in his wallet. Elliot would have to pay the maximum price. Normally this kind of hassle would sink a good mood. Yet it didn't bother him in the slightest. The most important thing at that moment was the pie he had bought earlier. It was on the floor of the passenger side, calling his name, but it would have to wait until he returned to work where he would try a slice. Or two. The thought of pie filled his heart with a profound sense of joy.

On the way into the parking lot Elliot hadn't noticed there was a parking attendant in a booth, but on the way out he noticed a beautiful human being lean out of his booth with a warm smile. As Elliot pulled up the man said, "When I saw you walking to your car, I said to myself, 'there is a guy who knows.'"

"Knows what?"

"Knows that today life is good."

"I do know that! Life is good today."

The man handed Elliot back his change and leaned out of his booth just a bit more, as if to share a secret with Elliot, "you know, sometimes people leave here sad. I can see it. Bad news from the doctor. But you had good news. I can tell." And with that the parking attendant gave Elliot a big smile and a thumbs up.

The truth of the parking attendant, at least his truth on that day, was made clear to Elliot. Whether or not the man liked his job, Elliot didn't know, but he did know, on that particular day, the man loved bringing his own bit of sunshine to other people. The sting of his tears surprised Elliot.

***

The smile on Elliot's face as he walked through the front door of their home caught Amy's attention because it had been a stranger to her for years. Seeing it upset her. Realizing she was having a negative reaction to her husband smiling caused her further discomfort. There was nothing wrong with him smiling, in fact, she should be happy to see something other than his mask of impassivity, and yet she wasn't.

Elliot said "hi" to her, and then because she wasn't responding, he said, "hello." Eventually she responded in kind, barely, because her conscious mind was absorbed by a memory from her youth.

When she was a teenager she traveled to Alaska with her parents. The main anticipated highlight was the aurora borealis, or as her Mother would whisper with an air of romance not customary for her, "The northern lights," while gazing off as if the dazzling light show was happening right before her eyes. The anticipated spectacle was the reason for the entire trip. Unfortunately they never saw the northern lights. There were grizzly bear sightings, glaciers and other natural wonders to enjoy but nothing stirred her mother's passions like the promise of the northern lights had. While waiting to board their plane home a married couple struck up conversation with her parents. They too had traveled to Alaska with their child. Predictably everyone was sharing their highlights.

"Oh! And on our last night we saw the aurora borealis!" The woman shrieked with delight.

Settling into their seats on the plane Amy sensed her mother's agitation. Then her mother scoffed at nothing in particular, shook her head in disgust, and she hissed to herself, "the northern lights." The romantic gaze the northern lights had elicited from her mother had been replaced with a burning stare at the seat in front of her. Amy couldn't understand why her mother was angry at the northern lights. Reading Amy's perplexed expression, her mother said through gritted teeth, "where were they when I wanted them," and then the anger dropped and she could see the heartbreak in her mother, "when I needed them."

"Are you there?" Elliot's question brought Amy back to the present moment and she realized she had been staring at him without being aware of doing so. Staring at his smiling face which was looking at her like she was the best thing in his world. The northern lights. It reminded her of the cute bookish young man she had fallen in love with and of the absent-minded yet brilliant young husband she had begun a life with. And it reminded her how all of that disappeared leaving a remote and disconnected nearly middle-aged man who seemed put off by anything outside of work. Yet here was the young man again. The one she had fallen in love with. Actually, the Elliot before her exuded something much more powerful than she had ever felt from him. It brought up in her both attraction and resentment.

"Are you there?" He had asked. To answer his question she might have said his smile and the way he was looking at her broke her heart because it wasn't there when she wanted it, when she needed it. That she wanted to blame him for things she had done, that she felt unworthy because she had long given up on him. But instead, she simply said, "I want to be."

"Well, I went to the doctors."

The way he said it caught Amy's attention. Then he paused which drew her in even more, and she asked, "is everything okay?"

Elliot didn't respond to her right away but he wasn't ignoring her. In fact, at that moment there was nothing else in his world except Amy. When he first met her he remembered thinking there was this secret beauty about her, one that a person might overlook, one that had to be discovered, and how lucky he was to have been let in. Earlier that day he had been lucky enough to be let in on another beautiful secret, nothing less than the indefinable infinite power of everything, which of course he wanted to share with Amy. Once again she said his name and so he said the first words that came to his mind.

"I'm dying," Elliot blurted.

2

Five years earlier Elliot and Amy had agreed to give marriage therapy a try. Their relationship had been skidding for awhile and had reached, what they both hoped, was their rock bottom. Sliding any further down would have made their relationship untenable. So on a cold and dreary January evening they found themselves in a waiting room full of water scene paintings. A door opened and a therapist poked her head out. Having imagined the therapist would be some wizened old woman they were surprised that Stephanie was an attractive woman in her 40's with straightened hair and form-fitting clothes who spoke with the slightest accent which was impossible to place.

After leading them to her office, and once everyone had settled in, Stephanie asked what had brought them in. The question, a perfunctory and uncomplicated way to start things off, stumped Elliot. Not that he didn't know why they were there, he had a pretty good idea about that, it was the idea of articulating those reasons which daunted him. To his relief Amy fielded the first question but when it became clear she would have to field the majority of questions, this pattern became very telling. In the preceding year Elliot had become accustomed to being withdrawn and uninvolved and so his best effort for therapy was to hope "being there" was enough, and it might have been an encouraging start, had a state of complete beingness been achieved. Instead he seemed rather fallow, as if there was something of him missing.

"We're just, we just don't have much of a relationship anymore," Amy said bluntly, and as way of his contribution, Elliot nodded in agreement.

"So, you both agree there isn't much of a relationship. Can you describe to me what the remaining relationship is like for you?" Stephanie looked at Elliot.

"Me?"

When Stephanie nodded her head, Elliot mumbled something about drifting and disconnection, and although Stephanie looked at him encouragingly, to let him know he was getting somewhere, he found himself unable to go any further and, once again, Elliot looked to Amy, so she fielded this one too.

Starting from the beginning, in a clipped manner, she described their relationship in a linear fashion. "We met in grad school. We were both working on PhD's. Mine in education. His in physics. After a few weeks of dating we made it official. Of course we both took our studies seriously but we somehow still saw each other almost every day. And, ah, yeah. . . " Amy faded out and paused for a moment.

The dispassionate way in which she was describing their relationship surprised Elliot because typically she was exceptionally articulate and enjoyed flexing that strength. Amy was also shocked at how little desire she had to recollect their relationship history. The reason for this was based on a resentment about his lack of passion and so she decided to put him on the spot. "You know what, I'm doing a poor job of describing what it was really like. And I think it's because I am always the one who tells our story. Always. And here I am again. I want to hear it from Elliot." Amy turned from Stephanie and looked at Elliot, and not in an aggressive way, but more in a resigned way, and indicated for him to continue their story.

"But, that's because you're better at this than me," he said, slightly annoyed by this true accusation and call to effort. Both Amy and the therapist wondered what he really meant by that. Was he referring to talking, to talking about their relationship, or about being in a relationship? Before

Stephanie could inquire about this, Elliot began plowing through the rest of the their relationship history like he was making a large order at a drive through. Sitting up straighter, his voice a bit louder than necessary, he continued with an even more mechanical bullet point style than she had been using, "ah, we moved in a year later. Three years after that we became engaged. We were married one year later?" He looked to Amy for timeline confirmation, she gave a slow nod of the head, he took a breath and trudged on, "yep, married one year later, after engagement, then we bought the house right after the wedding. Our careers started to take off. . .and, ah, life, went on, annnd," unsure of where to go, Elliot was stretching the "and," then he saw the finish line flash in his mind, so he gave it one last burst and took it right up to that day, literally, "yeah, and, ah, then we came here to meet with you." Elliot felt like a socially inept adolescent rather than a fully grown man.

"That was very, efficient," Stephanie observed.

"So, was that wrong?" Elliot asked.

"This isn't about wrong or right in here. I'm not judging you and I'm certainly not grading this."

"Oh," Both Elliot and Amy said in unison because they were actually surprised to learn there wasn't some sort of grading system.

"So, has there always been a lack of passion?"

"No," both Elliot and Amy said, again at the same time.

"Good. That's good to hear. When you think of your relationship, what feelings come up? Try to use emotional language. . . Who wants to dive in?"

They collectively sighed and dropped their shoulders. Then they looked at each other. Again, Elliot expected Amy to go first but she didn't. He wasn't sure what the therapist meant by emotional language. Amy knew what Stephanie meant and was afraid to go there. Stephanie waited patiently. The silence lasted for what felt like ten minutes but was only several, and once again, Amy broke the ice, "maybe that's it. Or at least a lot of it. That our relationship has become a list. And when you ask what feelings come up. . ." Amy hesitated, "I don't want to say it. I don't want to hurt Elliot. I don't want to make things worse."

"You have to start where you are, okay? Where you really are. If you don't, and you just stay on the surface, I can guarantee it will get worse."

Amy nodded, and then it poured out, "There is no passion. I feel alone. I feel ignored. It's like he doesn't see me. It's disappointing, in our relationship, in him, and in me. My self-esteem in the relationship is drowning and now it's effecting the rest of my life. When I try to engage he has so little to give-"

Stephanie jumped in here, "Tell Elliot. Look at him and tell him."

Amy shifted herself towards Elliot and looked at him. It was more difficult to say these things directly to him but she continued warily nonetheless, "when I try to talk to you about more than just surface stuff, you don't have anything to give. Either you're too tired, too disengaged, or lately you're just straight up impatient. Like sharing a life with me is a bother to you," Amy turned to the therapist, "I don't know exactly when it became like this because it happened slowly. We didn't start out like this. We didn't." There seemed to be more she wanted to say but Amy stopped there and grabbed a tissue from the end table to wipe away her eyes.

It seemed like a natural segue point for Elliot to jump in, or at least put a toe in, but he didn't. Instead, he stood at the edge and hesitated, rendering the plunge impossible. Instead, the thing he feared would happen, did happen. The invisible wall came up. Like thick bullet-proof glass that separated him from everyone else, the wall had first started to come up at work. That was easy to live with because his job allowed him to isolate, and isolating improved his performance at work, and so, in a sense, he was encouraged to isolate. Because he was finding himself more and more exhausted outside of work the wall came up at home. It wasn't that he was unaware of the negative effect the wall had at home, he was very aware of it. And it wasn't that he didn't care about this, he did. But by the time he was aware of the wall's negative effect he was trapped within its circular cause and effect death spiral. The wall had shut out everything personal which caused everything personal to become more difficult, and being that he was unable to face his personal life, he relied on the wall as a solution to the very problems it caused. Worst of all, for some reason he couldn't understand, Amy had become a symbol of the emptiness he saw outside of the wall and so he thickened the wall between himself and her. This all contributed to what he thought of as the expansion of emptiness outside of the wall and the contraction of fullness inside of the wall where he existed. Unfortunately, by that point, he believed there was nothing he could do about it. Talking about these kinds of things had never been on the agenda for Elliot. Who would understand?! So, when he found himself deep in this morass, the only way forward, he believed, was to stop feeling things.

"Elliot, would you like to say something?" Stephanie asked encouragingly.

"I don't know how." It was not for lack of want.

***

Once upon a time at a university library there was a young man who built up the courage to ask a studious young woman if he could sit at her table. "Of course," she said barely glancing up. If she had looked up she would have noticed the other tables in the library were empty.

Elliot had noticed Amy in the library the night before. She had an understated beauty that kept drawing him in. But it wasn't her beauty that attracted him the most. It was the way she focused while she was studying. There was an energy that surrounded her. Then there was her disposition. There was a seriousness about her but when people spoke with her she was warm and sociable. Elliot decided he wanted to know this woman who was beautiful, focused and friendly. So far, it didn't seem to him like he was off to a great start. She hadn't looked at him and the focus that had attracted him earlier, now felt like a defense system.

With a looming exam Amy couldn't seem to prepare enough. She found herself in the library three nights in a row. There was something about the library that helped her absorb material. Besides, her roommate's long distance boyfriend had just arrived. He was a bit of an oaf whose clunking around the apartment she found distracting. When the guy with glasses politely asked if he could sit at her table she said, "of course." *A guy with manners,* she thought to herself. It was refreshing. The night before she had noticed him looking at her. She didn't mind. He was actually kind of cute. Peeking across the table she tried to see what he was studying but she couldn't tell, but what she could tell is that he had an impressive mind. It was as if he created an energy field when he concentrated and she found that very attractive.

They kept sneaking peeks at each other and finally about two hours in they both peeked at the same time, their eyes met, and they both blushed.

"Hi," Elliot whispered and with that, the most common of words that has begun more relationships than any other word, began another. After he asked what she was studying they ended up talking for the next hour. When the library closed they made plans to meet there the next night. They ended up meeting at the library for the next two weeks straight. Then while standing outside of the library one night something romantically synchronistic happened that removed any doubts they might have had.

"Why don't we meet sometime," they both blurted out at the exact same moment which caused them to pause before adding simultaneously, "you know, somewhere else," and this was followed by a giggle which led to them both saying, "yes," at the same time. This delightful word collision caused them to fall into each other with laughter. When their laughter faded they realized they were holding hands, and so at the same time, they leaned in for their first kiss.

This destined young couple, once magnetized to each other, would one day sit in a therapist's office struggling to connect. But ending up there didn't happen overnight. It was gradual and it took time.

After that first kiss they began spending all of their extra time together. Some nights they would lay in bed talking until the early morning hours. They told each other about their hopes and dreams. They laughed about silly and inane things. They fell asleep holding each other. Eventually they moved in together. They gave each other plenty of space which their personalities and habits required, but they were always sure to make quality time. They both valued routine and fairly quickly one emerged. The bulk of their days were filled with an almost fanatical work ethic. While the long periods of work and study were mostly sexless, their getaways were another story. They punctuated study and work with quick sex filled trips. Hours in a hotel room or tent were spent fucking. On every level they felt satisfied by their relationship. There was support, communication and affection. Soon they had careers. They spoke about having children, but there was difficulty conceiving, so they put that off. Besides, they were giving their jobs their all, which left nothing for their relationship. That was how, one day, they woke up and realized they were alone together.

***

The first therapy session was winding down and Stephanie was giving them an activity to try at home. "The seduction must happen at different times during the relationship. Not just when it's time for sex. Rather, there is a buildup. When you first started dating and you would wait all week and then go on your outings, was there some physical affection and flirting during the week? Of course. And before the physical affection and flirting there was intimacy? And that is where you must begin again. With intimacy. And with the very basic feelings."

The issue they had wound up discussing was their sex life. There wasn't one. So, it made sense they would go back to the basics. Asking them to have sex now would have been "like trying to sail without wind," is how Stephanie put it, "of course, stranger things have happened and if you do happen to spontaneously have sex, by all means, sail away." In lieu of a windy day, Stephanie suggested they spend fifteen minutes every night that week sitting together somewhere comfortable in their home with no distractions whatsoever. All they had to do was be with each other. "Talk with each other. Look at each other. Whatever comes. Let's see what happens. Once this happens, then you move onto this same exercise while completely naked, physically. In fact, if this goes well this week, and you want to do it naked, go for it!" So simple yet so difficult. It was very telling that they both felt fifteen minutes of undistracted time together seemed a daunting assignment. So, daunting they didn't even try.

After their session they rode the elevator down in silence. There was a lot to process from their first time in therapy. "She knows what she's talking about. I mean, it makes sense, the homework." There was a hint of concern in Amy's voice as she eyed Elliot.

"Yeah. . .It does make sense. I understand what she's asking, but. . ."

"But?"

When the elevator door opened their conversation was cut off by a mother and her crying toddler pushing their way into the elevator. Then stepping into the lobby a small group of people were laughing loudly about something.

"So, I'll see you at home. My car's this way," Elliot said as he drifted away from her.

"Sure, see ya there."

"Want me to pick something up for dinner?"

"No, I'll just make something."

"Right."

It did not go unnoticed to Amy that Elliot had avoided discussing their therapy homework, which proved why they needed it. *Probably the first time in his life he's been afraid of homework*, Amy thought to herself.

***

There was always the potential for Elliot to implode personally and tie himself to the yoke of work. Much of his surface identity had always been derived from his mental gifts which had also factored into his most valued social relations. Friends had gravitated to him because of his brains, he was "the smart guy" in the group. Much of the respect his older siblings showed him grew from their recognition of his intelligence. Scholastic achievement brought high praise from his parents and it might be said he conflated that with their love. One of the things that Amy was initially attracted to was

Elliot's cerebral confidence and achievements. So, in adulthood when his personal life became increasingly unmanageable he subconsciously grabbed onto the immense mental challenges that were coming his way at work. Unfortunately, his work, unlike his friends and family, would do much more than appreciate and celebrate his mental energy, it would eagerly absorb every last drop of his brain, perhaps even his soul, if given the opportunity. And without understanding boundaries in this area, this is how Elliot found himself empty.

This perfect storm of personal collapse was realized when LDE, the company he worked for, was purchased by another company, and soon pressure at work began to ratchet up. For his entire career the company he'd worked for, LDE, had been a private contractor for NASA. Things were demanding and high stakes during that time. But that was manageable compared to the demands of his new boss, Talbot Helms. One of the world's richest men, Helms bought LDE which he then folded into his newly founded space exploration company, Target Aster. Helm's stated goal was not just to normalize space travel on the outskirts of our own atmosphere, nor just to the moon, he wanted to go beyond. He wanted to send people to Mars. He wanted to beat NASA there, beat the Russians, beat the Chineses and beat anyone else. More than anything he wanted to beat the other billionaire space racers. He wanted to be first. To be first meant he demanded impossible results with impossible deadlines.

Elliot had thought they were impossible deadlines but he soon realized their deadlines were possible if everyone at the company dedicated their entire lives to their work. Although Elliot had already become a bit of a workaholic, he was soon consumed, body, mind and spirit. Target Aster began demanding more and more. Elliot was a key employee when it came to proofing anything physics and math related the engineers were working on, and there was endless work in that area coming across his desk. From propulsion to landing, and everything in between, Elliot was involved in checking the math. While others worked in teams, his was a solitary role. For hours on end he wouldn't speak. Only work.

The company culture before the Target Aster purchase was one of passion for space but also stressed a balance with life here on earth. Target Aster's company culture was about making Talbot Helms happy, or at least, staving off his wrath. In the first year Helms made frequent visits. In meetings he would overly praise teams that had met their project deadlines and belittle and humiliate the teams that hadn't made their deadlines. Initially there was some pushback but when certain people were fired the pushback stopped. The signal was received loud and clear by the employees. They were on notice. They had to go above and beyond to prove their job. This was a company filled with many people who were inherent overachievers so they naturally rose to the challenge. Praise was important. Accomplishment was important. Keeping their jobs was important. In short, many of these employees were already conditioned to work themselves to the bone to prove they were geniuses. They were more than happy to sacrifice everything and soak up the glory the company was offering. The financial incentives didn't hurt either. Besides, many of them eventually found a way to have some measure of a work and personal life balance. Others, however, were not faring as well.

One engineer had gone into such a severe manic state he suffered a psychotic break right there in the office. Trying to finish a key feature on the landing mechanism of a Mars scout rover he pulled an all-nighter. Then he followed that with another all-nighter. This on top of working weeks straight. The employee, a tall, hairy man with a shaved head, had the habit of "doing it on his own" and "not asking for help." Those qualities didn't serve him well when he began to crash. It was a Monday morning and as employees arrived they heard extremely loud music blaring from his office. It was The Gap Band's *You Dropped the Bomb on Me*. Opening the door to his office they discovered him sitting in his desk chair which was set on top of his desk. He was naked, except for his socks, furiously typing away on his laptop. When he looked up and saw several concerned co-workers staring at him, he stood up and exclaimed, "The rocket is ready for lift off! The rocket is ready for lift off!"

As for Elliot, at first he took the challenge. He thought that the pace would let up sooner or later. That this initial push was to let the world, and stock holders, know Target Aster was serious. This wouldn't last forever, he reassured himself, and when things did let up he would be recognized as one of the people who rose to the challenge. Unfortunately things never let up. Once anyone proved they could perform at a mind-breaking level, they were held to that standard. Of course people were burning out. It didn't matter though. People were being replaced and replacing people in their fields isn't typically easy. Yet, somehow the company managed to find replacements. Knowing they really could be replaced was another reason people began to adjust to their new normal. Work was life. Like his colleague who had cracked, Elliot was also known to work alone and do it all himself. Like his colleague who had cracked, this wasn't a problem before but it was now. Elliot was overwhelmed. He couldn't do everything they were asking unless he worked more hours. So he began working late almost every night. He rarely had an entire weekend off. When one challenge was met at work, there were ten more right behind it. He was too busy to realize he was miserable.

This experience exasperated certain innate traits in Elliot. He became withdrawn, isolated, and socially anxious and it was during this time he built the wall around himself believing it was the solution to his problems and not a manifestation of the problem itself. When the thought occurred to him that he should reach out and connect, he found he simply couldn't. The social and emotional atrophy was too great to reverse. Soon it became easier to let himself shrink and drift away inside his small contracting world. The effort to return from it was too much. Then one day Amy told him they were going to marriage counseling, to which he simply said, "okay."

***

"The goal of all this is not sex. Let's forget about sex for now. Instead take this time to rediscover and redevelop your intimacy. Take care of that and the sex will come naturally." This is what Stephanie had advised on their first therapy visit, the day she sent them home with the intimacy homework, the homework they didn't even attempt. Intimacy for them, it would seem, proved impossible.

However, after five weeks, Elliot and Amy had made some very important discoveries about themselves and their marriage. Elliot feared he was impotent. Sex loomed frightfully in the shadows. He also realized sex wasn't his real issue and that his real issues stemmed from things within himself he felt were too heavy to even take a crack at. Amy realized that her frustration with Elliot had grown into a resentment so large that she was no longer attracted to him. She no longer cared if he gave her attention or not. Like Elliot, she too realized, this wasn't her real issue and her real issues stemmed from things within himself she felt were too heavy to even take a crack at.

If they had only shared everything that was really going on inside of them, then perhaps their relationship might have improved, but instead they barely scratched the surface.

"I don't know if I have ever said this to clients, but I will now. Please, argue," Stephanie said in all seriousness.

It became clear they were starved of passion to such a degree they couldn't even argue. There were other suggestions the therapist offered. Things to try at home. They did eventually try several suggestions at home but when things would quickly became too uncomfortable, they simply shrugged and gave up. Once, Amy did try to argue with Elliot. She yelled at him. A monologue about loneliness and lack of passion and how he basically pissed her off. When she was done he nodded his head and told her that he had work to do. Then he went into his home office and shut the door. For a moment she considered going in and continuing to yell at him but she didn't. Looking back, that was the moment she gave up. This was the night before their fifth and final session.

As their fifth session was winding up Stephanie offered a succinct summation of their relationship from what she had observed so far. "Somewhere along the line you both made an implicit agreement that it was okay to give up on sex, friendship and life sharing. What you should be doing now, what you should have been doing this entire process, is asking yourself what this relationship is and what you want it to become. But if you have been doing that, I am not seeing it. I don't see you doing anything, quite frankly, other than you both keeping your appointments. But I suspect that is only because you are both innately conscientious people and not because you believe this marriage can improve. Maybe the relationship is no longer capable of a level of intimacy and emotional involvement necessary, not only for it to thrive, but also for it to simply survive. Because that is where the relationship still lives, with survival in question. Unless you are both willing to really let it all out then I can't help you. . .But if you can do that, then I can help you. I do believe there is a love there great enough to bring you both back. Yet, we must work from where we are, right? So, I ask you one last question, is the relationship you have right now enough?"

And with that their hour was up. The therapist had held the mirror up, a starkly dire, but not surprising, image of their marriage was thrown in their faces. They walked quietly down the hallway to the elevator. Even though it felt like they had been fired by their therapist, which they hadn't, they were ready to quit. They knew she was right. It was going to take more than dutifully showing up and giving surface answers. There was a level of willingness they were not able to give. They also wanted to avoid responding to her last question. Was this relationship enough? As bad as it was, they didn't want to answer "no" but they would be lying to say, "yes." They pushed the button and waited for the elevator. It arrived and stale air wafted out when the doors opened. They stepped inside. The doors closed. It was just the two of them, which had a magnifying effect on their silence.

"Everyone needs someone to put down as their emergency contact," Amy muttered sarcastically.

"Huh?"

"Our marriage. We're still each other's emergency contacts. At least we have that."

"If that's all we are then I can put one of my siblings down."

"You aren't even close with them anymore."

"That's not true."

"Fine, invite them over. And your friends."

The elevator opened and Amy walked away leaving him standing there. She had stung him, and it stung because it was true. While he stood there licking his wounds the elevator doors began to close, he aggressively thrust his arm out in between them and they jarred open again. With a hurried walk he caught up to Amy.

"It's not like your some socialite." It was a weak comeback to which she scoffed at.

"Invite somebody into your life, Elliot," Amy snapped, "if not me. Then somebody!"

"You're the same as me. When it comes to work. When it comes to us. And you know it. Tell me you're not."

They were just outside of the building, standing toe to toe. Their voices raised. She wanted to deny him, to keep blaming him but he was right.

"Yeah, I am the same as you. But not as bad."

"What!"

"Yeah. I've been trying. I was the one that initiated therapy and I was the one who initiated in therapy and I was the one who initiated the homework. I tried to argue with you but you couldn't even do that. But yeah, finally I walled myself off too. So, there."

"Oh, okay! You win! Winner, winner chicken dinner." He was actually yelling the words. And he was animated. He had flung his arms out in a gesture meant to indicate she was the winner. He even did a strange chicken wing thing for an instant. For a moment Amy began to feel something. It was anger, and a mocking embarrassment, but at least she felt something.

"Well, actually, I will give you this, we finally did one of the homework assignments," Amy said.

"What's that?"

"We argued. Thank you for finally joining me on this

journey."

Needless to say they didn't return to marriage therapy, but considering that divorce was on Amy's mind even before therapy started, it certainly was a feat of apathy that they made it another five years living alone together.

3

"I'm dying." From the moment Elliot had walked into their home they both sensed a change in their shared energy but immediately after those two words were said that shift became seismic. Their long lost magnetism drew them together physically. When he sat down on the edge of the coffee table she scooted to the edge of the couch. They took hold of each other's hands and an electrical charge shot out through their bodies. Even their knees, which were now touching, created a charge. Their eyes connected and remained fixed. Without words they were able to communicate all that needed to be said right then.

The feelings inside of Amy were extraordinary. They were so many and so powerful it would have made their description impossible. There was so much to process about what Elliot had just said that it overwhelmed her thinking mind, so she just sat there, basking in the warmth and openness which surrounded them.

The culmination of a transformative day had left Elliot feeling more alive than he had ever felt. Those illusory walls he had built to imprison himself disappeared. Nothing stood between himself and everything that was. A newfound strength and vitality coursed through his veins. All those years sinking deeper and deeper into isolation led right into the pandemic, which crushed him. It was so painful he had even considered suicide. Now death had freed him from all of that. Gently, he reached out and touched Amy's face.

"I will call my family. And I will call my friends," Elliot looked around the room with a prescient gaze, "there will be a gathering here, in this very house." Realizing his delivery sounded slightly theatrical, like King Arthur forming the knights of the round table, he almost laughed. But the silliness of how he spoke didn't negate the premonition of people from his life gathering in his house at his request.

As Elliot spoke of the gathering, the first words either of them had said since he announced he was dying, Amy found herself nodding in reverie. All of her emotions were settling enough to recognize a feeling of awe. There was also a sense of shock, not just that he was dying but shock from the feelings she was suddenly having for him. For the first time in years she was passionately attracted to Elliot. This made no sense to her. He just told her he was dying. Empathy, compassion, love, would have all been understandable, but attraction? How was dying attractive? Especially given she couldn't even remember the last time she desired him. What was happening to her? Perhaps, she thought, it was the beginning stages of some grief induced psychosis. But that's not what it was, and she knew it. This wasn't some scattered, unbalanced expression of tangled thoughts and emotions she was experiencing. This was the coalescence of all she had ever felt for Elliot and more. A warm line of tears gently rolled down her face.

"I don't understand," her words whispered so softly Elliot couldn't hear them or read them on her lips, and yet he was able to receive them. In response he squeezed her hand and smiled again. This smile was different, it was the most reassuring smile anyone had ever offered her. The thought that dying did him well occurred to her. It was a thought so contrary and so strange it unfortunately caused her mind and emotions to return to their conditioned state of resistance. The fear, resentment, doubt and despair of their relationship past began coloring the picture of their present moment together and it began telling the story of their future. Of course she would stand by his side till the end but she wasn't going to get her hopes up that their relationship would somehow be fundamentally different during his remaining days. After all, were not she and Elliot the very same people they were just the day before?

***

Telling loved ones you are dying should not be done happily. So, Elliot paused and reigned in his demeanor before calling his sister because there certainly was something about Elliot that might be mistaken for joy. Coming at them with an attitude so entirely contrary to what they would expect to accompany such news would only add to the potential anguish it carried.

In the best of times his sister Karen's emotional reactions were extreme. Even during times of light turbulence her typical mood pinballed between moderate to severe depression and anxiety. So, for her sake, Elliot delivered the news in a sober tone reminiscent of the way a kindly family doctor might.

Straight away Karen burst into tears. Although it was a completely normal reaction, the immediacy of it startled him. Amy had shed tears but they had come after a moment of shock and processing. This was a sudden burst, like a downpour of rain that soaks everyone as they try to run for cover. Then, as sudden as it started, it stopped, and there was a sturdy blow of the nose. And then she began peppering him with questions, most of which he answered by saying, "I don't know." This kind of not knowing felt great. It absolved him from the weight of pain, allowing his mind and spirit to remain light and nimble.

"When will you begin to feel sick?"

"I don't know."

"What do you mean you don't know?! You keep saying you don't know," she said, as if it were accusation of negligence.

"Karen. I just don't. One step at a time. Please."

"But-"

"Karen. I need you to be calm. Can you be calm, for me?"

"I think so," she audibly took a breath, "it's just, how do you not even know the exact diagnosis details."

"I think I blanked out. I'll be going back. Obviously."

There was a deep breath on the other end with a long and slow exhale, and then it was quiet for a moment, and in a calmer voice she said, "well, I admire your calm, Elliot. You've always had a level head. Steady emotions."

Predictably she offered help while at the same time making excuses why she might not be able to help. Elliot didn't take it personally because he knew her excuses hid a painful truth. Her emotional life was potentially erratic when faced with adversity like death. She may show up like a champ one day but have to bail out the next because the sadness she felt about the situation might render her incapable of getting out of bed. Having worked hard to pull her life together after several breakdowns in her late twenties, she built a good life for herself, and maintaining that life took precedence. Her family, her routine and her job were vitally important to her.

"Right now I have it all handled. So, you're off the hook. I have faith you will do what you can. That's all that matters," he said.

"And I will. I promise," she began to tear up.

"On a positive note, next Sunday I'm having a small gathering. Just family and a few old friends. I would love for you and Doug to make it."

"The whole family is coming?"

"Yes, Karen. I want to see everyone at once. It's been how many years?"

"Brian and his family?"

"Yes, that would be the whole family."

For the first time since leaving his doctor that afternoon

Elliot began to feel uncomfortable. There was tension in his gut which threatened to spread throughout his body. One of the big contributors to the distance within his family was a sibling rivalry between Karen and their brother Brian. It had been going on for years and had also served as an excuse for Elliot's isolation. An excuse he no longer needed as he no longer desired isolation.

"Uh-huh. Well, Katie will be in town. From college. So…"

"Great, it'll be good to see my niece. I probably won't even recognize her it's been so long."

Karen kept tossing out excuses, seeing if Elliot bit on any. In days past he would have caved at the first one but he didn't. Instead he summoned his newfound strength and courage. *Fuck it,* he thought to himself with a chuckle, *I'm dying. Even she can suck it up for one night.*

"It's my wish to see everyone together. It's been ages. I'll see you Sunday."

"Okay. Okay. You're right. I'm terrible. I'm being selfish. I'm so selfish. I'm sorry."

"No, don't worry. Don't be sorry. You are not terrible, you are wonderful. Just be here Sunday."

Despite more assurances that she was not a terrible and selfish person Karen continued to flog herself. It spiraled to the point where she was sorry for being sorry. Finally, she caught herself and laughed wildly with a grand flourish, and said, "You're right! Goodbye! I love you!"

***

Having boldly refused his sister's excuses gave Elliot added confidence, which he would need because his brother Brian surprised him by being the most obstinate of his siblings. When Elliot brought up the Sunday gathering Brian bluntly rejected it, "if Karen is there we can't make it."

Elliot persisted, "you would put, what I would argue is a

minor difference with your sister, above your dying brother's wish."

"It wasn't a minor difference. That's what you don't get. You don't have kids. Sorry but if you did you might understand."

"Perhaps, what I mean is, the issue or issues you and Karen have are minor relative to death. And I think in the grand scheme of things the differences you and Karen have could be surmounted. At least for one evening. For your dying brother." He would play the death card again and again if need be. It felt great to assert his needs and to use all available resources to achieve them. It was much easier than he had imagined. His only regret was that it had taken this long for him to discover this power. But as easy as it was for him to employ this attitude, he learned it didn't guarantee an outcome.

"It's just the way it is."

"Brian, it's not a complicated request."

"Well, that's where you're wrong."

"Okay, tell me how I'm wrong."

For the first time in the conversation there was hesitation on Brian's part and Elliot sensed there was an opening. Rather than jumping at it, he relaxed and let it happen. Brian's blunt tone softened and Elliot sensed regret coming from his brother, "Okay, you know, it's a bit more complicated than just me, okay? Just, you know, look, I'm still at work. Let me get home, mull it over and I'll call you back tonight. I gotta talk with Mona," even though Brian was at work he lowered his voice, as if Mona might hear him. It was a testament to the power Brian's wife held over him or more accurately the power he assigned to her. "It's really not me that still holds the grudge. I mean, don't get me wrong, its not all water under the bridge as far as I'm concerned, but you know."

"I know. But I really think Mona might actually be more reasonable about this than you give her credit for."

Brian scoffed at that, "I mean, first of all Mona is not more reasonable than I am. About anything. And second of all, Mona isn't wrong. Karen was harsh. Sure there was some validity in her opinion of how we're raising Dulce. A grain of truth. I'll admit that. Like I said, I'm reasonable, Elliot. But Karen was too harsh, you know. And what about how she's raised Katie? Let's not even go there."

"Let's not, please. Let's just all gather next Sunday at my house. . .Brian, you're my brother and I need my brother there."

There was a sigh and a long pause on Brian's end. "God, you're right. You're right. I'm a pussy. Mona's become unyielding. I am afraid of her. There's other stuff going on with us, a lot of other stuff, and just the fact that I would even hesitate about this, really tells me something. This request from you has brought up some issues. Really."

"I certainly don't want to make waves. Not trying to raise any issues for you. Just asking to have a family thing."

"For fuck's sake, after what you just told me, I made it about my relationship!" At that point Brian choked up. When he tried to continue his voice strangled the words and he had to stop and let out a groan before continuing tearfully, "I'm so sorry to hear the news Elliot. I think when you told me I wanted to think of anything else so I just seized on the only fucking thing that seems to occupy my life anymore and that's all this personal bullshit. So, of course yes, yes, we will be there. Or at least I'll be there. With my daughter."

***

Davey's chuckle brought so much back for Elliot. Good things. It reminded him of times when he was young and happy. "Man, I'd be there for you in a heartbeat. Dying or not. I'm just glad to know you're actually still alive." It turned out Davey had just moved back to the area and was thrilled to reconnect with his old friend. "We were becoming long lost friends!" Davey joked but there was truth to it. Elliot was shocked to discover Davey had been living in another state for the last five years. "Got married and got divorced out there. All kinds of shit to catch up on," Davey laughed. Laughter in the face of anything. That was who Davey was and had still remained. Confidently accepting the absurdity of being human. It was a quality Elliot had always admired and being around Davey it rubbed off.

When they began hanging out it was the dawning of adolescence which was a time for Elliot when his social gauntlet of awkward nerd hell was only worsening. This future had brought to Elliot a burgeoning sense of hopelessness but for some reason Davey befriended him and his life changed. "Having a smart friend is cool," Davey would often say, and Elliot would say, "having a cool friend is cool." Soon Elliot had a safe place in the social ecosystem and his future no longer seemed hopeless.

Gordo was another key relationship to Elliot's formative years. Gordo was the nickname his older brother had given him. It was meant to be ironic because in actuality he'd always been flaco. His real name was Arturo but even his parents began to refer to him as Gordo. As with Davey, Elliot lost contact with Gordo somewhere in their early thirties. When Elliot called him, Gordo was "pumped" to get together, so pumped in fact, that although it was almost eleven on a Thursday night, he was ready to come over right away and hang out, to have a drink, and to commiserate about Elliot's situation.

Laughter was the defining characteristic from his

relationship with those guys. Sure, some of it was juvenile humor but it was also medicine that took them through their teenage years and into early adulthood. *Without that laughter, what would I have become?* Elliot knew the answer. He would have become the man he'd been the better part of the last ten years, a withdrawn, depressed, emotionally flaccid workaholic. Only he would have become that man sooner, and had that been the case, perhaps he might not have had his friends, his family, and his wife to reconnect to. With whatever time he had left he was going to continue being the person he discovered the day he announced he was dying. He was going to have the relationships with friends and family he'd always wanted, and was going to have the marriage he had always wanted. It had been there before and so it could be there again. And it could be even better!

Lying on their bed in the dark an elusive thought nagged at Elliot. There was a loose thread from his day and he was trying to figure out what it was. While searching his mind, another thought came to him, *Amy!* Without realizing it, and by force of habit, Elliot had gone to bed without a word to Amy. Without hesitation he got out from their bed and went to find her. The house was eerily dark and empty. Oddly he couldn't find her anywhere. A morbid thought of losing Amy flashed through his mind, not just of her being out of his life, but of her not being alive. His heart jumped into his throat cutting off his airway and it felt like fire ignited around the rim of his eyes. He wasn't religious, and God didn't make sense to his scientific mind, but he believed in his own idea of God nonetheless. Standing in their living room, in total darkness, he closed his eyes and he prayed. He asked for as much time with Amy as possible before he died. When he opened his eyes he saw her standing outside, bathed in moonlight, holding herself as she stared into their fountain.

Stepping outside into the cold night air he too was quickly holding himself.

"I was about to go to bed but wanted to say goodnight before I did."

Slowly she turned towards him. Her wet eyes glinted in the moonlight. "Thank you. I'd like to say goodnight to you too." Gently she raised one hand out to him, he took it and wrapped his arms around her. Time dissolved while they warmed each other with their embrace. Unable to grasp onto and organize the many thoughts bouncing around in her head Amy had followed an instinct to wonder outside where she began to empty her mind and focus on her breath. When Elliot appeared she was grateful to share with him the peace she was standing in.

4

Entering the room her gaze dragged along the now familiar brown and beige carpet. Her purse was slung over her shoulder. It was heavier today. Everything was heavier today. She didn't quite know what to do with the door key she held in her hand. It had been three days since Elliot told her he was dying. The moment was still playing on repeat in her head. Behind her the heavy door closed loudly, the noise of which startled Amy. She looked up and saw he was laying on the bed. Already naked.

"Someone is excited to see you," he said as he glanced down at his erection, "And I am too."

This sort of thing used to make Amy laugh. Todd was goofy and that helped her feel alive when she had, for so long, felt otherwise. Their times together reminded her life could still be silly and playful. Naughty even. But at that moment their relationship was frivolous to her. It had been feeling that way for awhile.

"Actually I was about to take a shower and I started to masturbate," he said with a shrug.

Looking around room 304 she was suddenly swamped by memories made within its confines. Memories made with a man other than her husband. Sex with Todd happened in that bed so many times she couldn't count them. The ghosts of their sex moved before her eyes. They'd had sex on the ledge by the window. On the chair. On the bathroom counter. In the shower. A haphazard and disorganized style of fornication defined the early part of their affair. The frenzied rush of adrenaline he brought in the beginning helped sweep her past a threshold of moral resistance. Penetrating the fortress around her sexuality was a challenge for him. He was aggressive but in a playful way, "Put your glasses on," he would tell her, "like a librarian. Now tell me to be quiet."

Over time, as she relinquished all resistance, she was able to assert herself more into their dynamic. Her patterns, her rhythms and her movements began to dictate more of the action. For a time her steady, methodical temperament fused nicely with his impulsive, hungry style. She thought of it as organized disorganization. Closed off for so long, those early moments in room 304 were liberating. It used to feel like a supercharged form of electricity running through her entire body and that feeling was addictive.

Like anything addictive it began to have an adverse effect. Over time she became aware of a split within her. It was as if someone else, not her, was having the affair. Recently, she had become so aware of that split that it led to a very bizarre experience. The last time they had been together, while they had sex, she had watched herself with Todd. It was only a brief moment but after it happened questions began to surface from her subconscious. She asked herself what she was really doing with Todd? Then, in the parking lot afterward, he broke protocol with a kiss outside of the hotel room. That day was a turning point for her, not just for reasons related to the affair itself, but most of all because that was the day she learned Elliot was dying.

This was the first time she had seen Todd since that day and he was standing there indicating a small gift bag on the console. From the gift bag Amy pulled out a very thin and delicate gold chain.

"Want to undress and try it on? It's a body necklace."

***

Every year the office holiday party was held at a TGI Fridays adjacent to a Hyatt hotel. It was a routine get-together they had every holiday season. Of the several dozen or so staff that made it, less than half were joined by their significant others. So it wasn't a big deal that Elliot wasn't there. Not that Amy really cared anymore at that point. It certainly didn't make her uncomfortable to be without him. In fact, what would have made her uncomfortable is if he did show up. That's what living with an invisible man had brought her to. It had been almost a year since they gave up on marriage counseling and in that time they had become strangers.

Considering where the marriage was, she wasn't surprised to find herself receptive to another man's flirtations. Todd had worked in the same office with Amy for several years but had been transferred recently to another district office. So it was natural he would drop by to see some of his old friends and colleagues. When those old colleagues all said goodnight Todd and Amy stayed on and continued talking. Although they had not known each other well during the time they worked in the same office, the night of the Christmas party was another story. They moved from the bar to a booth. When Todd teased her for always being so serious she laughed mischievously, a way she hadn't laughed in years. When Todd mentioned that he would be getting a room at the Hyatt and casually asked if she would like to join him for one more drink, in his room, she said yes. And saying yes made her feel even more mischievous.

As they walked out of the restaurant and towards the hotel Amy could feel her heart begin to race and her diaphragm tighten. She had to consciously make herself breath. Stepping out of the elevator onto the third floor they walked down the hallway toward room 304. The hallway seemed to stretch out for miles. By this point Amy's heart was pounding so loud she wondered if Todd could hear it. As he opened the door to room 304 a flood of adrenaline temporarily rendered movement impossible and she realized this was the moment when she was about to cross a line.

"I'd offer to carry you over the threshold but it would probably kill the mood," he had one leg inside of the room and was using that foot to hold the door open. "Fuck it," he said with a grunt as he swooped her up into his arms and carried her into the room. The door slammed shut behind them. They fell onto the bed and began pulling each other's clothes off.

That first night something about Todd reminded her of an explorer. Together they would adventure to undiscovered lands filled with new and surprising experiences. There was no path, there was no plan, there was no thought. There was only the moment. The whole thing was spontaneous, daring and forbidden. It was an escape from the structured life of routine, consistency, and predicability she had locked herself into.

When they had finished and she was leaving, she immediately thought about her home and her structured life. The thought of it gave her a certain reassurance. For the first time in years she yearned for it, perhaps because it was the necessary contrast to make what she had done so appealing. It was exciting knowing she could live in two worlds. To have dipped out of her contained life and into this passionate moment was thrilling to her. To have something to sneak away from had always been a turn-on for her. To have rules to break, lines to cross, secretly thrilled her. And in this arrangement she found something else that suited her. When it was done she could walk away, leave it in that hotel room, locked away. As for any guilt regarding Elliot, she could just lock that away too.

Amy and Todd would meet four or five times a month, during the week, when she was "grabbing lunch with a friend" or "running personal errands." Sometimes she "worked late." Their affair became routine and eventually it began to lose something because of that. It became too organized, too structured, too monotonous, even for Amy. Then something unexpected happened with Todd that changed the nature of their relationship.

***

It was noon on a hot summer day. The heat hit Amy like a furnace blast when she stepped from her car. The asphalt had a cooked smell which caused her head to tighten. Squinting against the bright sunlight she fumbled for her sunglasses. She was meeting Todd. Room 304. Once again. Going through the motions, she didn't expect the nature of their relationship to change that day.

The affair had always come with compromises. She knew certain things were missing in her "relationship" with Todd but they were balanced out by what she was getting. Yet as time went on, the affair's emotional charge was weakening. The escape was no longer an escape. It was becoming part of the ordinary. The adrenaline rush was waning. Occasionally there was a growing emptiness which accompanied her. It had began to nauseate her at times. So she threw herself further into the only thing they had, the erotic. Yet the more she pushed the limits of their sex, the greater the emptiness. Somewhere inside she knew she was hopelessly trying to solve her problem with her problem. This was something she was stubbornly unwilling to admit. Wrapping her mind around the possibility of an affair not working was too much. Examining that emptiness wasn't something she was going to do. She was not going there. Not if she could help it. And so she rehearsed the same script in preparation for the event. The script began with her entering the hotel where there was a Pavlovian response to the familiar stimuli in the physical environment. The sudden wave of cool air scented with vanilla. The dim lighting. Modern jazz music at a low volume. All of it helped prime her for what would come. It was just enough to give her a slight surge. Enough to torque her mind to where she imagined what fucking Todd in the elevator would be like. The thought of getting naked right away caused her breath to shorten, her pulse to quicken and her throat to dry up.

And this is where she was, the scene playing out as it had been rehearsed, but then, as had begun happening, the emptiness rose up. So she took hold of that feeling and forced it below the surface. Then she focused on the rush while striding down the hallway and with her eyes straight ahead she reached room 304. Key in hand, smoothly slid in and turned. Door open. Into the room. Sunglasses off. Ready to wordlessly pull each other's clothes off. To feel warm flesh against hers. To grapple and fumble about till they found the right position and he inserted himself into her.

But when she stepped into the room something stopped her. An energy hit her, one that matched her own buried emptiness and all the momentum ceased. There was Todd glumly sitting at the edge of the bed. She had never seen him like this before. He looked sad. Immediately, she knew there wouldn't be a reckless adventure in the hotel room that day. What happened next completely surprised her, and for a time, it filled just enough of her emptiness to make the affair worthwhile.

When Todd saw the way she came in, the way she deflated upon seeing him, he dropped his head, and took a deep breath. When he raised his head up she saw tears in his eyes. She had never seen him cry before.

"Today I can't be that guy you want me to be. I just can't."

Without hesitation she sat down on the bed and put her hand on his. They laid back and she held him in her arms.

Soon he began to quietly cry into her shoulder. After some time the tears subsided and he reached over to grab some tissue. Once his nose was cleared she asked him, "What happened?"

"Molly served me with divorce papers. She took the kids and all our stuff while I was at work."

They lay there facing each other. The silence between their words was filled with noise from the room's air conditioner.

"I'm sorry for your pain."

"Thank you. I'm sorry you have to experience my pain."

"It's okay."

"I didn't want a divorce but I've done what I've done. . .She found out about it."

"About us?"

"No."

"She didn't. . .find out about us?. . .Then what did you do?"

That's when the dime dropped. She wasn't the only one. He was having another affair. This was the exact moment where that shift happened in their relationship that fundamentally changed it. Rather than a reactionary rush of anger and jealousy. Rather than screaming at him, storming out or both, Amy simply remained calm and present. She didn't pity him, she didn't condemn him, she simply understood him and accepted him for what he was. They had never talked about exclusivity. Everything had been somewhat unspoken. They kept it very simple. It was a purely physical relationship. Their lives outside of room 304 was their own business. But until right then she hadn't actually realized what their life inside of room 304 really was. Finally they were revealed for who they truly were, two lonely people meeting in a hotel room. Seeing this changed how she felt about the affair. It was much deeper than lust. It was a kind of love. Certainly not the kind of love she would consider throwing her life away for, but a kind of love nonetheless. Pulling the covers on their relationship she realized how basely human it all was. It almost made her laugh.

"What's her name?"

"Stacy."

"Do you love her?"

"It was…" He trailed off with a slight shake of his head.

"Like us? A fun diversion?"

"Yeah," he said with a catch in his throat. His eyes closed, pressing a tear out. It slowly rolled across his face and onto the pillow, "yeah, a diversion."

"Does Stacy know?"

"Oh, she knows. When Molly found out she went to Stacy's work and she made a scene. It was bad. Like fucking reality TV show bad. And it's all my fault. I've hurt them both. And the kids…" The words caught in his throat and he couldn't continue.

After that they didn't speak about it anymore. Not that day or ever again. They just held each other until they began to have sex. Amy was correct earlier, they weren't going to have one of their reckless sexual adventures. Instead they had a slow, quiet joining of bodies. Deep, clutching sex that didn't move all over the place but remained intensely locked in one position until they shared a climax that came from somewhere much deeper than they had ever experienced together.

Driving home that day something inside Amy pushed to the surface. Something long given up on began to rise. Something she didn't want to want. Not again. For so long she had believed she would one day, somehow, leave her husband and create a new life. She had imagined dozens of different future lives without Elliot. But sitting in her car, in their driveway, seeing him in their home, she suddenly imagined not leaving him. The intimacy she had just shared with Todd is what she desperately wanted with Elliot. It's what she had missed. Sex with Todd was just a half-measure way to fill that void. If she and Elliot had that kind of intimacy she would never consider a life without him. She would never be having an affair.

For a moment, she imagined a life with Elliot and she allowed herself the feelings that thought brought with it. Then the moment passed. She turned the car off and walked towards their front door. When she entered the house they didn't acknowledge each other. Nothing unusual there. After some time he said, "there's food. Take-out."

Feeling hopeless, Amy stabbed her fork into a dumpling, put it into her mouth, and swallowed it. She couldn't believe the naked honesty she had experienced earlier with Todd had given her a flicker of hope for her marriage. When she heard Elliot crawl into bed, turn off his bedside light, and go to sleep without word to her, she knew that flicker was gone. Once again, she began to consider leaving him.

***

The affair continued. Todd would go through a drawn out and difficult divorce which caused Amy to call a time-out in their relationship. This was at the onset of the coronavirus pandemic when people were under lockdown and avoidance of physical contact was normalized. Meanwhile, Amy and Elliot were temporarily working from home. They functioned surprisingly well like two well-mannered acquaintances sharing a rented work-space but that kind of success only underscored how apart they had grown as a marriage. They were the only couple who couldn't muster an argument during the lockdown, and not because of their romantic harmony, but because of their lack of passion.

41

The affair with Todd resumed, and for a second, the old thrill of it did too. But then the thrill began to wear out again and once more Amy began to question the affair. She had also begun to seriously question her marriage again and she finally came to a resolution. Without Elliot's knowledge she made an appointment with a divorce lawyer. It was a brief consultation and she said she would need to think about it. Less than week later Elliot told her he was dying. And it was three days after that she found herself back in room 304 with Todd, holding a gold body necklace which she placed back inside the small gift bag.

"Okay. We can just hold each other," Todd suggested as he stood up and moved towards her. She backed up slightly and he stopped.

"We can wait. I have time."

"Not today."

"Wanna talk?"

"Yes. No. I don't know. I can't stay."

"I don't understand. Is it something with us?"

"No. It's not about us. It's about Elliot. He's dying. My husband is dying."

The tears surged up. Todd offered his hand and she took it. She leaned in, sobbing into his naked body while he held her, and when her tears ran dry she gave him a soft kiss on the cheek before she left him alone holding the gold body necklace. Another memory for room 304.

5

The bullpen area overflowed with Target Astor employees waiting to hear whatever announcement the last minute general assembly had been called for. Several dozen more employees were present through video conference. Elliot stood with a scattering of colleagues in the adjacent hallways to the bullpen. In the center of the bullpen a raised platform had been quickly assembled for the "Vices," as they were called, to make their announcement from. The Vices looked over the room which was now slowly hushing as the music they had chosen to enter with was carefully faded out. The only vice president Elliot had personally interacted with was Don Davis, who with his ever present computer tablet by his side, stepped up and   raised a hand to indicate quiet. Then Don stepped back and rejoined the other Vices flanking Advik Verma, Executive Vice President of Operations, who sported an old school combover, thick glasses and a suit that looked two sizes too large. He was well known, almost legendary, for his work in the early days of Silicon Valley. He had the technical brains of the best software engineers but was equally savvy at management. Since he had the most power of any of the Vices it fell to him to make the short and unpopular announcement, which he did in his characteristic impersonal style laced with an ironically droll attempt at pep. There wasn't much suspense as to the content of the announcement. The gist was that their deadline for the rocket design rollout was moved up six weeks. Expected but not welcomed. There were several audible groans from those in attendance. Elliot felt his lower back painfully tighten.

Verma wrapped up the announcement with his stab at gusto, "this is why Target Aster has the best people in the world. For moments like this. Let's show them what we are made of. We can do this! Now we have a few more announcements from the other departments."

Don was the first of the other Vices to speak. He smoothly tagged Verma's announcement, with both an offer and a threat, "if you need additional help to meet your goals, please ask right away. We are all here to support you in any way we can. But, keep in mind, we can't help if you come to us too late in the game. There will be no ability to bail you out at that point."

A business knowledgeable engineer in front of Elliot whispered to another colleague, "it's the stockholders. Helms wants to make a big splash by coming in early, dazzle 'em and then tell 'em to fuck off. All this because he's launching a new AI development and floundering out of the gate, word has it. So a success here, helps him there. With the board. Basically, we have to suffer because his other company is floundering."

As another one of the Vices was prattling on about something, Elliot drifted back to his office having just realized he couldn't care less about it all. The moment he stopped caring his lower back released all tension. Within an hour after the announcement Elliot's desk was piling up with additional work. Suddenly everything was a priority. There was a predictable panic. All thanks to Talbot Helm's need to distract his board. Rather than struggling to wrap his head around how he would get everything done, he began wondering if he even wanted to, and that's when Don walked into his office, or "popped in" as Don called it.

Don Davis had come on board recently to speed things up. His title was Executive Vice President of Project Management. Although Don had no experience in space travel, aviation or satellites, that didn't matter. "Don't know a motherboard from an ironing board. But I do know how to iron out the kinks in any system," Don liked to say. What Don did have was the reputation of a guy who made sure things got done. Period. No excuses. He had a surgically smooth quality when firing someone. Over time, his performance at various technology companies that Talbot Helms owned, earned him the nickname "the velvet guillotine." Above and beyond his management skills, Don's real skill, as everyone began to realize was making Talbot Helms happy. If Talbot said "jump," Don would ask "how high do you want them to jump?"

Personally Don frightened and angered Elliot. He came off like a friendly guy who stepped out from the corporate world of the 1950's. There was this spiffy, peachy-keen old fashioned manner that belied a cold interior. One time Elliot overheard Don matter-of-factly tell an engineer, "you made a commitment to this company and, quite frankly, you're not living up to that commitment. If you can't deliver, then perhaps we should all seriously consider your resignation." The engineer, one of the best, had been doing his best. He ultimately got the job done and when he did, it was as if Don got the credit, not the guy who actually did it. Don oh-so "humbly" reveled in undeserved credit. With a twinkle in his eye, and a studied wave of the hand, he pretended to shrug off the the accolades the engineer had actually earned. There was a hopeful rumbling that Don was only a specialist, brought in to squeeze as much juice out as quickly as possible, then leave the company before long term moral sank too low. Unfortunately Don was now standing at Elliot's desk asking him questions. Clearly trying to squeeze out more juice. That was the moment Elliot's slow growing epiphany about work coalesced into action. It was connected to something that happened at home that morning.

***

That morning it had had been almost a week since Elliot had told Amy he was dying and the initial momentum and optimism around their recoupling was flagging. The reason they were slumping was Elliot, he was distancing himself again, but only in regards to his health. Naturally it was a subject Amy would bring up and when she did he would deflect her inquires and once again work was his shield. Rather than taking this as her cue to slip into her own bad habits, Amy decided she would remain present and patient, not only because the circumstances influencing Elliot's behavior were different, but because she had found a desire to improve her own well-being. But aside from the health issue, Elliot was completely engaged in their relationship and their chemistry was flourishing, so there was still tremendous hope. But that morning they came dangerously close to tipping their marriage back into the quicksand they had just been delivered from.

At five am, as per usual, Elliot's alarm clock went off. From there he went about the same routine he'd had for years. He immediately got out of bed, went directly into the bathroom to relive himself, comb his hair and apply deodorant. His closet was well organized, it helped him dress quickly, which he did so. Moving into the kitchen, he put on the coffee, fried an egg and toasted a slice of bread. He sat down to eat while checking the news on his phone. While sipping coffee and browsing a tech story, Amy walked into the kitchen. They didn't even say as much as hello to each other, which was an echo of their past routine. The worst habit of all from the past, which they almost fell back into that day, was leaving the house for work without speaking. But something special happened that morning which caught their collective attention. Amy was at the counter cutting a piece of fruit and Elliot was at the small kitchen table when it happened. At the very same time they turned to greet each other and with genuine warmth simultaneously said, "hey, we almost forgot to say good morning." This was followed by their laughter and when their laughter died down Amy shifted to a more serious tone, "I want to ask you something." Elliot sat forward, and although he feared she would again ask him something about his health, he nodded for her to go ahead, so she asked, "do you love your job?"

This question surprised him and he didn't know quite what to say at first. Then the answer clearly came to him but he didn't know how to say it.

"Okay, I'll take that as a no," she said and he nodded his head, "so, then let me ask you, why continue working?"

"Right. I see what you're saying." All week the only thing that had changed at work for him was that he was leaving for work later, leaving work earlier, and was thinking about his life outside of work more often. But the question she had asked, which made perfect sense to consider, was more complicated than she realized.

"With your limited time left-" her throat caught and she swallowed, "it's something to consider. Anyway, I'd also like to know more about what you're facing. You know, the details. Maybe later tonight?"

Once again she made the entrée to a more detailed conversation about his illness. The idea of that conversation made Elliot nervous, but she wasn't hoping to talk about it right then, and her warmth made him feel incredible, so he took her hand in his, and they gazed into each other's eyes for a moment before he left for work.

***

Leaving the warm sunshine of his love with Amy, Elliot arrived at work to the self-created strum und drang of an "all hands on deck" announcement in order to meet an artificially moved up deadline. Then he found himself sitting at his desk with Don standing over him asking Elliot for an update on all the existing projects, plus updates on any new projects that had landed on his desk since the announcement, plus he asked when Elliot thought he would complete them all while actually telling Elliot when he needed to complete them. That's when the epiphany came.

"Well, I don't exactly know about all of that but there is something I do know about," Elliot was surprised with his frank, even slightly sarcastic tone, because he typically replied robotically, and without hesitation, to Don with a list of his projects and their estimated completion dates.

"Okay," Don's eyes perked up, his hand poised over his tablet, "tell me."

"I'm going to be heading home."

"Home?" Don asked almost as if to himself as he took a beat to set his steely gaze before continuing, "when?"

"Now."

"May I inquire as to why?"

"You may."

"Fine, why?. . .Medical?. . . Personal? " Don's annoyance showing through by his clipped tone.

"Nothing specific."

Although Don's eyes didn't move, Elliot could see the wheels turning. Then Don took a breath and looked down at his tablet, taking his time while he spoke, "looking over your schedule, and what you're working on, and the corresponding deadlines-"

"Don," Elliot cut in, "the work will get done. And if you're concerned, let the whiz kid take a stab." The whiz kid was a junior associate hired right out of MIT who was doing some of Elliot's overflow work. When he was first brought around and introduced it was tacitly implied by Don that Elliot should take heed that his job wasn't locked in for life. "Of course, we hope that Wilson will be working with you, not replacing you, but he's a real whiz, so you never know," Don said with a laugh.

Now Don was making excuses why Wilson wasn't going to be doing Elliot's job, "well, Wilson does have his desk full too, with the ramp up. The deadlines are approaching. There's no pushing them. Especially not now. Plus I need you to go-"

"The ramp up," Elliot cut him off again. Something was stirring in Elliot and it felt good. "Right, speaking of the ramp up. I'll need some help. I'm asking now. Like you said in the meeting. So, if we can get someone else in here."

"That's what we brought Wilson on for."

"But his desk is full, right?"

"Right. Right, we'll see what we can do."

"I'm counting on you Don," Elliot had never been a smart-ass, until now.

To counter, Don whipped out his old chestnut, "you know, Elliot, I appreciate your call for help and we will answer that call to the best of our abilities. But leaving early on the day the company has asked for you to step up, well, I'd like to remind you of the commitment you made to this company and if you're not able to live up to that commitment, and," Don paused, wound up the delivery and tried to nail Elliot with a challenge to his work ego, "if you can't deliver the goods, then we need to sit down and seriously talk."

"You softened it a bit. Because I thought you were going to do that one where you threaten someone with forced resignation instead of 'we need to sit down and seriously talk.' Hmmm, we must really be under the gun if you can't risk someone calling your bluff and losing them. That or I'm more valuable than I thought." Elliot could not believe the words that were coming out of his mouth and the attitude they came with. And by the look on Don's face neither could he. But Elliot really didn't want to be a dick and poor Don looked like he was about to jump down Elliot's throat, so Elliot decided to diffuse the tension, "okay, I appreciate the nudge Don and I will certainly get this work done, and before the deadline. I always do. I'm on it."

"Well," Don started, then stood there momentarily with glazed eyes before swinging back into his rhythm, "I'll expect the fully updated project report in my inbox before you leave today." And with a sharp tilt of the head Don popped out of Elliot's office.

***

The wind had picked up and was blowing with considerable force. From his lounge chair Elliot was marveling at its effects. Trees swayed and shook. Some of the remaining dead leaves were pulled into the sky, where the wind tossed them about. A palm frond flew by and landed in their yard. When he looked at their fountain Elliot noticed the wind created little wavelets which were colliding with the water cascading from the fountain's pedestal creating miniature turbulence.

How long had it been since he sat in his backyard and appreciated his surroundings? He couldn't remember. Months, maybe even years. For the last decade his weekends had been spent hiding. Often he would go into work. Other times he would bring work home with him. When there wasn't real work he would make busy work. Need to find a way to isolate in the home office? Go through the mail and read the fine print of credit card offers. Those were the types of things he would do. Shuddering, he remembered going into the garage to look at his surfboard and realizing he didn't surf anymore. To justify this violation of living, he told himself he was never a good surfer anyway. As if that even mattered. Or he would say he was being a responsible adult. What should have mattered is taking time to live. That is the true responsibility a human is entrusted with. Not to throw their life totally out of balance for a cause they don't even care for. It matters to take time to play. To enjoy the world for a minute. Occasionally he did slide the stationary bike out from the back of the garage. That was his big adventure. Riding for miles but going nowhere. And even that he'd stopped doing.

All that would change, Elliot thought to himself, from here out he would appreciate and participate in life. Surveying the backyard was another lesson in this regard. Amy had planned the backyard's landscaping and together they had planted almost everything. That was over ten years ago and everything had filled in beautifully. Elliot noticed there were new succulents meticulously placed along the small path. How long had they been there? A faint memory surfaced of Amy telling him about the succulents. This was years before. Her words had gone in one ear and out the other. One of the countless times he'd responded to her engagement with nothing more than "uh-huh." There was a time when she would call him out on his vacant responses. Then she stopped calling him out. Then she stopped mentioning things like the new succulents in the yard. But she had never stopped caring altogether. This was something he'd come to realize over the past few days. Telling her that he was dying had brought them back together. Reflecting on this ironically auspicious turn in his life, his eyes peacefully closed, and he drifted into sleep.

It was one of those dreams where no matter how hard Elliot tried he couldn't succeed. He was in a large cathedral, it had tall ceilings and was full of sunlight. Behind the alter there was a floor to ceiling mirror. Elliot was desperately trying to paint over the mirror using a flimsy paint roller that made the job extremely difficult and as he rolled the paint on the mirrored wall it would evaporate revealing his reflection. The paint kept changing colors. It was black, then red, then white. When the paint went on the mirror the light in the cathedral would darken. When the paint evaporated the light in the cathedral would brighten. This went on and on until he heard Amy's voice, "Are you feeling okay?" *What's she doing here?* He wondered in his dream consciousness. Then the dream itself slowly evaporated.

The wind had stopped and the sun was dipping below the tree-line. There was the sound of birds hurrying to find their place before last light. Slowly Elliot stretched himself out of the painful pretzeled position he found himself in.

"Are you feeling okay?" Amy asked again.

"After I came home from work early I was relaxing back here and just fell asleep."

"Did you come home early and fall asleep because you felt sick?"

"No, why?" For a second he forgot why she would ask if he felt sick. When she cocked her head to the side he remembered. He was supposed to be dying. "I'm fine. Just tired. How was work?"

"Meh."

"What do you mean?. . .Tell me."

"Okay, I'll try. It's like this feeling I have, a general, sense of something. And I'm not sure what to do with it."

"What do you mean?"

"Maybe, I'm inspired, I think."

"And that's a problem?"

"Maybe. First of all, you're sick and I'm feeling inspired?"

"If you feel inspired, then nothing would make me happier. That's living."

"Right, that makes sense and I get that. But then it's also because I'm not used to feeling inspired at work. I'm used to being this machine. A task master. The brain I have developed at work doesn't know how to integrate inspiration so it's a bit of a blocked feeling but I think I need follow this inspirational thing. I'm tired of rubber stamping life."

"So, is this a generalized inspiration or are there specific desires?"

"That's another thing. I don't know exactly what I'm inspired to do. And the not knowing drives me crazy. But. . . it shouldn't. Needing a road map for everything in my life isn't always helpful. For someone like me that's hard to accept. But sometimes roadmaps don't get you to where you need to go. Does that make sense?"

"Makes perfect sense. Just enjoy the inspirational feeling. I mean, isn't that the whole thing anyways."

"What?"

"The vibration you have. Isn't that what it's all about anyway. That's what leads you, that's what gets you there, that's what will keep you going after you get there. So, just enjoy."

"Thank you, wise sage."

"For what?"

"I needed to hear someone else say that to give myself permission."

The gift of feeling understood by your person, as Amy felt right then, made her want nothing more than to be close to him, and so she laid her body down next to his, facing him, their eyes connecting. Everything around them went out of focus. What remained were the details of their faces, the soft sounds of their breathing, and the feel of their bodies together. Then a gentle hum became part of their moment. As the hum grew louder, it became a soft, rapidly vibrating buzz. Simultaneously their eyes widened and they looked up. Merely two feet above them a hummingbird hovered. Then it darted away, a flash of green and red reflected from their patio light. *Magic*, their look to each other said.

"Do you want to talk about what's happening with you?" Amy asked.

"Not yet. Let's just lie here. Just like this," he whispered.

"Fine, but we need to talk soon, like this weekend. Okay?"

And to that, Elliot said, "and right now, I want to kiss you."

They shared a kiss that started gently and built into their first expression of sexual desire for each other they had experienced in years. Then they stopped and continued to hold each other. Something wonderful had been awakened, within each other and within their relationship, but it came at a painful price. For Amy that price was sorrow, for she knew she would have to somehow reconcile her feelings around the affair she had been having. For Elliot that price was something more complicated. Elliot's problem was the trap he had caught himself in. He had told a lie. A big one. He wasn't dying.

6

The first call to Elliot came from Gordo. It was late Sunday afternoon, the day of Elliot's gathering, and Gordo had been getting ready to leave his house to go over to Elliot's. He would be riding solo because the baby sitter canceled at the last minute. They rang family but no one was available.

"If you drink too much, call me. Or call a car. I won't be mad. It's a night with old friends. But I will be fucking pissed if you drive drunk," Gordo's wife Yessie warned.

"I'm not drinking anyway."

"But if you do, don't drive."

"I won't."

"Promise me."

"I promise you. Look, you're acting like I'm guilty or something. Do I look like Tommy?"

"Actually, you do."

"Whatever, just cause we look alike doesn't mean I'm gonna get drunk and crash my car."

Gordo's cousin Tommy had just totaled his car in a drunk driving accident. No one was injured but it was a close call and Tommy had spent a night in jail. Potential legal consequences were still on the horizon. The whole thing had caused a panic with his family. Somehow this event had spawned a global concern about everything and everyone in the family. Yet the one person they should have been worried about, aside from Tommy, was Tommy's father. But he seemed to be getting a pass. Tommy Sr. was a legit drunk. That man drank and drove on the regular. By the grace of God no one had died at his hands. But as it so often goes, everyone is afraid of telling the truth to the one who needs to hear it. Instead a responsible guy like Gordo had to hear it every time he cracked open a beer. Which, admittedly, was a bit too often lately, but he wasn't getting drunk and never did drink and drive. He would just call for a car.

However, when he left home, he did drive straight to the liquor store his cousin Tommy owned. Yes, the same cousin who had the drunk driving accident, and had an alcoholic father, also owned a liquor store. Gordo knew how it looked going to the liquor store right away but his intention wasn't to get blasted that night. The tequila he was there to buy was meant to give the guys a good laugh. There was a crazy story they shared thanks to a certain top-self tequila. It was to remind Elliot of the good times. The fun he'd had in life. The thought of Elliot having fun in his life struck at Gordo's heart and caused him to shed some tears.

To cover his bases Gordo decided he should tell Yessie what he was doing. If she heard from his cousin that he had bought a bottle of tequila it might worry her, or worse she might flip out. Plus, because they were bickering, they hadn't really said a proper goodbye when he left. When he pulled into the liquor store's parking lot he called her. To her credit and his relief she thanked him for the call and said she understood.

"I trust you always and I'm sorry if I stressed you earlier."

"You're just looking out for me. That's what we do for each other."

"Baby, I'm just glad you are alive and well. It could be different. Look at Elliot," Yessie took a breath, there was a moment of silence as if paying respect to Elliot and to honor the gratitude they felt, "okay, tell Elliot I love him and that we will definitely get together soon. I love you, baby," she whispered softly.

"I love you too."

A powerful emotion filled Gordo's entire body when he hung up. Love. It was love and it was nearly overpowering.

He loved his wife dearly. He loved his children dearly. The man truly loved his life. For Gordo this was a familiar feeling and he was constantly grateful for the love in his life. Counting himself lucky he smiled and looked skyward. At that moment the thought of Elliot burst into his mind. What a nice guy Elliot had always been. The quiet one of the group but also so solid when it came to being responsible. Always there when you needed him. But then he disappeared. Well, almost everybody from back in the day had disappeared. It can happen when you grow up but for the most part they were all still alive. Now Elliot was going to die.

We're all going to die. . .Yeah, but he's going to die soon. . .You could die at any moment. . .Yeah, but he knows for sure. His time is up. With young children, a boy eleven and a daughter eight, Gordo was thankful he hadn't been given the same death sentence. How would he deal with it? Just the thought of leaving this life and leaving his family was bringing tears to his eyes again. *Please God if you're planning to take me early, let it be instantaneous. . .No wait, let it be slow too. I need to say goodbye to everyone.* He wiped his eyes, thanked God and got out of his car.

The tequila was literally a top-shelf bottle, eighteen feet up from the ground. Being that it was his cousin's store, Gordo was free to climb up the ladder they used to get the bottles from high up. The ladder was hooked over a track on the wall twenty feet up and a person could slide it from one end of the wall to the other. When he reached the top of the ladder he realized he wasn't in the right position. He was lined up about three feet to the left of where he needed to be. When he tried to pull the ladder a bit closer it didn't slide. For some reason it was stuck. Rather than climbing down and readjusting, he did something he would regret. He extended his right hand out as much as he could but he was barely able to touch it. To get his hand solidly on the bottle he leaned out a bit more than was safe but he was able to grip the neck of the bottle. It was an unfortunate moment for his lower back to lock up, but that's exactly what happened. Because of the position he was stuck in and his inability to move a muscle, he was unable to look down. Perhaps it was a good thing he couldn't look down because below him were shelves upon shelves of glass bottles. Falling would not be a picnic. It would be a disaster. But he didn't have to look down to know what was waiting for him. He imagined his body bent by the metal shelves, crashing into the glass bottles, all of them breaking, puncturing him, stabbing him, slicing him, and finally his head hitting the concrete floor and exploding like a melon. A wave of dizziness washed over his body leaving him helplessly light-headed but somehow he maintained his grip on the ladder and his grip on the bottle. From playing sports he knew to breath. When they were stretching, the coach always told them to breath to get oxygen to the muscles. For some reason, the way he was extended, prevented him from getting air deep into his lungs but he kept trying. Then he remembered the power of visualization. In his mind he pictured his arm pulling the bottle back to his body and miraculously it worked. He was able to pull the bottle off the shelf and bring it to his body. Hugging the ladder, with the bottle in hand, he thought out his next move. Slowly and carefully he would have to back himself down the ladder, one step at a time, without dropping the bottle of tequila. The bottle cost well over two hundred bucks, even with his family discount.

"Fuck," Gordo muttered.

"Are you okay?" It was his cousin Tommy, he finally noticed Gordo hugging the ladder. Gordo hadn't wanted his help because Tommy's help often complicated things.

"Yes. No. My fucking back locked up," because of the tension he could only hiss and grunt words.

"Don't curse it."

"What?"

"You said 'my fucking back.' If you want your back to relax, be nice to it, don't curse it."

"Fine. My wonderful back locked up."

"Better?"

"No," Gordo wished he had the ability to yell at him.

"Should I climb up?"

"What're you gonna do, carry me down?"

"Right. Okay, what then?"

"Catch me if I fall."

"Seriously? Okay,"

Still leaning into the ladder, with his left arm tightly wrapped around it, he slowly took a step down. It worked. After repeating that eleven times he finally he reached the ground. His back was still bad though. Slowly, step by shuffling step, he made his way into the back room. When Yessie arrived a half-hour later she found him laid out on flattened cardboard. With her assistance he made it into her car. A barrage of at home treatments ensued, including ice, heat, compression, anti-inflammatories and rest but first he had to call Elliot and cancel.

"We'll still get together. You know what, Davey and me were going to surf soon. Haven't seen him either in years. You gotta come."

"What about your back?"

"The back will let up. It's been doing this lately. Well, not this bad. But I'll be fine by next weekend. Look, the main thing is I'm sorry for tonight. I really wanted to be there."

"Don't apologize. I'm the one whose sorry. You were up on

that ladder because of me."

"Why are you apologizing? It's not your fault. This is just a minor back thing. What you got going on with your health is a lot worse and you got every right to ask people to show up for you."

Gordo was wrong. About several things. First of all, his back injury was worse than what Elliot had going on with his health, because Elliot actually had nothing going on with his health. Second, and most concerning, was the cause and effect issue. If Elliot believed his lie had been the root cause for bringing him and Amy closer, then it would logically follow that his lie was the root cause for Gordo's injury. This was an unavoidable hypothesis for Elliot.

**

The mug didn't break when it hit the wall. It broke when it hit the ground. Coffee splattered across the wall, on the floor, even the ceiling. The screaming stopped suddenly. The quiet followed the storm. Brian and Mona both knew, this time, something was different.

"Guess you really enjoyed that cup of coffee."

"I guess I did."

"Thank God that Dulce is still at her friend's house."

The coffee explosion was the climax of a fight that seemed like forever, and although it had only been an hour, it really was, in certain respects, a fight that had been going on forever. As was their habit, the fight led them deep into the forest where they were soon lost. Aimlessly hacking away with their words they found themselves so deep they forgot where they had started.

The fight had started while Brian was getting dressed for Elliot's get-together. That's when Mona informed him she wasn't going.

"Are you getting dressed? We have to go soon because we

need to pick up Dulce from her friends?"

"Please let Elliot know we'll both come over another time," she said softly. The tone in her voiced pissed him off, delivering upsetting news in a baby whisper. The heat rose in his chest. Of course she thought she was being sensitive and delicate in her delivery.

"I'm not feeling well, " she added.

"Bullshit."

"No, not bullshit."

"Maybe you should just suck it up and show up."

"We went over this already."

"No, you said you might go. This is the first time you've said you won't go."

"Tonight, I won't go tonight but I will definitely go another time. It doesn't have to be tonight. I'll see him soon, okay."

"Soon? Soon may be too late. He's dying."

"This doesn't have to be a big deal."

"Exactly!" His voice raised triggering her voice to raise. Soon they were trapped in a circular argument. Using different words to say the same thing over and over.

"Stop yelling!" She screamed.

"Stop screaming!" He yelled.

"We don't need to fight about this!"

"Actually we do!"

This particular fight had been brewing ever since Elliot called Brian to invite them over. Right away Mona expressed her reservations. For the following week Brian would broach the subject and she would deflect. She was on the fence. If he could bury the hatchet with Karen, if only for a night, then so could Mona. Instead of becoming frustrated and angry Brian let his hope build up. Unfortunately the higher the hopes the farther the fall and then this particular fight unleashed years of related marital issues.

The entire sibling rivalry that Mona found herself trapped in was exhausting. It was fair for her to avoid the situation if she wasn't feeling well. It had been five years since Brian and his family had seen his sister Karen and her family. Although the roots of Brian and Karen's issues began much earlier, with the onset of their mother's dementia, they didn't totally blow things up until much later. For years before it blew up Mona had tried playing the peacemaker between the two but as can happen, the peacemaker got drawn into battle. And of course Mona had slowly let herself become personally drawn in. Karen had problems totally unrelated to Brian but she would assign him the blame anyway. Brian did the same thing with Karen. Mona grew sick and tired of their shit and began calling them both out on it. Soon she was fighting more with Brian and she also had a brewing conflict with Karen. Finally one day Mona blew up on Karen because during one of her typical rants about Brian she took it somewhere new. Somewhere unforgivable according to Mona. Karen went after Dulce, Brian and Mona's daughter, who was only nine at the time. Basically Karen said that the dysfunction Dulce lived in would start manifesting soon with boys and drugs. According to Karen it was already happening by example of the clothes Dulce liked to wear. Brian and Mona were not great spouses but they were actually solid parents and despite the constant strife of their relationship, Dulce was an incredibly stable kid. She was smart, kind, funny and emotionally well balanced. Essentially she was the only really true bright spot in a difficult marriage and Karen was throwing shade on her. Mona wasn't some angry hothead looking for a fight, but when a fight came to her, watch out. And once she crossed that line she was extremely stubborn and unforgiving. Whatever rift Brian and Karen had was nothing compared to the one Karen opened with Mona.

Almost immediately Karen knew in her heart she'd said something wrong. Something she didn't even mean. But she was also stubborn, and she was extremely defensive, which made it difficult for her to apologize. Especially when someone came at her fast and hard like Mona had. And especially when Mona regrettably dragged Karen's daughter Katie into it.

"You want to criticize how we raise our daughter, you want to tell me the problems she will have in life because of us, then do the same with your kid. Look at how your endless stream of neurotic bullshit its drowning her. You should look at yourself, Karen, because there is a whole fucking mess there you are passing onto Katie. Like some fucking genetic defect."

Afterwards Mona felt sick that she had punched back using Katie. It was no better than Karen using Dulce. They both felt sick about it but they were too entrenched to admit this. So they found their justifications and they stuck to them. *She started it, this is all her fault*, was how Mona saw it. *She totally overreacted, this is all her fault*, was how Karen saw it.

Elliot made a few attempts to get everyone to reconcile but gave up on that fairly quickly. It wasn't the first time his siblings had bickered. For much of his childhood he felt caught in the middle. He never really knew what to do about it then and he still didn't. Feeling terrible about it all, Elliot did what he always did when he didn't know what to do. He put his head down and went to his desk. He had drifted away in his marriage and he did the same with his family. Soon after the rift, the pandemic arrived, and they were all officially isolated.

So all of that led to Mona telling Brian she wasn't going with him to Elliot's. They were at a serious impasse and Mona began to regret telling Brian she wasn't going. *I'm just being selfish*, she admitted to herself. She did feel kind of sick but there was a part of her that wanted to change her mind and go and naturally she wanted to see Elliot. Then, just as she was about to tell Brian that she would actually in fact go with him to Elliot's, their fight blew their entire marriage to pieces.

"There wouldn't even be an issue with Karen if it weren't for you!" Brian said as he thrust his index finger towards her. This, he said, just before Mona was going to change her mind about going to Elliot's, and of course, thanks to his escalation of words, she never did change her mind.

"After all the times I tried to help you and your sister make peace and you're blaming me for it! No you fucking don't." Now she waved her index finger back at him.

And so it went, back and forth, fingers pointed at each other, until Brian stormed out of the room. The fight might have ended there but he just had to get in the last word, "I'll tell everyone you were too fucking selfish to show up for my dying brother!"

"That is fucked up!" She was right on his heels. "You know I love your brother. I will go see him on my own. Without you. Why should we stress him out with our toxic energy."

"Oh, right, so it's better you don't go? You're doing him a favor because, oh, we're too toxic together. Our energy," he said mocking her.

At this point they had reached the kitchen and Brian announced, "can I just have my fucking coffee!" There was a break in the battle. From coffee brewed an hour earlier Brian poured himself a cup. While he stirred in a dab of cream and a pinch of sugar he deliberately ignored her. She stood at the kitchen entrance, fuming, allowing his every movement to fill her with an anger so strong it bordered on rage. Eventually he turned around to face her. Seeing how pissed off she was he decided to get further under her skin. He leaned back against the counter, relaxed his stance, almost like he was casually standing at a bar, and although the cold coffee tasted like shit, he looked at her and said, in an over the top, indulgent way, "mmm, so good." When she began to say something, he cut her off, and calmly said, "seriously, can I at least enjoy my fucking coffee?"

"Enjoy it or not. I'm talking."

"Well, I'm done listening."

"What I wanted to say is that I was about to change my mind. I was about to say I will go with but you had already started your yelling and your blaming me for everything. You made it about everything. You blew the whole thing up. And now it's too late."

"Wait, you're claiming you would have gone but you're not because it's my fault?"

"Yes."

"You make me crazy."

"And you make me crazy and I can't take this anymore," She waved her hand around indicating that "this" meant them.

"Me neither. So what are we going to do about it?" He dared her. They were locked in a stare down. It was dual. Who would shoot first?

"It's over. We're done." She said matter of factly.

"Good. Done." He said without hesitation. When he tried to walk out of the kitchen she blocked his path.

And that is when the coffee hit the wall and everything else.

"God fucking damnit then!" Brian screamed as he spun around and hurled the mug of coffee against the wall.

"Guess you really enjoyed that cup of coffee."

"I guess I did."

"Thank God that Dulce is still at her friend's house." He had nothing to say to that. It was the only thing they did agree on that day.

Finally they left each other alone long enough for Brian's heart to sink even further when he thought about the call he needed to make to his brother Elliot.

***

When his phone rang Elliot could see it was his brother Brian calling and instinctively Elliot knew Brian was canceling because something bad happened that could be traced back to Elliot's lie. After he answered the call, the first noise Elliot heard over the line was a banging sound, then Brian groaned and asked Elliot to hold on. The phone was muffled and scratchy, there was the sound of a door slamming in the background, and then the call disconnected from Brian's end. Pacing the room Elliot tried his brother back several times, then after about a minute Brian called back. He sounded breathless and distracted. In a rambling stream of words he explained that all hell had broken loose in his life.

"This is it little brother, this is the end," he said as if he were an outlaw pinned down by the sheriff and his posse. He did have reason to sound dramatic though. The banging and clanging noise was Mona hauling things out to her SUV.

"What happened?"

"It's over. Wait. . . hold on. . ."

"Brian?. . .What happened?"

"Okay, she's gone. Well, you invited us over. That's what happened. All week she was undecided about going. You know, because of the whole Karen issue but I thought, no way she is going to miss this. I mean it's not about her, it's about you!"

"It's not about me."

"Yeah, it really is. This is about you. And today she made her decision, she said she wasn't going. 'Oh, I'll see Elliot some other time.' You know what, there may not be another time! Sorry. But, it's true."

"It's really over? Like over-over?"

"Oh, it's beyond over."

"Maybe it's just a time out?"

"No more time outs. Look, we're both tired of this shit. How long have we been doing this to each other?"

"Don't give up. Not now."

"It's done."

"I'm sorry, Brian, I really am. I feel like this is somehow my fault."

"What?! Why are you sorry?"

Elliot could hear a door slam on the other end.

"Fuck, she's back. Look, I gotta deal with this shit. I can't make it tonight. So fucking sorry. I swear we will see each other soon. This week?" Again Brian muffled the phone. There was an exchange of words between Brian and Mona. It sounded like she wanted him to tell Elliot something. He was saying something about it being her fault. Then Brian came back on the phone, his breath short, "she says hi and, yeah, I don't know. Look, I gotta go. Love you," and with that he hung up.

Elliot sank back into the couch and put his hands over his face.

"What's wrong?" Amy asked as she entered the room.

"That was Brian. He's not coming either."

"Why?"

Just then, Elliot's cellphone rang. It was his sister Karen.

***

There was something cool and hard in Elliot's hand which he was holding up to his ear. Then he remembered it was his phone. There was a voice coming from his phone. An unfamiliar voice at first. Then the voice registered in his mind. Katie. It was Katie, his niece, on his phone. Karen's daughter Katie. Why was she calling on Karen's phone? What was she saying? *Car. Panic. Accident. Flowers. Mom.*

"She's dead." Elliot muttered.

"What did you say? I can't hear you." Katie's voice sounded stressed.

What the hell was Katie telling him? What the hell happened? The moment he answered the call, expecting to hear Karen's voice but instead hearing a voice other than Karen's his mind temporarily blanked out. From that point on his basic cognitive functions felt tangled and sluggish. Unable to comprehend complete sentences, he handed the phone to Amy. His balance faltered despite the fact he was well ensconced into the couch.

The trouble for Karen began when Elliot told her he was dying and then invited her over. Dread of seeing Brian and Mona had been building inside Karen all week. This was either a perfect opportunity to prove her emotional stability or the perfect storm to prove her emotional instability. On one hand, it had been years since a panic attack. She had even gone without medication for some years now. However, stability without medication was predicated on the idea she would take care of herself and that her life would be relatively uncomplicated. But lately she hadn't been taking care of herself and her life had become increasingly complicated. When she went down the checklist she knew she was on thin ice should anything upsetting come her way. No meditation. No spiritual life. No physical exercise routine. Poor diet. Increased caffeine and alcohol intake. The pandemic's toll. Work had become stressful. Katie had gone away for college that year which had created waves of depression she hadn't seen coming. The depression increased her anxiety. And to top it all off, the thing that had the potential to tip the scales, her little brother was dying. But, somehow she had been weathering these stresses but perhaps her resilience had been worn dangerously thin, and perhaps she should have taken greater heed. So, on the verge of cracking, Karen got in the car with her family, and headed to Elliot's. Katie, her daughter, had come home from college for the week and was in the backseat. Her husband Doug was driving. Doug was a continued blessing, a husband who had always been so solid and supportive but he couldn't, and shouldn't, be responsible for her sanity.

"Damnit!" Karen cried out. Startling Doug and Katie. "I forgot the gift."

"Let's turn around," Doug suggested. He was already signaling to exit the freeway.

"No. No, no. There's a place we can pick up flowers."

"Are you sure?"

"We'll be late if we turn around."

"I'm sure it's fine if we're a few minutes late," Katie suggested.

"You know how I am when I'm late."

Yes, Katie knew all too well what it was like when her Mom was late but she still made that suggestion anyway. It was her passive aggressive way of poking at Karen's neurotic behavior. After a lifetime of feeling like a hostage to her Mom's mental health Katie had developed unhealthy coping skills in regards to their relationship. Being late triggered a general anxiety for Karen, which was unpleasant under the best of conditions but under the stress of a family conflict it was a potential bomb. Turning around was a bad idea so they forged ahead with a quick stop to pick up flowers.

The florist was in a tiny store within a tiny corner strip

mall. The parking lot was ridiculously small and crammed with minuscule parking spots. Most of the parking spots were full which made Doug's task of parking their oversized suburban all the more daunting. Karen insisted on large cars because she felt there was a better chance of survival in an accident. After having managed, with some difficulty to pull into one of the minuscule parking spaces, Doug hopped out with instructions on what kind of flowers to buy.

"Hurry!" Karen commanded. Doug rushed off, not noticing his parking job used up two spaces.

Trying to tune out her mom's palpable anxiety, Katie absorbed herself in her phone. The stress of the impending encounter with Brian and Mona was building for Karen. It had been five years since she had spoken to Brian and three years since she had spoken to Mona. All of a sudden they would all be face to face. Not to mention the reason for this encounter was because Elliot was going to die. While Doug was in the flower shop Karen was deep breathing. Nice and slow. In through the nose, out through the mouth. In her mind she told herself that everyone would get along well enough. That being there for Elliot was so important it would help them all rise above. It really did put it all into perspective. Ideally, this sort of rational thinking should remove or lessen anxiety but no matter how much something might make sense intellectually, that doesn't guarantee it will translate to the body. Karen knew herself well in this regard and she was aware of the fact that she was probably not going to shed her anxiety in fifteen minutes. In fact it would probably increase. These were the stories she could not help telling herself. Desperately she wanted to believe a different story, one where she would somehow float like a butterfly. But that story wasn't holding and so she prepared for the worst because the worst was all she could ultimately imagine. If she arrived and was truly struggling she knew she could still make it. Something she had learned through experience was that if she simply willed herself into the situation, it worked out. It might not be comfortable but it was survivable. And she could always bail out at the last second.

"Got 'em!" Coming out of nowhere Doug's voice and his jerking open of the car door blasted Karen.

"Whaaa!. . .Oh, my god. I thought you were a car jacker!" Doug handed her the flowers. They weren't what she'd described for him. This bothered her but she appreciated his going in for her so she smiled and thanked him. Besides they were a few minutes behind schedule and couldn't afford the time it would take to go back in. Doug started the car and began strategizing how to successfully back out of the spot. It was tight. With a car on either side, he felt pinned in, and there wasn't a whole lot of room behind him either. This would take a few turns to get out.

"Just hurry," Karen said.

Perhaps it was the fact that Doug's neck had been bothering him lately. Perhaps it was the ridiculously small size of the parking lot. Perhaps it was the hurried way the other driver backed out. Perhaps it was Karen's order to hurry. Whatever it was, it happened. The collision came out of nowhere. A sudden and considerable jolt. It shocked everyone, particularly Karen, who cried out with a piercing shriek, followed by three more shrieks, each more breathless than the last, until she was gasping for air. Then it was as if she was holding her breath. Everyone in the car knew immediately what had happened to her. She was having a panic attack. Katie deflated and felt both horrible for her mom and angry at her mom. She also felt guilty because she'd prodded her mom about showing up late. She wished she hadn't come for a visit that week. Doug immediately had all his attention on Karen, his hand on hers, trying to give her calming energy.

"Breath," he advised.

I fucking would if I could, she would have said if she could have. But since she couldn't catch her breath she couldn't speak. He meant well but his attention was a bit too intense and it only made her feel more panicked and more helpless. What she wanted him to do was go and see how the car was. With her eyes she indicated for him to get out and check. He got it.

"Yes! Be right back, okay? Okay."

While he dealt with the fender bender situation, Karen was realizing this was worse than she initially feared. Her body had seised up. It looked like she was pressing her back up against her seat. Her eyes were peeled wide. Her heart was beating a mile a minute. There was an aggressive and uncomfortable tickling in her chest. Her brain was racing. She could only manage short breaths.

"Mom, you'll be okay," Katie set her hand on her mom's shoulder for a moment.

"I, don't, know," the words barely sputtered out.

From experience Katie knew that she had just done all she could. The best thing for her was to stay out of the way and take care of herself. Getting pulled into her mom's spin cycle didn't help anyone. Sometimes she wished her Dad knew this but instead he went into hyper mode during these crises moments, only making Karen more anxious. At that moment, Doug yanked open the door and plopped back in the car, again startling Karen, who let loose a painful groan-shriek

"Sorry," Doug said realizing his entrance had, once again, been unwisely aggressive. "Well, good news there. No damage to either car." He sensed this might sound minimizing to Karen's distress, so he added, "but it felt a lot worse, for sure."

"Urgent care," Karen muttered.

"What?"

"Hospital!" Karen hissed.

"Sorry. I didn't hear you the first time. Not questioning you. Are you sure?"

She managed to turn her head just enough to stare daggers at him, "now you are questioning me," she said through gritted teeth.

"Right. But-"

"I feel like I might have had a heart attack. Is that enough for you?"

Having learned his lesson Doug decided not to mention the fact that Karen's previous panic attacks had also felt like heart attacks. Karen managed to slip her phone from her pocket and dial Elliot.

"Katie, grab my phone. Tell uncle Elliot we can't make it.

When Elliot answered his phone Katie began to tell him, very clearly, what had happened. When Elliot responded, Katie wasn't sure she had heard him correctly.

"She's dead." Elliot muttered.

"What did you say? I can't hear you." Katie now sounded stressed having heard the word "dead."

Having been handed the phone Amy put Katie on speaker. Katie repeated what she had told Elliot. Hearing it a second time Elliot was able to make sense of the words Katie was saying. There was a moment of relief. Karen wasn't dead. Then the reality of what had actually happened became clear. She had a panic attack and was heading to the hospital. This terrible turn of events, Elliot quickly calculated, had been caused by his lie.

***

After the call from Karen ended Elliot and Amy sat quietly on the couch trying to make sense of the sudden misfortune Gordo, Brian and Karen had just experienced. Although Amy and Elliot both had very different contexts shaping their perspectives, they both came to the same conclusion.

"Honestly, I don't think this was a coincidence that all this happened to everyone on the same day. It's just too strange to be random. And I know this sounds crazy but there has to be meaning. Have you considered that?" Amy turned to Elliot as she asked this. He was looking back at her with an expression she mistook for confusion, "you know, one person after another-"

"I understand what you're saying. And yes, I certainly have considered it."

"It's like that concept of synchronicity, do you know-"

"Yes, I understand the concept of synchronicity. Defined as meaningful coincidences. It's definitely something I am. . . pondering, at this moment."

"What's it telling us?" Amy asked.

If I wasn't dying this wouldn't have happened, that's what it's telling us, Elliot thought. Without his realizing it, this was the first time Elliot thought of his lie as the truth. This wasn't intentional on Elliot's part. Instead it was a psychological trick his mind was playing on itself. A cognitive sleight of hand. Perhaps it was a defense mechanism to avoid the feelings of guilt he would have otherwise had to grapple with. And, for that moment, believing he was dying, he was better able to accept what had happened to his friends and family, and that allowed the peace and serenity he had recently discovered to once again flourish. Soon he began to feel better and a thought bubbled up from the good feeling, *since I'm dying I am going to live feely and happily.*

Still puzzling over the sudden misfortune that their friends and family experienced, Amy felt horrible for everyone, particularly Elliot because she knew how difficult it was for him to reach out like he had. The way he had withdrawn from everyone was a major source of their marital problems and his recent efforts to grow out of his self isolation were inspiring to her. Particularly in the face of death. He had been so brave recently and she feared this would be a setback. So, when Amy turned her body to Elliot and put her arm around him as a way of comforting him, she was surprised to notice how peaceful and relaxed he seemed. This calm energy in the face of bad news was reassuring to her. It was the energy he brought home with him the night he told her he was dying. His passing would be difficult but she wanted him to live as freely and happily as possible before that happened. Then it occurred to her that she wanted to live the remainder of her life as feely and happily as possible. It wasn't until Elliot responded in kind that she became aware she pressing her body into his. Soon they were writhing, and fitting together, moving their hands along each other. Hungrily kissing. She whispered into his ear, "I want to fuck you right now because you're so brave." Then Elliot became aware of something happening to him which hadn't happened in a long time and when Amy's hand reached down to his pants she realized it too. She slide on top of him and was straddling him.

"You want to have sex right here?" He asked.

"I don't know."

"We don't have to go anywhere?" It was a serious question given her sexual particulars.

Just then the doorbell rang.

"Davey," Elliot said with a rueful smile, "well, at least he didn't die on the way over."

7

On the walls there were several black and white abstract photos. To Amy one photo looked like an old tower over a lake and the other looked like shapes of whirling humans. Her eyes drifted over to the literature rack full of brochures pertaining to everything from eating disorders to chakra healing workshops. At some point she became aware of a soft hum with occasional gentle bells and gongs. There was a sweet and woodsy smell imbued in the room. The whole atmosphere was soothing, peaceful. This was Amy's first visit and before she even sat down across from her new therapist she was feeling better.

The impetus for the visit happened just after Elliot told her he was dying. Amy had been at work staring at an email that was about to be sent out to students and parents. It was a weekly flyer with various updates about the school district. There was a sentence she had seen dozens of times in these emails but today she was stuck on it. It read, "if something doesn't feel right, talk to someone about it." Even before the pandemic the school district had been spending considerable time and effort making mental health education and access a priority for their students. Although Amy wasn't overseeing the mental health initiative it did come across her desk at various stages. Part of the philosophy their initiative was putting forward encouraged young people to view mental health the same way they would view the health of the rest of their body. You have a fever you take care of yourself. You break an arm you get a cast. You have anxiety and depression, you do what? You don't understand your own behavior, you do what? It might seem like most kids just stuff it, like the kids before them did but the truth was, in her opinion, this generation's attitude towards mental health showed a significant and positive change because they were seeking improved solutions. There were not too many instances where she felt her job was affecting positive change and was not simply a machine of bureaucracy with standardized test scores and budget cuts. The flyer she was looking at that day, reminded her, that at the heart of her profession, were people trying to level up humanity, to better the lives of others. As her boss put it, off the record, referring to the push for mental health advocacy within the district, "we're simply doing our part to stop the cycle of people being fucking crazy. And in doing so we are shining a light, and in doing so we are going to hear people saying more people are crazier than ever, but that is only because we have shined the light on what was hidden."

Amy was proud of the mental health initiative. It was inspired in the way that she wanted to be inspired at work. She wished she had been a contributor to its creation, not just a witness. But she could be a beneficiary of its wisdom. That's when the impetus for the therapy hit her. If something doesn't feel right, talk to someone about it. The words from the school flyer stuck in Amy's mind. They were leading her somewhere but she couldn't see it. Instinctively she sat with it. Then a cascade of realizations flooded her mind.

For so long something hadn't felt right within her. She was quick to point out how Elliot buried himself in his work, his routine. How he disappeared but she was the same. She had buried it all with routine. When she did recognize her unhappiness she put it all on him. She had sat in therapy with Elliot and demanded, "connect with me." Yet neither of them could connect with themselves. For so long her motto might as well have been "don't ever stop and let it catch up to you." That attitude fueled her part of their marriage problems, it had turned her into a robot at work, it had sought satisfaction through an affair and she needed to talk with someone before it broke her. So, she did what they were preaching to the kids. She was going to take care of her mental health. Most of all she realized she needed an inner well-being that didn't depend on Elliot, or anyone else. Or anything else.

"Okay, maybe you want to start by telling me what brought you in," Elaine, her therapist, asked once they had gone through the intake formalities and both sat down.

"I have this need to compartmentalize my life. Perhaps it served me well at one point but," and she paused waiting for the words to form, "it's fucking driving me crazy now. I'm not a whole person. And I think that might be what's prevented me from the kind of connection I want from my life. Yeah, I think maybe I have been feeling that way for a long time and maybe my husband finding out, just this week, that he is going to die soon was the catalyst for wanting to feel better, and so yeah, that probably is a lot, if not all, of what brought me in."

From there talking about her life was like lifting up a large rock and seeing all that lived underneath. In doing so she could feel her breath come and go easier. Her mind and body felt lighter. As the session was wrapping up, and Elaine was walking Amy out, almost like an afterthought Amy said, "oh, and I've been having a long term extramarital affair. Just thought I would mention that too."

"Oh by the way," Elaine said with humor, "well, it sounds like we certainly have some more to discuss next time."

It was the first time Amy had told anyone about the affair. Words that had been locked in her mind had now been vocalized. It was liberating. Throughout the rest of that day and into that night various memories flooded her, like dots connecting, they seemed to be part of a larger picture, one which would help her gain a greater understanding about who she was.

***

At age thirteen Amy had hardly given boys a serious thought. Sure there was the occasional crush she kept to herself but she was not one to have a boyfriend or even flirt. And her parents were definitely on the conservative side and were very strict about that sort of thing. Besides, she was obsessed with getting good grades and keeping up with all the activities her parents arranged for her. A workaholic in the making.

Then one day Haley, her best friend, invited Amy to spend the weekend at her families cabin near the lake. Amy anxiously asked her parents fearing they would say no, but since they knew her friend's parents, they let her go on the trip. It was Amy, Haley, Haley's parents, Haley's older brother Johnathan and his friend Roger. The boys were fifteen, only two years older than the girls.

The kids spent the first day playing around the lake. They went canoeing, they swam out to the floating dock and they explored in the woods. Over the course of the day Amy had developed a crush on Roger. This was exciting and scary because she'd never had such unfettered access to a boy she had such a huge crush on. Not only that but she could tell Roger was interested in her. Although it was all a bit overwhelming for her, she promised herself that if she had the chance she would let Roger kiss her.

Being a bit of a ladies man, Roger could tell Amy had a crush on him but he could also tell this was all new to her. So, he had to play his cards right and he thought he knew just how to do that. As the sun was beginning to set, the kids asked if they could get a fire going and toast marshmallows over it. The parents agreed that if the kids collected the kindling, and only after they ate dinner, they could toast marshmallows. So, out they went to find good kindling. Naive as she was, Amy thought it was serendipity that she and Roger somehow ended up alone behind an old woodshed. "Oh, hey," he said as he ran his hand through his hair. Amy had never flirted but Roger was a talented flirt. Amy loved his attention and when the moment came she let him kiss her. There wasn't any tongue or anything. Just a regular kiss on the lips. They held it for a few seconds. To her this felt exhilarating. It was just so wild and spontaneous. Then she leaned in and this time she opened her mouth and their tongues touched for a moment. It felt like a slimy piece of rubber. But just the fact that she was doing this excited her. So many different feelings were dancing around. She felt electric. It was wonderful. Her heart was racing. An unfamiliar warmth spread through her body. When he told her that she had beautiful breasts she almost burst out laughing. It hadn't occurred to her that he might have been checking her body out and the idea that her breasts were beautiful, well, all of it was almost too much to comprehend.

"How do you know, you haven't really seen them," she unwittingly teed up the big move he wanted to make.

"Well, you're right. I haven't see them. Do you wanna show me?"

"I can't do that."

"Why can't you?"

This question made her think for a second. Why not? This would be a major line to cross but it also felt like it would be fun. Somehow it could cause trouble, but then again, how could this really cause trouble? She was away from home and away from school. It was a different world here. It would be just a moment in time. Just between the two of them. It would stay right where they were. Contained.

Compartmentalized.

"Do you like me?" She asked in all earnestness.

"Yeah," he responded quickly.

"I mean, do you like me as in do you have a crush on me?"

"Of course," he would have agreed to anything at this point and who knows, maybe he was telling the truth in his own way. But they would never find out because the ensuing embarrassment and shame would end any chance of a relationship between Amy and Roger. And, for a long time, between Amy and any other boy for that matter.

Slowly she lifted her shirt over her breasts. She kept her eyes on Roger the whole time and he kept his eyes on her breasts. The sound of a twig snapping underfoot caught their attention. Roger turned to see who it was, leaving Amy visible to Haley's dad who rounded the side of the woodshed. The sight of Amy's exposed breasts stopped him in his tracks.

It all happened in a matter of seconds. Amy felt paralyzed. She would try to explain this to Haley who complained, "why didn't you just put your shirt down so my dad didn't have to see your tits?!" Needless to say this caused a great deal of trouble but the worst of it was the shame. Shame because Haley's dad had seen her breasts. Shame because everyone on the camping trip found out, worst of all Haley's mom who gave Amy disapproving looks the the rest of the trip. Shame because everyone was upset with her for ruining the camping trip. Shame because Haley's brother told everyone what had happened and she had to deal with the gossip fallout at school.

But the worst shame was at home, in the way her parents treated her. Amy was grounded for what seemed like forever. Her parents couldn't even make eye contact with her for weeks. There was a lasting effect on her relationship with her dad in particular. It altered the way he behaved around her.

Suddenly there was a distance between them, a type of formality interjected into their interactions. This was painfully awkward for Amy. She wished she could have just told him that he was making things worse for her, that it caused her a terrible self-consciousness about her sexual thoughts. Why couldn't he just act normally, like he always had? Was it the fact that she crossed this rubicon earlier than he would have wished? Was it the shame of another father seeing her breasts? Was it the idea of his daughter as the object of sexual gossip? Of course there was no talking about it, at all, which meant there was no fucking way in hell she would ever learn to deal with it in a healthy way. It occurred to Amy, for a brief moment, that her parents could have told her it was okay. Not to be embarrassed. And taken this opportunity to open up a dialogue with her about boys and sex. And why couldn't Amy have just listened to her own voice inside that was telling her it was okay? Well, for some reason she couldn't, at least not then.

So what did Amy do? How did she deal with this? She kept getting straight A's. She kept doing her best at whatever activity she was forced to do. And she hid the entire Roger incident from her day-to-day life within a secret room in her mind. This room was off limits while she was at school, while she was at her activities, and while she was with family, but not when she was alone. She hid Roger because she wanted to protect and preserve that experience from further damage. From further shame. She also hid the memory so she could feast off it. Not the part with Haley's dad. That was horrible. She tried her best to cut that out. It rarely crept in. Most of the time it was just her and Roger. She allowed herself to fully live in that moment with Roger. It felt wonderful. They flirted with each other. They kissed each other. And sometimes they did everything with each other.

***

Now Amy knew. Knowing is better but it is not always easy. It was scary how much it made sense. How this one event had shaped her sexual behavior. First there was the sexual pattern she had with Elliot when they first started out. Day to day there was no sexual activity. Maybe some flirtation. Maybe some mild physical contact. They were both so engrossed in school and work she hadn't given this a second thought. Then they would have weekend getaways and overnight jaunts with explosive amounts of sex. It was satisfying, it came to them naturally, and it worked. Then they got busier. Careers came first. Their need to achieve was wearing them out. The flirting during the week stopped, physical contact during the week stopped, the getaways eventually stopped and with that went the sex. Basically, Elliot began having an affair with his work and Amy began having an actual affair. For a time she was aware Elliot had a masturbation habit that was increasing in frequency but then she became aware that it might have stopped completely. As for Amy, the affair suited her perfectly. Elliot replaced her parents as the entity she was hiding her erotic side from, especially when she believed he wasn't even masturbating, which helped to further her association of him with her parents, who she imagined as sexless. During the affair her sexuality was contained to a room. Literally compartmentalized. It never left there. It was physically, emotionally, and mentally separated from her work and family. Another peculiarity was the fact that the risk of being caught, and therefore shamed, both thrilled and depressed her. She found this to be a disturbing and frustrating contradiction. It was incredible what just one day of therapy had unlocked for her when she was open to it but it was saddening to think how little was gained in six marriage therapy sessions with Elliot because they had both been so resistant.

"I went to therapy this week. My first appointment," Amy gently touched her foot to his under the blankets.

"That's right. How was it?"

"Amazing."

"So, am I supposed to ask what you talked about? Or am I not supposed to ask?"

"Both. Neither. I don't know."

"Any takeaways?"

"Lots. I'm starting to meditate. Her suggestion. First time today. It was hard. I didn't realize how much my brain wants to go, go, go."

"So, you like it?"

"Meditation or therapy?"

"Both?"

"I think I love them both.   Maybe you could see someone?"

"Better late than never?"

"You never know. Maybe you'll live forever," she hugged on him and gave his body a kiss, and as she held him she continued talking, "did I ever tell you about my brother?"

Ever since Elliot told Amy he was dying he began thinking about her brother. When Amy and Elliot were falling in love and having long talks till the early morning hours, the story of her brother's death was a big moment. She had cried when she spoke of it. That conversation, among all the others, was one that stood out as a bonding moment.

Amy was ten years old and her brother Alex was fourteen. The parents didn't discuss his illness. She was kept out of it and then he was suddenly gone one day. Perhaps her parents did this to protect her but later in life she wondered if they didn't speak about it to protect themselves. After his death they made a point of piling Amy with activities. It was not just "life goes on," it was life gets so full you don't have time to stop and reflect that sometimes life ends.

Laying in bed Amy once again told Elliot about her brother's death because she wanted to share her new perspective about it, a perspective which had brought her the peace and closure she needed. Most importantly she wanted Elliot to understand what this meant to her in relationship to his death.

"I never slowed down to grieve. They didn't want me to feel it because they didn't want to feel it. I understand it must be devastating to lose a child but I lost a brother I loved. They didn't want my tears but I needed to have my tears. 'You need to stop crying about it,' that's what they actually said. So, I did. I became their good little robot again. But, I'm not going to do that with you. I'm going to feel things. I love the way you're fully living through this. Like you have taken this and let it expand your aliveness. At the same time, I want you to be okay with me having more difficult moments, to realize that aliveness is not always going to be joy and serenity, that sometimes I will have those contrasting emotions. Certainly not to be stuck in the quicksand of pain but you know what I mean, right?"

"I think it's wonderful that you're going to allow yourself to feel things."

"But also," she took a breath here, "we haven't really talked about your illness. We have to, Elliot," she could feel him bristle at this but she gently continued, "I want to know more of the details. What exactly is happening?"

Since the night of Gordo's back spasms, the night his brother's marriage exploded, and the night his sister went to the hospital with a severe panic attack, Elliot had been believing his lie, believing he was actually dying. It had absolved him of any guilt that their misfortune was triggered by his lie, but then, right there, he remembered the truth. With the truth came a dreadful feeling inside himself because he was looking right into Amy's eyes which were staring right back at him with so much love and pain. The love seemed undeserved and the pain certainly unnecessary.

"Please," she gently pleaded, "just tell me what you know."

He remembered that he had researched various causes of liver disease and had settled on the most likely for himself. Cirrhosis was unlikely given he was not overweight, hardly drank alcohol, and didn't do drugs. For a second he did consider cirrhosis as a result of hepatitis C but then realizing it was contagious he scrapped that idea because that would have dragged Amy in for testing. The most obvious choice was a very rare congenital disease that people are born with.

"It's called Wilson's disease. I was born with it. Not that anyone knew."

"Can we get more opinions?"

"There have been."

"Can we find a cure?"

"How?

"Can we exhaust every option and get every opinion available, until. . . either we find something, or, or, we don't?"

"I can tell you this. Dying can wait for now. Let's focus on living. And I love you."

"Just tell me we're going to try?"

"We are going to try."

"I love you so much."

Although, to Amy, it felt like he was constantly trying to shut the door on the conversation, patience was advised by Elaine. So Amy took the positive out of it. The door was open and they were actually talking about it. That was progress.

"I'm truly sorry this brings back the pain of your brother's death," and he truly was, he was sorry for causing it to resurface, "but I'm glad you are stepping up to deal with any bad emotional habits you created to survive those difficult times. I'm proud of you."

"Thank you for hearing me, Elliot."

"Thank you for letting me be the guy who gets to hear you."

Their bodies moved closer to each other. They continued talking for a little while longer. And then, for the first time in a long time, they fell asleep in each other's arms. Despite how emotionally difficult it was for Elliot to reconcile his lie with its various consequences, in that moment as he fell asleep in Amy's arms, he could not help but feel like it was worth it.

8

The morning marine layer had just began to slowly lift, releasing the trapped fog, and leaving a sliver of visibility for Elliot to glimpse the waves and see they were big. Not that he needed to see them to know they were big, he could hear the booming rumble of the large surf. That thunderous bass was matched by the booming in his chest made by his frightened heart.

The chortling of his friends, Davey and Gordo, called his attention, and seeing their casual interaction settled his nerves. It struck him how much they had aged. Receding hair, sprigs of gray, and bodies no longer in the prime of their youth. The reflection of a man in the side window of his car surprised him. Then Elliot realized it was himself. He too had aged. It was like seeing one of those artist renderings where they imagined how someone might look in the future. But that future was now. Perhaps he should have feared this, fought this, cursed this, hid from it, or denied it, but he didn't. Instead he chuckled at the sight of who he was, thinking he looked kind of cute, an observation which amused him. There was even a glimpse of what he would look like as a much older man, the way one glimpses the man a child will become, and seeing this stirred something deep and primal. Perhaps, he didn't fear the inevitability of death as a result of the gift he had recently been given. The gift of treasuring every day he had.

"Man, I really gotta start eating right and working out," Gordo grunted while he struggled to pull his wetsuit over his upper body, "finally living up to my name," he said slapping his protruding belly.

"Like a marshmallow with four toothpicks," Davey joked.

Gordo gave Davey the finger while he continued grappling

with his wetsuit.

"Is your back okay?" Elliot asked.

"Guess we're gonna find out. Are you gonna suit up?"

"Yeah." Elliot tied a towel around his waist, slid his pants off, and began to put his wetsuit on. Davey was already suited and had his surfboard, the "spooner" as he called it, under one arm. He went over to take a look at Elliot's surfboard.

"Mini log. Nice. Brand new?" Davey asked.

"Not brand new."

"It looks like it's never been ridden."

"Well, it hasn't."

"When did you buy it?" Gordo was out of breath. He had finally managed to pull his wetsuit on. Without injury.

"Present to myself on my 33rd."

"Dude that was years ago. And you haven't ridden it?"

"That's tragic," Davey said seriously.

"It was. But today is a different story," Elliot declared.

"Fuck yeah, you're right, it's not sad or tragic cause you're riding waves today. Let's get out there fellas," and as it had been when they were young Davey led the charge with Gordo right behind him and Elliot trailing.

The sand was still cold from the night. Elliot sat down and began to put booties on his feet. The ocean had a lot of energy and movement. Powerful waves were pushed further into the beach sweeping water across the dry sand. Sensing Elliot's apprehension the guys stopped before they paddled out.

"If you feel too rusty, just remember you can always sit in the bay and pick off smaller ones," Davey said.

"I don't think I was ever really a great surfer, even when I wasn't rusty, so yeah."

"You were never a bad surfer either. In fact you were pretty good for a minute. Before you disappeared building rockets and shit," Gordo said.

"It is kinda big today though."

"It is but it isn't, you know. I mean it's not Pipeline out there. It'd take a freak accident for someone to die here. It's impossible. Almost."

"Just get in the water. That's all you gotta do today," Davey said simply. Then he turned and sprinted towards the waves. In one clean movement he dove over the incoming whitewater, with his surfboard held underneath his body, and landed smoothly on the water using the momentum to begin paddling out.

"Remember, you might be dying but you're not old yet," Gordo said over his shoulder as he walked into the water.

***

Davey and Gordo had timed their paddle-out to avoid any sets of waves and they easily duck dove under the several small waves that passed by them. By the time Elliot was ready to paddle out another set was approaching so he waited for it to pass. Despite the heavy crowd at the main take off spot, Davey and Gordo each picked off a wave. Davey had immediately paddled deep and lucked into one that broke further out from where everyone was sitting. His surfing had always been excellent but with age his style had gained considerable power. Making a large and tricky set wave look easy, he drew beautiful lines while flying across the face of the wave. He finally kicked out in the bay where the wave died out. Gordo had sat on the inside, pouncing on a wave that closed out on another surfer who took off too deep. He still had his characteristic smooth and mellow style.

Seeing his friends out there brought back the fun of surfing for Elliot. He could feel it in his bones again. His muscle memory began to kick in and his fear was being overridden by his stoke to catch a wave. The set passed and he had his window to get out there without getting flogged. The cold water washed over him when he pushed under a small wave. The shock of cold was so invigorating he felt as though he was born again. That feeling alone made the day worth it. There was a mist over the water's surface and a sizzling sound from the aerosolized whitewater the waves left behind. The current was strong, so he began to dig deep with each paddle. Soon Elliot had made it past the break line and was gliding over the slate gray ocean surface.

Then something made him stop. The pack of surfers ahead. Social panic surged within his body. Anxious thoughts began to creep into his mind. Was this an aggressive hoard of men huddled in the ocean waiting to judge and harass him? Another surfer unexpectedly paddled up from behind and passed him up. He nearly gasped. The whole scene started to feel rapid and staticky. All of a sudden he became uncomfortably aware of the fact that he was out of his comfort zone. And for a moment he could feel something pulling at him to be small again, to hide at his desk and to shut the world out.

Fortunately he feared losing his newfound mojo more than he feared anything else at the moment. He simply wanted to feel good bad enough. So he shook it off, sat up on his board and started to take slow, deep breaths. He focused his gaze on the horizon which was an ethereal blending of sea and sky in shades of gray. His focus shifted to his sensation of touch. The air itself felt like water, as if there was no separation between the two. The flavor of the ocean passed through his nose and with it was everything under its surface. He could taste the kelp, the fish, the crustaceans, all of it. *I am one with the ocean. I am one with life.* With that truth in his heart, he fearlessly paddled over to his friends.

"Every Sunday morning, let's meet up and surf. Rain or

shine. If there's no waves we paddle out anyways. Why? Because we can. Do it while you still can," Davey gave Elliot a knowing look. The subtext of what he had said was clear, *we could die at any moment,* and Elliot was proof of that. It was relieving for Elliot to see his friend inspired from the fact that he was dying. It was also relieving to see Gordo surf without throwing his back out. Suddenly, it felt like there was a mojo to this whole thing, like he had created this lust for life all around him. Now all he had to do was catch a wave.

After a half-hour Elliot still hadn't caught a thing. If he chased a smaller wave and didn't catch it, he ran the risk of getting mauled by a bigger one behind it. Paddling for a bigger one was tricky because, first of all, it was big but also because there were so many surfers going for the bigger waves. But he knew from experience a wave would come his way. Every surfer knows to keep their eyes on the horizon. That's where the waves come from. Turn your back on it for too long and you might miss your chance. Or worse, you might not see the wave coming that drills you down to the ocean floor. A good surfer can spot a set coming long before a layperson would ever see it. And suddenly another set was coming.

Davey and Gordo immediately made strategic moves to get in position for a wave. Wave after wave passed, each with a surfer taking off on it. Elliot kept waiting. He had been paddling further out as each wave was breaking farther out.

The set subsided and assuming he was safe Elliot sat up on his board. He turned to look back towards shore to see what happened to Davey and Gordo. They were nowhere to be found. Then he realized he was alone. It seemed like everyone else had caught a wave. The nearest surfer was about ten yards away. Looking away from the horizon and back toward the shoreline, he could see the back of the last wave that had passed as it peeled down the beach. Every now and then the surfer on the wave would throw a massive arc of spray from his turns. Unfortunately Elliot marveled for too long. Long buried surfing experience finally kicked in, but a little too late. He snapped his head back around to the horizon. There was a wave coming. It was big and coming in fast. His options flashed across his mind. Option one, stay here and it would break on him. That would send him through a violent washing machine and he would dragged towards the shore. Frightening, exhausting, humiliating, and possibly dangerous. Option two, paddle hard towards the horizon and scratch over the wave. It was the safe move but there was only one problem and that problem was option three. What option three offered was glory. Paddle hard towards the fast approaching wave and get himself in position to catch it before it broke. Catching it was no guarantee but it was certainly possible. According to the surfers code this meant one thing, Go! In fact Elliot could hear some unseen surfer calling out, "Gooooooo!" Elliot had somehow scratched into position, and as the wave stood up even higher, he turned and dug into the wave. Turn and burn as the old guys used to say. All of this, from the moment he had seen the wave until the moment he paddled into it, was probably five seconds. But in those types of moments time perception does incredible things. It goes faster and slower all at once. So you see what is happening in slow motion but in reality it is happening at lightening speed. As it was all coming together, Elliot realized the wave was not makable, not even for an experienced surfer but at that point it was too late because he was already totally committed and he was loving every second of it.

Sure enough, just as he was standing up the bottom of the wave dropped out. Rather than a round shape, the wave squared up over a reef and Elliot was air dropped to the bottom. Somehow he stuck the landing. It was indeed heroic but it didn't matter because the entire wave closed out. No one would have made it. The lip of the wave came crashing down on his shoulder. It drilled him straight down into the water. For a second he was pinned to the rocky bottom of the ocean floor. *Don't panic,* a flashcard from past experience thankfully popped into his brain. What happened next was that he was sucked back up towards the surface and then thrown back down again, falling head over heels underwater as the wave continued to push him down. The spin cycle began to slow so he decided to put his feet on the ground, it would help him kick up to the surface, but when he kicked his feet out there was nothing but water. No ground. That's when he realized he was upside down, and that sensation of not knowing if he was right side up or not, totally disorientated him. Luckily he wasn't surfing a true big wave spot, otherwise this would have only been the beginning. Instead, the ocean calmed and buoyancy finally took over. His head broke the water's surface, he caught a breath, and reeled his board in. With the coast clear he began to paddle back out to the take-off zone. He was utterly and completely stoked by his wipeout.

The thing about surfing is that one minute you get thrashed and the next minute you get the ride of your life. After earning some praise and chuckles from Davey and Gordo for his last effort, Elliot was ready to go again. When the next set rolled in he was right there with the rest of the crowd, jockeying for position. As a surfer deeper down the line took off Elliot held his ground just in case the surfer didn't make it. The surfer was good but when some kook dropped in on him, they both wiped out. This left the wave empty and Elliot seized the opportunity. He easily stroked into the wave and was quickly up on his feet. Just like that, Elliot caught one of the best waves of the day. Wild eyed, he flew down the line, pumping for speed, hooting and hollering, a grin plastered across his face.

***

As far as Elliot could see Gordo's back was okay. He'd seen him surf and he'd seen him change in and out of his wetsuit but he wanted to make sure.

"The back, it's okay?"

"Actually I think the paddling helped it."

"Oh, that's good to hear."

"The whole thing with my back, it was a good thing. Fucking my back up on that ladder was the wake up call I needed. So, thank you God for that. Maybe if I put it all off any longer something worse happens, you know, because the truth is I've been letting my body go. Eating ice cream all the time. Drinking too much beer. My diet sucks. I hardly exercise. I can feel it. I'm getting injured doing things like climbing a ladder? Come one, it's depressing. Time to start eating better, drinking less, getting off the couch, exercising-"

"Surfing more," Davey added.

"Surfing more!" Gordo echoed, "so, dude, don't be blaming yourself because I hurt my back on my way over to your place."

Elliot looked around at the radiant energy of his friends and the energy of nature vibrating all around them. No, Elliot was no longer blaming himself, he was now giving himself credit.

***

After Elliot returned home from surfing Brian unexpectedly dropped by, triumphantly holding up a six pack of beers as he entered the house. It had been a week since his tumultuous split with Mona, but unless Elliot was mistaken, he seemed happy.

"Are you allowed to have a beer?" Brian asked as he handed Elliot one. In his other hand Brian had a joint, "this is probably good for you, right? Can I smoke in here?"

"Let's go outside."

"Want some?" Brian sparked up the joint as they settled into chairs on the patio. Elliot waved it off. "You sure?"

"No thanks."

"First of all, how are you?" Brian asked.

"I'm doing good."

"Feeling okay?"

"Yeah, I feel great actually."

"Brave face. That's inspiring. So, I don't know, I feel like I should ask you more but I don't want to upset you. I'll just put it out there, you know, I'm here to talk about whatever you want, okay."

"Thank you. The same goes for you. Whatever you need to talk about I'm here."

"So, you're good?"

"As they say, the present is a gift. So I'm just doing my best to enjoy it."

"I feel ya."

"So, how are things at home, Brian?"

Brian kept his eyes on Elliot while he took another hit from the joint. He nodded approvingly while holding the hit in, then he exhaled the smoke slowly and said, "great." Then he stubbed the joint out and offered it to Elliot.

"Here, keep it."

"I'm good. Pot's always made me paranoid."

"For Amy then."

"Sure. You never know. Thanks. So, things are great?"

"I feel good. I've been smoking a lot less pot lately. Drinking a lot less too. Bad habits seem to be manageable."

"Oh, for how long?"

"Like a few days."

"Oh, the way you said it, it sounded like a long time, you know."

"Time is relative. You know that. You're the physicist."

"So, things are great, huh? What's going on with you and Mona? Last time we spoke on the phone it was, ah, a little crazy over there."

"Yeah, the coffee incident. So, here's the update with my situation. Life is a fucking trip. That's the headline. And yeah, great might seem like a bit much given the implications but things are great."

After the coffee incident, and "the fight to end all fights," Mona immediately packed luggage for herself and Dulce and left. Within a day she had found a furnished luxury apartment she could rent month to month. For all the times they had a "fights to end all fights" no one had actually moved out. Usually it was Brian who was forced to leave the house for a night before they made up. This time it really was for real. The first couple of days Brian was miserable. Not because he was sad about Mona, but because he was devastated about Dulce.

"She is such a good kid but I'm thinking 'could this be the thing that fucks her up?' You know, her story becomes, 'I was a great kid until my parents split and then it all changed and that's when I headed down this dark path that led me to God knows what.' And for the first couple of days, with Mona and Dulce gone, and with an empty house, I would return home from work and start drinking right away. Two nights in a row I woke up on the couch after passing out. The television would still be on. I'd been drinking myself to sleep. Then in the middle of the week Mona texted and said on a Friday she would drop Dulce off after school and she'll spend the weekend with me. So, I cleaned up the mess of beer cans, ash trays and take out containers."

"You said you cut down on the drinking and smoking?"

"Well, I mean I have. Since then."

Then when Brian came home from work Mona stopped by. Watching Mona walk up to the house gave Brian chills. They hadn't spoken since she left. They had only exchanged a few text messages about where Mona would be staying and about Dulce coming over.

"Can I come in?" She asked gently.

"Of course, it's your house too."

"I know, but I just want to be respectful."

"Oh, cool. Yeah. Thanks."

While retelling the story Brian stopped here and said to Elliot, "can I just say, in that moment, as she stepped inside the house, I wanted to fuck her. It's weird, man, I know. She'd been driving me crazy for so long, right? But then she was so hot. And so cool. Her whole vibe."

"Did you guys?"

"No."

When she came into the house, Mona and Brian sat at the dining room table, and she started by saying how she wanted the process to be civil. He emphatically agreed. She told Brian that she needed a week or so to get her mind straight before they began the legal process. She asked if he would hold off till then. That was fine he told her. Truth be told he hadn't even begun to wrap his head around the idea of lawyers and court papers. It felt like a cold and distant planet he wasn't prepared to visit. Mona wanted to clarify their living situation. Dulce would stay at the house full-time, while the parents would alternate between being at the house with Dulce and being at the furnished apartment.

"So, Dulce is always here, but you and I take turns being

here?"

"Do you agree to this?" Mona asked.

"Yeah."

"You don't need to see the apartment first?"

"No, I'm sure it's fine. The price is doable and it's only temporary until, you know, we figure out the rest."

"Exactly."

"Honestly, I think it's a great idea, letting Dulce stay here full time. How did you come up with that?"

"Actually. . ."

"It was Dulce's idea?"

"Of course." They both laughed. Dulce was a logical, composed, and wise twelve-year old. Sometimes Brian and Mona wondered if she was actually their child. Dulce also had a dark sense of humor and could be mercilessly sarcastic which seemed to verify she was indeed their child.

They agreed on some basic ground rules as it related to Dulce followed by an awkward moment of silence. That's when they politely wrapped up the conversation.

"Dulce wants to come in for a bit and see you. Then we have to go. She has to finish a project for school."

"Of course. Yeah." Brian walked Mona to the door and said goodbye. It was a painfully hollow feeling. Till that point in the break up the only sadness Brian had felt was for his daughter. When it came to Mona his feelings weren't nearly as tender but something about seeing Mona walking all alone back to the car nearly destroyed Brian. A deep sorrow suddenly gripped his heart so hard he thought he would keel over. Tears and snot seemed to erupt from his face. It was messy. He had to step inside and go blow his nose. By the time Dulce was inside the house he thought he had removed all evidence of his crying.

"You've been crying," she said matter-of-factly.

Before he could lie she put her hand up.

"Don't be embarrassed. She cried the second she got back to the car. She's been crying a lot. Honestly I'm relieved that you've cried. You should. If you didn't you would be a psychopath."

"Have you?"

"What?"

"Cried?" He didn't want to say it, but it suddenly occurred to him Dulce might be a psychopath.

"Why are you worried I'm a psychopath?"

"No."

"Would you be relieved if I cried myself to sleep the last few nights?"

"Relief is not the right word."

"Well, I did," when his face reflected sadness hearing this, she added, "and now you can think of the bright side. Your daughter might be sad but she's not a psycho."

"Do you want to sit down and talk about things for a second?" Although it wasn't actually a question Dulce told him no, she didn't want to.

"It wasn't really a question, Dulce."

"I know."

"I need to say a couple things."

With an impatient breath Dulce followed Brian into the living room and they both sat on the couch. Brian told her the standard things a parent should tell a kid when they are trying to divorce responsibly. It's not Dulce's fault. He will always love her mom, they just had a difficult relationship, and again, that it has nothing to do with Dulce. Things might be hard for a bit but they will be okay. They will get her a therapist to talk with if she needs. Other kids she knows have been through this, maybe she could talk to some of them about it.

"And most of all, if you ever need to talk about anything, I'm here to listen. No judgement. So, is there anything you want to say, or ask me? "

"Well. Thank you for saying all that. And I know you're there to listen if I need. And," Dulce scrunched up her face, she did this when she was considering whether or not to say something.

"You can say anything?"

"Obviously I'm sad in a lot of ways but I also feel guilty."

"Why? It's not your-"

"I know. I know. It's not my fault. Trust me, I know that. I've been in this house too. Now, I know you guys stayed together for me, I know this-"

"Well, it's more-"

"Let me finish," her face scrounged up again. It had to be something awkward for her to hesitate like this because she was typically blunt and direct. "Okay, so, I know this might sound terrible, but I'm also kinda relieved and kinda happy you guys are divorcing. I used to pray you guys would just get it over with and divorce. I mean, after I gave up on praying for everyone to get along."

Brian was stunned. Not just that she had these conflicting feelings but that she understood them and was able to articulate them. Of course, it was a bit sobering to hear that his own daughter had rooted for a divorce.

"Is that okay, dad?"

"Yeah," he said almost as a question.

"It's just weird, the thing that makes me happy also makes me sad, and vice versa. Do you know what I mean?"

Brian and Elliot were still in the backyard. Brian had relit the joint at some point and it was almost finished.

"Sorry, I know I said I would leave some for Amy."

"Not a problem."

"Elliot, the kid blows me away. You know what else she said and mind you she said this as she wrapped up the conversation, not me. She said 'the positive thing from this is that you guys can now become better versions of yourselves,'" Brian started to choke up, it took him a moment before he continued. "Just, wow. That kid," he took a deep clearing breath, "so as the child said, or something like what she said, I'm really happy even though its a sad thing. Life is a trip. And you know, what's also weird, is that if you-" Brian stopped himself.

"What?" Elliot asked.

"It's insensitive."

"Never stopped you before?"

"Really?"

"Kind of."

"Sorry. I need to work on that. Never mind then."

"I know what you were thinking, Brian. I've been thinking the same thing. If I wasn't dying then I wouldn't have called you and you wouldn't be getting the divorce you needed to have."

Brian nodded his head, sat back in his chair, and looked up at the stars.

***

Karen did not hesitate to attribute her situation to the cause and effect of Elliot dying. She told him so, after apologizing several times for not calling him sooner. The past week had been so hectic, between hospital visits, work, and her own emotional ups and downs, that she lost track of time. Perhaps it was the current state of mania she was in, or perhaps she didn't trust that people were actually listening to her but Karen told Elliot her story twice.

Following the panic attack in the parking lot Karen went directly to the psychiatric wing of the hospital. It was determined she was not having a heart attack and that she was having an acute panic attack. After a psychological assessment by the psychiatrist on staff, Karen voluntarily checked herself in for the night. After saying goodbye to Doug and Katie she was taken to her bed and given some sleeping pills. When she woke up the next day she was immediately seized by a terrible pain in her stomach area. Between the mysterious stomach pain, and a slight benzo hangover, it took her a moment to remember what had happened the night before and realize where she was. She pressed the call button for the nurse and immediately began to doubt if the pain she experiencing was real. Last night she had wrongly believed she was experiencing a heart attack. This morning she was pretty sure her gut was exploding. But was it? Or was this another physical manifestation of a nervous breakdown? The nurse entered the room and asked if everything was okay. When Karen hesitated the nurse cocked her head and asked again. So, Karen told her about the pain in her stomach but added that maybe it wasn't as bad as she thought. The nurse assured Karen that she was going to get a complete physical before discharge and they would look into it then.

Another hour or so passed while Karen lay in bed. At some point it began to hurt so badly that she started crying. Again she called for the nurse. By the time the nurse entered the room Karen was balled up from the pain. Immediately the nurse paged the doctor on staff. Right away the doctor ordered Karen to be moved to the medical intensive care unit so she could receive an endoscopic exam. The exam revealed what the doctor had suspected. Karen had undiagnosed peptic ulcers that had burst. After a few days in the hospital and what seemed like a ton of medication, she was discharged.

"I would have called sooner, but as I said, so much was happening and, you know, I really didn't want to add my troubles to yours."

"Karen, you can always call me. I want you to call me. I want to be there for you. We're family."

"I will, I will. I know, I know. And I want to say the same goes for you. Really. Please know I am there for you. We all are. And Elliot, I just want to say, and I'm sure you being a scientist and all that you believe this kind of thinking is crazy, or maybe you don't think its crazy. But I believe there really is a logic to it all."

"A logic to what?"

"You really did save my life."

9

The main building where Elliot worked was a sleek, modern, silver structure built onto the front of the older building which was an atomic era building. The older building was originally built to design and develop weapons during the second world war. The entire structure was tucked against a hillside that abutted thousands of acres of undeveloped land. It was an absolutely cloudless clear blue sky which Elliot happily noticed after parking his late model Chevy Volt, which was by far, one of the oldest cars in the lot. *Soon, I'll be the only guy without a Tesla,* he thought with a laugh as he strolled towards the entrance.

Thanks to all the good news his friends and family reported over the weekend Elliot had been flying high all morning. So far that morning his thoughts had not turned to work which was antithetical to his old habit of obsessing on work, even in his dreams. And nightmares. It wasn't until he saw his reflection in the building's glass exterior that work fully entered into his mind, and his libido drained. The weight of the small satchel slung over his shoulder had somehow quadrupled and each step forward became a laborious effort. The impulse to simply stop walking was strong enough that he had to consciously put it out of his mind. A hawk's piercing cry from above brought to his mind the image of carrion.

Why am I still working? The thought lingered in the back of Elliot's mind. It was Amy who had first broached the subject, asking him why he continued to work. This question jumped to the front of his mind as he walked through the office and noticed his supervisor Don surreptitiously eying him with a critical gaze. Elliot wasn't accustomed to that look at work but he was not surprised because although he was generally praised at work, as of late he had lost his desire and focus. After exchanging the usual morning salutations with co-workers Elliot finally made it to his office and sat down. This was the one area of his life where dying hadn't made things better, in fact it had made things worse, but perhaps that was a good thing. Perhaps things being worse were better because it finally made him stop and realize he had no interest in the projects the company was working on, nor in the overall mission of the company, and if he were really dying he would definitely give notice. Whereas the rest of his life had begun to feel like the best wave he had ever ridden, at work it felt like he was swimming against a riptide.

***

"If nothing changes, then nothing changes" was a bumpersticker Amy saw when she left her therapist's office and it was exactly what Elaine said to Amy just minutes earlier about her marriage.

"These new insights, these positive feelings, they are all wonderful but they're a starting point. You need to start allowing them to become actions. Otherwise it all stays in here, inside your head, and never connects to here," Elaine indicated her heart, "if nothing changes, then nothing changes." And that is why Amy found herself extending her already extended lunch so she could go visit Elliot.

The tickling of excited nerves in Amy's body were not just because she was going to surprise Elliot at work but also because this was her first visit in all the years he had worked there. It wasn't all on her, he had never invited her, and she had offered more than once. In the beginning when Elliot was invited to do things socially outside of the office he would decline. For holiday parties he would make a quick appearance without her. At first she objected to this. Presenting her objections on practical grounds, saying that developing relationships at work was a way to move up in the company. It was something she knew how to do, it came easily to her but Elliot told her people didn't expect a person in his department to be an extravert. Besides he wasn't interested in leading teams or overseeing anything. He was good at what he did, he was well paid and had job security. That was enough. What was not said, what should have been said, and what it was really about is that she wanted to be part of his life. And if work was becoming his entire life, and she was not part of it, then she was not part of his life. Well, that was going to change. Privately, Amy had accepted the irony that if Elliot wasn't dying she would have left him, but he was dying and she wasn't leaving him, so with whatever time they had left, she would be part of his life.

When the door opened and Elliot emerged she could tell he was just as excited as she was. They were like two giggly school kids on a first date as they greeted each other in the lobby. Meandering through the office with Elliot, Amy realized she'd never seen his work persona. He was polite but a bit clipped in his exchanges. With several people he was a bit warmer and made a point of introducing her. There was also a peppiness about him but perhaps that was due to the excitement of her presence. So she asked him.

"Are you usually so peppy at work?"

"No. This is a special occasion. My spirits are raised. Usually, I'm a bit in my head, a bit isolated. I'm sure you could imagine that," he said and gave her hand a squeeze. "I would give you a full tour but they're pretty concerned about trade secrets. Actually there's a whole vetting before the full tour."

"Really?"

"The corporate space race has created its own corporate espionage. Anyways, most of what goes on is pretty boring to the layperson. They actually build everything somewhere else."

They were alone in Elliot's office and Amy was sitting on the edge of his desk looking out over the quiet flow of activity in the bullpen area. Not a lot of interaction. Lots of people in offices with heads down, working. There was a larger office area that had a team of people watching a man furiously scribbling numbers on a grease board. It was an environment that suited Elliot but she also wondered if, in some ways, it might not have been good for him. It seemed too easy to become an isolated workaholic here.

"What's all that for?" Amy pointed to the larger whiteboard in his office which was filled with equations, "it looks a bit like a recurring nightmare I had in high school."

"That's part of a sequence proving the viability of a new propulsion system working within the moon's atmosphere. A lot of people don't think the moon has an atmosphere. Well, technically it does and I'm just proofing the calculations."

"And that one?" Amy pointed to a smaller white board crammed in a corner of the room.

"That. That is something I need to erase."

"Why?"

"Not for work. It's a theory I've been thinking about."

"You have a theory?"

"Hopefully."

"Since when did you have a theory you were working on?"

"I don't know, twenty years ago."

"And I'm just hearing about it?"

"Well, I kind of shelved it for like fifteen years but when it's ready you'll be the first to hear about it," Elliot said as he took his phone out and snapped a photo of the smaller white board with his theory on it. But before he could erase it, Don popped in, as he was wont to do, and warmly introduced himself to Amy. Don was an extravert all the way but as a somewhat controlled extravert he knew how to shift his own gears according to the needs of the situation. He could make small talk all day long. And some days he had to. And when it called for a quick exchange, he knew how to efficiently and effectively handle that too. Right now he was making small talk with Amy and although she was not a master like Don, she could certainly hold her own. All of this was as much small talk as Don and Elliot had shared in their entire history of small talk together. It wasn't all innocent though. Elliott had noticed that Don used small talk to gather useful information. He was sneaky like that. And Elliot had noticed Don's eyes drift over to the smaller whiteboard. Somehow Don had probably figured out that the work on it wasn't work related to Target Aster. And although he liked to say he "didn't know a mother board from a mother hen," Don actually knew a thing or two. Don was also sneaky like that. So, while Don and Amy talked Elliot erased the smaller whiteboard. Elliot was not sneaky like that. When Don initiated a tone that signaled the end of the conversation, Amy picked up the cue.

"I'm sure you didn't just stop in to talk to me, so I'll step outside and let you two talk business," with that Amy left Elliot and Don alone.

"New whiteboard?" Don asked rhetorically. Elliot didn't reply and just waited for Don to continue but all Don said was, "Uh-huh." Then Don took a breath and parked his skinny ass on the corner of Elliot's desk.

"We have to stay on target with the atmospheric propulsion proofs."

"Almost done."

"I noticed we're missing some key deadlines over the past week. The engineering team says it's been a bit slow on your end. Coming down to the wire here."

"I'm aware."

"Two things. First of all, I need you one hundred and ten percent focused on this project. There's no one better than you Elliot when it comes to proofing the calculations. And this is crunch time. Weeks away and then a breather." For the past couple of years, a "breather" had been the carrot Don dangled. There was always a breather, or a break, or a pause to look forward to. But the problem was that it was always just weeks away. And until recently Elliot hadn't been physically or mentally capable of slowing down if he had been given a break. Not only that, but until recently he wouldn't even have wanted that break. But now that he did want to slow down, and now that he did want that much promised break, he resented the bullshit. "Second of all,"Don continued with a nod to the small whiteboard, "anything you develop on site belongs to the company. Per your contract with Target Aster. Just a friendly reminder."

After this exchange, the shift inside Elliot that had begun over a week ago, finally shifted all the way as it related to work. Elliot opened the door to his office and walked out in the hallway. Don followed and was back in small talk mode as he and Amy exchanged goodbyes.

"Elliot's got a lot on his plate and he's really going to have to burn the midnight oil, so I encourage you to drop by more often. For morale."

"Well, I decided I better get down here for a visit before, ah, well, before," Amy searched for a way to say it, "he, ah, you know."

"I don't know." Don's brow furrowed and like a prairie dog sensing danger he darted his head from Amy to Elliot and back to Amy.

"Elliot's…." Amy sensed something was amiss by way of

Don's puzzled response, so she just let it hang there.

"Amy, I haven't told anyone at work," Elliot interjected.

"Told anyone what?" Don said. His eyes slightly bulging.

"Oh, I'd assumed. Sorry." Amy consolingly put her hand on Elliots arm.

"No, it's good you brought it up. I've been wrestling with when to say something and now that the proverbial cat is out of the bag, I think it's time."

Before Elliot continued talking, he gave Amy a quick look that was so full of confidence that it made her tingle. He had that new energy again, the energy she found irresistible. She squeezed his arm.

"Don, I'm giving my notice."

Don's eyes popped. Not what he expected. His wheels spun for a moment.

"I see. Okay. Uh-huh," Don began to do his constant nodding thing while he asked Elliot if he was "sure about this." When Elliot told him he was, Don told Elliot there would be some paperwork, as if this was a threat that might change his mind. Elliot replied he would like to get the paper work out of the way, but not until after he returned from lunch with his wife. Some niceties were exchanged during which Don continued to nod. When Don asked why Elliot was giving notice, Elliot simply replied, "personal health reasons."

Elliot left work arm in arm with Amy and at lunch he asked if she wanted to leave the next morning for a weekend getaway. Of course she said yes. And they both agreed that life was great.

***

The scenery began to change. Amy gazed out from the passenger window. The passing hills were dotted with wildflowers and snowcapped mountains rose in the distance.

Elliot's free hand rested between her legs in a warm embrace while she gently stroked his forearm.

"Why did we start calling them getaways?" Elliot asked.

"I don't know. I think I just liked how it sounded. 'We're going on a getaway.'"

"Was it because of that movie?"

"What movie?"

"The Getaway."

"Never heard of it."

"It's from the 70's. It's about a bank robbery gone bad," Elliot continued on with the plot summary, "at the center of it was this couple, Doc and Carol, who took part in the bank robbery. There are lots of shootouts. It's full of double crosses. Even Carol almost double crosses her husband Doc but, spoiler alert here," Elliot paused and waited for Amy, she laughed and told him it was okay to continue, "in the end the couple comes together and gets away with it."

Amy was focused on Elliot's retelling, not because she cared about the movie plot, but because she loved seeing him like this. So alive and happy. Watching him enthusiastically ramble on about an old movie, the way he stopped for a spoiler alert when he knew she'd never watch it and could probably guess the ending anyway, this was how he used to be around her. The two of them talking and laughing about things that were so random and trivial. It wasn't about the content of the conversation, it was about the chemistry between them.

After discussing the name origin of their "getaways," they tried to determine exactly when their last getaway was but they couldn't agree on the time. Not knowing something so trivial began to irritate them. They both liked to know things exactly. It was in their nature. Rather than letting that irritation grow into something larger they wisely agreed it actually didn't really matter. What mattered was that they were doing it, they were on a getaway and it felt great, and what mattered above all else was that they had chemistry again. To have lost it and then found it again was incredibly fortunate. It's a rare experience for a relationship to have this kind of renaissance after the of dearth passion they had. The renewal brought with it a depth of feeling and connection they could not have imagined. But there was still something important that hadn't happened. They hadn't had sex yet.

Their expectation of sex was natural but given their circumstances this expectation felt heavier than it ever had. The closer they got to their destination, the more pressure they both felt. For all the new intimacy they were sharing, there were significant truths they were hiding from each other. Each of them privately wondered if their secrets would sabotage their much anticipated sexual reunification. They each dealt with this pressure differently. It should have been easier for Amy to deal with the pressure because her main coping mechanism of planing and routine fit right into what they were doing. She tried to let schedules and logistics consume her mind. But, the route had been decided, the stops along the way, if any, had been decided, the check-in time had been decided. Even when and where they would get gas had been decided. There wasn't enough left to organize. Besides, she was trying to break away from her old coping mechanisms. She wanted to face this with a fresh attitude. But, the biggest challenge she was facing was an intruding thought she'd had. It was the thought that Todd was the last person she'd had sex with and the only person she'd had sex with in well over a year. This thought was deeply disturbing to her and kept encroaching on her despite her shunning it again and again.

The surface of Elliot's anxiety was good old sexual

performance anxiety. There had been a steady drop off in sexual desire from the time he and Amy first started drifting apart. Initially he masturbated constantly and as of recently he rarely did, so, Elliot genuinely questioned whether or not he would be able to do it. But, he knew his sexual performance anxiety was really a manifestation of the true source of anxiety. Despite the moments when he actually believed he was dying, the truth was always there, and that truth had not yet coincided with sex.

All at once a shudder passed through them and their hands recoiled, her hands folded back over her lap and Elliot's hands both regripped the wheel. A whispered look passed between them as a chill ran up their spine like a zipper exposing their insides. They both knew something shared had transpired but unlike their recent shared feelings, this didn't feel good, and they didn't discuss it. If they had discussed what made them shudder, they would have realized that their deepest secrets and fears passed through their consciousness at the very exact moment.

"I love you," they said in unison and then laughed. She took his hand back, placed it back between her legs, and once again gently stroked his forearm.

The impulse came to Elliot out of nowhere. It was a memory, but from when and where, he couldn't say. Supposedly, there was a beautiful, somewhat secret spot, along the way to their destination. It was one of those word of mouth spots off the beaten path. A place that very few people find. There was a lake that was fed by a series of small streams, which he figured would be running pretty heavy this time of year. The only thing he knew about this place was it might be somewhere off the exit right after the highway cut west towards the coast. After that he had no idea where it was other than it was supposed to be up the road few miles, somewhere off a dirt road. He knew from experience that getting off the beaten path would make Amy anxious. In the past Elliot had been fine with this, it had suited him too. But things were different now. He was different. It didn't suite him anymore and he had an instinct it didn't suit her anymore either. So following the impulse that came out of nowhere he put his turn signal on.

"Where are we going?" Amy's voice indicated a measure of alarm as Elliot took the exit and kept going past the general store and the gas station. She asked again where they were going.

"Somewhere beautiful," was all he said.

***

Looking around them the forest was dense and lush. The trees along the road seemed thicker and taller the further they went. They hadn't spoken for the ten minutes since he'd turned off the highway. Elliot needed to do this. No matter the outcome, he told himself, it would be fun. *It already was.*

Amy had registered her initial reaction to this unplanned turn off. It had caused her heart rate to increase. She was annoyed for a moment but was also excited. "Somewhere beautiful," he had said. Why fight that? Why fear that? They would both need to live fully and courageously until his death, and this was an opportunity to do so.

"Real talk. I have no idea where I'm taking us. We can turn around if you want to," Elliot said as he cut off onto a narrow dirt road, "or we can see where this road takes us."

"I think," Amy spoke slowly as she took in their surroundings, "I think this is wonderful."

They rolled their windows down and the smells of the forest rushed in. The cleansing air seemed to fill them all the way to their toes and fingers. Soon the road began to incline and a view emerged out of the trees. There before them was

115

an emerald landscape with a hint of a lake in the distance. Following his instincts Elliot pulled the car off the road and parked near a small foot trail that cut into the trees. Weaving their way through the trees the trail began to wind along the side of a mountain. They kept stopping and pointing out the different marvels along the way.

"Stream," Elliot called out, "I can hear it."

While he ran ahead, Amy stayed right where she was. The moss beds captivated her. She knelt down and gently pressed her palms into them. She sat and began to meditate. It was a meditation unlike anything she had ever experienced. It would have been impossible for her to explain what it was like. There was absolutely no sense of time. It might have been two minutes or two hours but when she finally emerged, she had no idea where Elliot was.

The faint sound of moving water had pulled Elliot towards it. He ran the trail, rounded the switchback, continued running until the trail dipped down and then he clearly heard the sound of rushing water. Jogging a few more yards he finally saw it through the trees. It was no babbling brook. This was a powerful stream of cold water blasting over huge rocks and banking around massive boulders. The section of the stream directly in front of him was particularly dynamic because the water was squeezed through a narrow gap. Downstream, where the gap opened up and grew wider, he could see the stream's personality changed. It seemed slower and there were large boulders and deep pools. He hiked downstream towards the large boulders and deep pools, and as he approached the area, a roaring sound surpassed the sound of the river. When he got closer he saw the reason. It was a waterfall that plunged fifteen feet down into a large pool of crystal clear water. The churning water at the base of the waterfall was hypnotizing. The memory of the wave he'd caught the week before flashed through his mind and brought with it a wonderful feeling. This was exactly where his intuition had been leading him and he knew exactly what he wanted to do. He was going to jump from the top of the waterfall into the water below. Thankfully Elliot's intuition was in harmony with his logic. He realized only fools rush to jump off cliffs into unchecked pools of water.

It took Elliot several minutes to scramble down the boulders and reach the base of the waterfall. He stood at the edge of a large pool of water he estimated it to be the size of a tennis court. Although it looked deep enough to jump into and he couldn't see any boulders under the water, he still needed to check. Knowing the water would be cold he wisely took a series of slow deep breaths and began stilling his mind. Once he was mentally prepared he stripped off all his clothes, and without hesitation, dove in naked. When he resurfaced he let out a hoot. The water was freezing. He took a deep breath, swam underwater, and explored the area he planned to jump into. The cold felt like a vice on his head and the deeper he swam the tighter it clamped. The pressure on his lungs and his eardrums began to grow heavier. It was definitely deep enough, he couldn't even swim down to the bottom. It was also clear enough under the water to look around and make certain no boulders hid just under the surface. Back on dry land his skin stung, his ears rang, and he felt wonderful. Totally energized, smiling like a maniac and completely naked, he quickly scrambled back up the boulders. By the time he reached the top his hands and feet were so numb they felt like stumps. He gave his nose a farmer's blow. Traversing through the shallow pool of water that flowed towards the waterfall Elliot carefully made his way to the jumping off spot. The water was up to his knees. The closer the stream got to the waterfall the faster the water moved and this gravitational force gave Elliot his first true butterflies about the jump. Safely he reached the jumping off spot at the edge of the cliff where waterfall was plunging over. As so often happens, it felt like a much higher jump once he was ready to actually do it. The butterflies in his chest were definitely increasing in size and activity.

Following the trail Amy easily found Elliot. As she looked downstream she noticed Elliot was naked, soaking wet, and slowly wading through a pool of water. She made her way towards him and when she was about twenty five yards away she hollered to him. By this time he had made it through the pool of water and was standing on some sort of precipice with his hands cupped over his privates. "Elliot!" The waterfall was loud, so she had to call again, even louder. Wondering what he was doing, intellectual thought instructed her towards fear but she found herself laughing instead. She called his name again, "Elliot!" He turned and when he saw her, he began laughing too.

"Hurry!" He waved her over but she stopped at the edge of the river. "Come on, take your clothes off!"

Between them was the pool Elliot had crossed. She continued to hesitate, "what are you doing?" she asked.

"Jumping. Do it with me."

"No! Really?"

"Yes. It's safe. Come on."

"Have you done it already?"

"No. But I went down and checked it for safety. That's why I'm wet. It is freezing."

"I can tell," she teased.

"Well, yeah, hopefully I'll do a wee bit better when the time comes."

It seemed insane but she took her clothes off anyway, and stepped into the freezing water.

"What the fuck are we doing? It's so cold!"

"Fully submerge! Do it. Seriously. It feels great once you do. And it's less cold that way. You're just torturing yourself right now."

"No!"

"Yes! And stay under a few seconds. Trust me!"

"Fuck!" And with that she submerged herself, and after a few seconds she surfaced with a scream, "You're right! It's better. It feels great!"

Soon they stood together, naked, shivering, holding hands and looking over the edge.

"We jump. On three."

Air rushed over their bodies, pressing against them, as if it were lifting them up. There was just enough awareness to think about what was happening before the water was right there, coming faster and faster until their feet pierced its icy cold surface. Their hands parted as their bodies were swallowed and thrust deeper and deeper until everything stopped and they were momentarily suspended in the silent stillness before swimming up to the surface.

***

A briny blast of ocean air greeted Amy and Elliot as they stepped from their car. It had been fifteen years since their last visit to the small seaside village and it still looked and felt the same. Amy was gazing up at the inn they had reservations for. It was a well maintained, grand old Victorian house built at the end of the 19th century.

"Do you wish we were camping instead? Like the last time we were here," Elliot asked her.

"I remember wanting to stay here last time and not having enough money. Besides this time has to be different, you know what I mean?"

"I do. This will be nice for us. Next time we can camp."

"Next time," she gave him a hopeful look, "next time for sure."

"It was fun back then, wasn't it though, on a shoe string budget."

"The kind of romance money can't buy."

"So, about that plan to take a meander before we check in," he said as he walked around the car to her, "Let's take a bath first," Elliot gently whispered into her ear.

"And then."

"And then."

Neither of them said anything as they walked up to their room on the second floor. They didn't say anything as they set their things down and undressed and they didn't say anything as they stood together naked by the window, cast in the golden afternoon sunlight, but afterwards, they couldn't stop saying, "we need to do that a lot more" and "why did we stop doing that?"

In the afterglow of their sex they strolled through the town. The used bookstore they loved was still there. For Elliot and Amy this was the equivalent to a cigarette after sex. Housed within another old Victorian style house, this one sagging with chipped white paint, were incredible books of all variety. On the front porch several people sat on old rattan chairs reading. Inside the warm pulpy scent of mildewy old books was like a pheromone for Amy and Elliot. If they hadn't made love before the bookstore visit they certainly would have afterwards. They drifted around and leafed through different books. Occasionally they would find each other and share a bit about a book they found interesting. The high from sex, followed by the intellectual stimulation, had Elliot feeling unhinged. All that plus the stale air became too much.

"I need fresh air."

"Did you find anything you want to buy?"

"I did," he held up three books, "This one about nothingness, then we have a historical account of the philosophical origins into infinity. And a John Grisham."

"I'm still going strong here."

"The sun sets in an hour and a half. Shall we meet in front of the hotel an hour from now?" Elliot asked.

"Until then."

"Until then."

The theory that had been formulating in Elliot's head for the past twenty years was starting to pop around inside his head a bit too rapidly in the bookstore. He hoped a stroll around the streets with all the old homes would help quiet his mind and streamline his ideas. If something salient emerged he could always run back to the hotel where he had a notebook. But the idea of streamlining his thoughts into a salient flow of ideas soon felt like an impossible wish. It was clear to him that his mind was refusing to quiet down and for the first time in his life he began to feel the desperate horror one experiences when their sanity begins to leave them.

10

The charged feeling hit Elliot after the sex and for a moment, while in the bookstore, he'd hoped to put that energy into his long mulled about theory. But at some point his fast moving thoughts began to scatter and as he unsuccessfully gave them chase he was left with a pulsing panic sensation within his body. Unsure of what was happening or why it was happening, he went for a walk but the nice quiet street with its variety of interesting old coastal houses did nothing to abate his discomfort. In fact, it was growing worse. It felt like there was something inside of him trying to get out from within his chest. Elliot was trying to pinpoint when the feeling began, thereby determining its cause, and then perhaps to discern a solution. Had it been kicked off with some chemical release during sex? And was it then increased by the "inspirational" thinking about his "theory" while in the bookstore? Was he basically overwhelmed by positive feelings? That didn't really make sense to him. He began to look further back in the day…the spontaneous drive out of town, the detour off the map, the naked waterfall jump.

Wait, he stopped walking, *these are good things*! He began to laugh out loud, *I'm so excited and I love my life so much that I can't contain it.* There he stood on the street laughing and looking skyward, wanting to believe all was well. But if he were to be completely honest, he had this slight nagging feeling that there was still a sense something unsettling and deep within was seeking his attention.

Remembering he was to meet Amy in five minutes, he began to walk quickly back towards the inn. Before Elliot reached the inn he spotted Amy window shopping a quaint store packed with local arts and crafts, local jams and salsas, all the requisite items for charming small town gift shops. Just as he was about to dash across the street and join her, she began talking to a man and woman she seemed familiar with.

The conversation became animated, with excited gesticulations, particularly from Amy. Something about the couple Amy was talking to gave Elliot pause. There was something familiar about them. Something he couldn't place. Then it clicked. It was the Algren's, Terry and Norah. They lived on Amy and Elliot's street, only a few houses away. Then Elliot's stomach began to tighten. Norah Algren was an attorney, she specialized in medical malpractice, but even worse was Terry Algren, he was a doctor. An internist, no less. Someone who knew all about liver disease. Someone Amy would seek advice from. With ninja-like stealthiness Elliot slipped into the nearest shop. Another quaint store packed with local arts and crafts, as well as local jams and salsas. Peering over the jam and salsa display Elliot tried to draw a bead on their conversation. Lots of lip flap, still a fair amount of gesticulation but nothing over the top. Then both Terry and Norah Algren's body language shifted. They looked serious. Terry's head tilted slightly, the way doctors do when they're intently listening to a patient, and Elliot knew, at that moment, Amy had told them Elliot was dying from a rare form of liver disease.

Finally conversation wrapped up and the coast was clear but rather than running excitedly to Amy, Elliot was seized with terror. For a second he considered making a run for it. Just go. Disappear. Forever. But he couldn't bring himself to do that. Habit helped his feet move towards Amy, and perhaps, he hoped, they had not discussed Elliot's health crises. But he knew, there was no way his medical condition didn't come up, it had to. When he rounded the corner her enthusiasm took him by surprise.

"Hi love!" He almost seemed to jump, so she asked, "did I

scare ya?" For some reason he threw his hands up, almost like she were the police, her excitement cut out and she asked with concern, "are you okay, Elliot?"

"Yeah. Totally. Let's hurry and catch the sunset," he nervously glanced around, looking for the Algrens, "come on," he tugged on her arm.

"What's the hurry? We have a half hour and it's a five minute walk," she stopped him and gave him a kiss, "hi."

"Hi."

Amy was giving Elliot a quizzical look, something was up with him and she knew it. Elliot could see all this registering in Amy's mind, so he tried to divert her towards her old habits, "Look, I just thought we have a schedule, you know. That's all."

"But you know what, I really want to loosen that side of myself up. Today was so great. If it had been up to me we'd never have found that waterfall. So, more waterfalls, less stress." They walked off holding hands. Amy on a pink cloud. Elliot under storm clouds. She squeezed his hand and said, "so, you'll never believe who I ran into."

"Really, who?"

"Our neighbors, Terry and Norah."

"Oh, Really. Wow, small world. Coincidence."

"Are you kidding? Coincidence? Come on, you're all about synchronistic events and this was definitely synchronistic-"

"Wow, look! The sky is on fire!" He interrupted her, pointing out the red hot sunset they were walking towards. She smiled, taking it in, as she continued talking. There would be no distracting her. It was coming and he had to accept it.

"So, we knew that Terry was a doctor but I had no idea that he was an internist. Did you?"

"Yeah. Yeah, I did."

"And you never thought to talk to him?"

"I, ah. . . " he threw up his hands.

"Sorry, that sounded harsh, but my point is, it's time to let me help. It's time to let the universe help, you know, you've been tremendously brave but there have been walls too. I'm sure it's been hard to go it alone. And you have been going it alone. In some ways. No more. Okay?"

"Uh-huh," Elliot nodded, his vacant eyes stared straight ahead, looking at nothing. His breathing became rapid and shallow, his heart rate accelerated. Suddenly the uncomfortable and irritating sensation began gnawing at the inside of his chest again, right in the center, but only worse. Not the butterflies, no. This terrible feeling, when it started felt like someone aggressively tickling his feet, but in his chest, and this was punctuated with little pin pricks, all of which seemed to grow and expand until it felt like an angry pile of scorpions were trapped within his chest. Then as a way to combat these feelings his body felt detached from his mind, and then his mind quickly jumped ship.

"I know," Amy exclaimed, as if she were reading Elliot's mind, but of course, she wasn't. The look she gave him broke his heart. She looked hopeful. The scorpions were replaced by sadness and guilt, and he realized these were the unsettling feelings which had begun growing within himself earlier in the bookstore.

If Elliot could have grabbed both sides of his rip cage and ripped himself open, he would have, just to release the pain that was inside of him.

"Terry Algren can help you," now she had tears in her eyes, "he'd like to have you come in to see him. He said you can never get enough opinions. Especially when it comes to the liver. And he said if he can't help you, he knows someone who can. One of the top hematologist in the country. In the world!"

"What's a hematologist?"

"He specializes in liver treatment. Elliot, we're talking about getting you a liver transplant if we have to," Amy continued talking but Elliot was unable to hear anything else after *transplant!* The word kept spinning through Elliot's mind. *Transplant!* Soon his body was spinning. To the point where Elliot actually had to stop, take a breath and steady himself.

"I know, it's huge. I know how you hate to let people help you. But this is why you have to. God brought us Terry Algren."

"Right."

"I know you don't believe in God. So the force, or the universe, random chance if you will. Synchronicity. Whatever. The point is, help is on the way and this thing ain't over yet."

"Okay." It was all he could say. It was neutral enough. He was hoping this would be the end of it for now and he could somehow gather himself. Get clear. Find a way through it.

They had reached the headlands and walked right to the edge of the bluffs. They were overlooking the ocean, which at high tide, felt like it was directly below them, crashing against the base of the cliff they stood upon. The sun was just about to touch the horizon. A cold onshore wind was blowing gently off the ocean. The incoming swells from heavy surf roiled the kelp beds creating a dramatic rust colored water surface. With a final blip, the sun was gone. Amy stood in front of Elliot and nestled herself into him and pulled his arms around her. He obliged to this and finally went with it, holding her tight. For just an instant he was totally in the moment with her, the stress wasn't gone but it was at bay. Then it came right back when she said, "we're meeting them for dinner tonight."

"Tonight?"

"Yes, tonight."

"The Algrens?"

"Yes, the Algrens. Who else?" she chuckled.

"But we have reservations at-"

"So do they. At the same time," she turned herself around and looked right at him "synchronicity. I mean, we've always said we should have dinner with them."

A strange noise left Elliot's mouth. Amy took it as a strained laugh, and so she snickered, "right? All these years. So, what better time for that dinner than tonight."

The fire in the sky had subsided, it was twilight and the stars and moon were now the show.

"We should go," she said. Elliot didn't want to leave. He stood his ground, kept her in his arms. Another couple of minutes went by as they stood silently, "okay, not to hurry us but, we should get going. We're going to be late as it is."

"I thought you wanted to be less plan-y."

"Well, yes, but I don't want to be a flake either. I think there's a balance," she gently extracted herself and was starting to walk away but the slight groan from Elliot stopped her, "are you upset?"

"No. No, not upset."

"You're okay?" she said giving him an expression he couldn't place and his thoughts began to run with paranoia. Was she suspicious? Not knowing what to do or say, Elliot simply nodded. Her expression fully revealed itself, it was concern. Again, her concern increased his guilt but it came with a chaser of relief. At least she wasn't suspicious. Together they walked down the darkened path back towards the inn.

***

Either way he was going to lie. The way Elliot saw it he

had no other option but to lie. He could either go to dinner with Amy and the Algrens and lie all night or he could skip the dinner with only one lie to Amy. He chose the latter. "I'm not feeling well, so I'm going to stay in." He felt terrible the instant he said it but it was better than feeling terrible all through a dinner. It had occurred to him that there was a third option, which was to tell the truth about everything but that was quickly scuttled for a number of reasons, top among them was relationship suicide and public humiliation.

Amy had just come out of the bathroom, wrapping a towel around her head to dry her hair. She stopped and stared at him. The disappointment was obvious but it soon turned to concern.

"Really?" She walked over to the bed and sat next to him. She examined him with her eyes.

"Yeah. It just hit me. Like a ton of bricks." Elliot was slumped out on the bed, his shoes off, and his head propped up with pillows. Gently she put her hand on his forehead.

"Hmm," was all she said when she removed her hand.

"You can never be too careful."

"True. You're not hot though."

"A low-grade headache with nausea," he said, then added almost sounding hopeful, "and aches and pains." *Maybe, I don't actually feel great*, he wishfully thought. There had been a great deal of stress from the Algren complication. There really was a kind of mild throbbing ring of pain around his head and maybe there was a sort of mild nauseous feeling in his gut. So, maybe he wasn't really lying.

"Bummer. I was looking forward to this but, yeah, if you're sick, you're sick. I'm sorry."

"Don't be sorry. Really. It's not your fault. Are you still going to go?" He secretly hoped she wouldn't go because it would slow down the talk about things like liver transplants, but he knew it would raise an alarm if he actively dissuaded her from the dinner.

"You wouldn't be upset?"

"I would be upset if you didn't. I don't want to spoil your night but I would also understand if you wanted to stay here with me."

"One of us should talk a bit more to Terry about your liver. And, of course, it's been our dream to eat at this restaurant. I can't pass this up for a lot of reasons. I mean, we are living our life to the fullest now, right?"

"Right. Right. Someone should live the dream. And it was more your dream than mine."

Fifteen years ago they had stood in front of the restaurant and peered inside through the window. A Michelin rated restaurant. They had never been to one. It looked beautiful and charming inside. The smell was not just enticing but intoxicating. When they looked at the menu they changed their minds. It was a quarter of their rent. They decided to return sometime soon, when they could better afford it. Sometime soon never happened. Ever since they had regretted not splurging on that dinner, particularly Amy.

It should have brought great relief to Elliot that Amy had gone to dinner and left him alone in the room. Instead of relief he felt what he could only described as soul sickness. After telling this second lie, the much smaller lie he told to avoid dinner, he began to feel dirty and small and was actually starting to feel as sick as he'd claimed he felt.

The big lie, the one where he told Amy and everyone else that he was dying, had made life better and so he had allowed himself to forget about it. Until today. Until the Algrens and the notion of a liver transplant. In all his life he'd hardly ever lied. At that moment he couldn't even remember telling a lie but he figured he must have told a few small ones here and there. Essentially he was not a liar. He was an honest person. At least he used to be. This entire thing, he realized, went to the core of who he believed himself to be, to his soul. And now that lie had him feeling soul sick.

Again, his thoughts began to attack him and he sought escape from them. The books he had purchased earlier that day seemed like an obvious distraction. Yet when he picked them up he couldn't bring himself to start reading them. This had never happened to him. He had always been able to read, even when he didn't want to. There was a television. After ten minutes of flipping through the channels, nothing interested him, and so he turned it off. His phone, designed to be the ultimate distraction machine brought nothing, it was as interesting as small brick in his hand would have been. And if he had a brick in his hand he might have thrown it through the window or smashed it against his head. Anything to snap out of the funk of despair he was falling further and further into. It was still early but not so early he couldn't try falling asleep, so he turned off the lights in the room and lay in the dark. After about five minutes he realized sleep wasn't going to happen, his mind was a battlefield.

Thought attacks continued. Try as he might to force his thinking in a new direction, it kept coming back to the big lie. It was as if the things in his mind felt bigger and looked bigger, like they were being seen extremely close up. Like they were in his face. This was the deep within thing that had been trying to get his attention all afternoon since he'd had sex with Amy. What was happening was inevitable, and deep inside he admitted this, but that didn't mean he was ready to face it.

***

One of the byproducts of their increased intimacy was a psychic connection. This intuitive ability had begun to reemerge in the revival of their relationship. Amy and Elliot had noticed it in the synchronistic events, in the way they finished each other's thoughts, in the way they predicted what the other was doing. The more Amy began to meditate and open her mind, the more connected she felt to this phenomena. But, when it came to Elliot's illness, and although she sensed something, she felt a blockage. Perhaps it was such a heavy subject that the thoughts and feelings surrounding it weren't able to fit through whatever part of the mind these things flow through. As she walked to meet the Algrens for dinner something related to his illness once again began to push upward. Like something slowly rising from deepwater there was only a faint hue of it. A shadow from the abyss. Then it caught the light. Shape and color began to emerge, but still abstract and inaccessible to the conscious mind. Perhaps it was just a trick of light. Maybe it was nothing. She let it go as she sat down for dinner and trusted whatever she was sensing would reveal itself in time. It wasn't until dinner was over and she had almost reached their room that it became clear to her, suddenly popping up, right there on the surface, in the light.

Elliot was still awake, sitting up in bed. There was a book in his hand but he didn't seem engaged in it. Instead he seemed more focused on Amy, in what she noticed was a sort of nervous energy. She quietly said hello to him as she set her purse down and then stood at the foot of his bed. Sensing her seriousness he straightened up. He asked her how dinner was and rather matter of factly she told him it was delicious. With that, their back and forth abruptly stopped, and considering their high earlier in the day, this certainly qualified as an awkward silence. It was where he should have asked what Terry had to say about his illness but he couldn't bring himself to. Instead, she sat on the edge of the bed, near him, but not close to him, and leveled unflinching eyes on him. Bad news was coming, this Elliot knew, and he didn't need a psychic connection to know that. It also seemed obvious this bad news would be whatever Terry had told her about his illness. But something didn't feel right to Elliot. It felt as though Amy was coming at him with something else. Like he was in trouble. Perhaps there was some psychic connection or perhaps it was his growing paranoia. Either way, he was freaking out, and wanted her to speak and just get it over with.

"So, there's something we need to discuss," she finally began and then took a beat, still looking him straight in the eyes, and seemed to wait, as if he should take it from there, her eyes drifted down to her hand which she was absentmindedly moving in a circle over the bedcover. Breaking the feeling of eternal silence, she began speaking again, but taking her time, and leaving cliffhanger pauses which Elliot became increasingly anxious about.

"Something my therapist has been telling me…" She started a lot of sentences theses days by quoting her therapist, which had seemed hopeful until tonight. "So…She says I need to listen, to really listen, and that sometimes it may take awhile before I'll hear what is being said. . . What is really being said. . .To know what is really happening," and here she looked up from the bedcover and bore her eyes deep into his.

"I don't think I understand. What are we talking about?" He winced as he asked this. The longer this took the more he suspected this wasn't bad news from Terry but something worse, something she had pieced together. His lie.

"Ever since the night you told me you were dying. There was something I couldn't put my finger on. I was so impressed by your positive attitude towards everything. Your courage, your strength. . . And this is my mistake because in some ways I gave those qualities complete credit for our relationship miracle. I didn't want to see this because I didn't want anything to threaten that miracle," once again she paused but this pause felt extremely dramatic and he knew this was it. It was the cliffhanger moment for Elliot, but he knew where this one was going, and so he braced himself for the drop, "you lied. I know you aren't sick. "

From his reflection in her pupils he thought he saw his soul evaporate. His head dropped and he stared at his lap. What could he say? Deny it, plead his case, beg for mercy, run for it, or do nothing. Not knowing what to do he chose the do nothing route and just sat there, waiting for it, whatever it would be. But she too did nothing, she too waited. It wasn't so much that her intuition was wrong, it was her interpretation of that intuition that was wrong.

"You made it up because you just didn't want to go to dinner tonight. That's why you lied about being sick tonight. And you didn't want to go to dinner because you're afraid to get your hopes up. Because you feel like if do get your hopes up, and God forbid, you're once again told there's nothing they can do, well, then you have to accept dying all over again. And it's that courage and dignity you've shown which I have found so attractive, and I will be right there with you, facing death, accepting death, if that is where this ultimately leads you. But first let's give this a fight, okay? And let's direct that courage and dignity of yours towards that fight." With tears in her eyes she moved closer to him and took his hand into hers. The almost over-the-top, straight from the heart quality of her words, the sincerity in their outpouring, only compounded the already heavy load of guilt Elliot was carrying. "And Elliot, I will be with you every step of the way, and I love you. And I'm sorry."

"Please, please, don't say that you're sorry. Why are you saying you're sorry? You're not the one who should be sorry."

"Okay, okay, shhh-shhh, quite now. Rest. Just rest," she said in a soothing whisper as she climbed into the bed and tenderly cuddled up to him.

11

On Amy's phone was a text message notification from Talia, but Talia was just a cover-name, in actuality the message was from Todd. The status of their affair was not exactly clear after Amy told Todd about Elliot. What she had said to him was, "I need space. Please don't reach out to me unless I reach out to you." At the time she had hoped this would be a soft ending to the affair. That it would simply fade away. But she also wondered if there wasn't a part of her that still wanted to keep the option open. Regardless, she was clear that he shouldn't contact her until she contacted him first. This request was ignored by Todd. He had texted three times.

Per usual, his messages were coded. *Wondering if you want to reconsider application for funding grant*, read one text.   Another read, *deadline for funding grant is approaching. Need confirmation.* The most recent text, the one she responded to, read, *exciting update from district head, let's do lunch to celebrate.* Amy replied, *I have time Tuesday.*

After she pulled into the parking lot at the Hyatt she turned the car off and waited. For thirty minutes she waited in her car, unsure what to do. Todd texted twice, *here waiting,* and then, *getting hungry.* To which she replied, *taking care of something,* and then, *still taking care of something.*

From the time she responded to Todd and up until the moment she pulled into the parking lot Amy had been clear to herself about what she was going to do. But then something happened upon seeing the familiar scenery. Her heart rate increased, she felt a rush in her body, and reflexively she began seducing herself. It wasn't even about Todd. It was about the feeling she'd feed on since the affair started. *Indulge yourself. Escape.* This was the pitch from a voice in her head. All she had to do was slip out of the car, walk right into the hotel, go straight to that room, and shut the door. When it was done it would stay in that room and she could go back to her life. But she knew that wasn't the reality. The feeling some small part of herself was trying to sell didn't exist anymore. The thrill was gone. The closest thing to a thrill was a momentary compulsive rush quickly followed by depression, emptiness, and self-loathing. So, why not start the car and drive away? She owed Todd nothing. As if it would help, she began playing games of chance to make the decision for her. If the next car to pull in was white she'd drive off. If a car leaves the parking lot before another enters she'd go up to the room. That game didn't help, because no matter what decision was made for her she would talk herself out of it, and so she remained stuck. The entire situation was beginning to make her stomach churn.

Fortunately her car had automatically begun playing meditation sounds from the time she left work and as she sat there in the parking lot her mind finally gave in to those sounds. Closing her eyes she began to slow her thinking. *You can never go back to not knowing.* She opened her eyes and texted Todd.

After Amy texted Todd the change in plans, he texted back *but I already in room!* Not only was it sloppy texting, but it was a reckless and egregious violation of one of their rules. They had an agreed upon text format. A simple and clear coded way to communicate. *Come up, ready to eat. you.* He was being reckless which infuriated her. But she didn't reply. Instead she walked into the TGI Fridays, the one where they had started their affair all those years back, and sat in the very back booth.

The restaurant was quiet and mostly empty. The lunch rush was over. In its wake was the oily scent of the restaurant's deep fryer mingling with beer and whatever cleaner the busboy was spraying on the tables. This wasn't helping Amy's nausea. The busboy picked up a stack of dishes topped with food scraps and wadded napkins and walked past her going into the kitchen. The entire scene came into her mind, like a bird's eye view, and she knew the woman she saw sitting alone in the back booth waiting for Todd was not the woman she wanted to be. While she waited she tried to calm herself. Her body was hot with anger. A touch of anger was effective to some degree because it removed any softness but too much anger would be ineffective. She wanted to control her emotions, not let her emotions control her. She didn't want this to be a fight. There was also a level of respect she wanted to show, that was the reason she was doing this in-person and not via some unceremonious text message.

The waitress looked like she was still in high school but was probably in her twenties. She had streaks of red in her hair, dark eyeliner, red lipstick and an expectant look on her face. While the waitress was topping off Amy's water she asked if she was ready to order. Todd entered, bringing the hot air from outside with him, and he slide into the other side of the booth with an annoyed breath.

"You know, I don't have all day. So, are we gonna eat first, then go up?"

The waitress was about to scurry off for another menu and glass of water but Todd stopped her.

"Hey! Hi, yeah, we're kind of in a hurry. Um, I know what I want so let's just order right now. A spicy buffalo sauce burger with onion rings and a side of ranch, for me," he looked over at Amy.

"I'll just stick with the water, thank you," Amy said politely. When the waitress was out of earshot, Amy said, "don't ever text me like that again."

"Like what?"

"I think you know like what."

"Don't blow your cover?" he said with a hint of sarcasm.

It hadn't occurred to Amy until right then but Todd had nothing to lose personally if it all blew up. He was already divorced. But he did have something professionally to lose.

"If we can't respect each other's personal lives, let's at least respect our professional lives." Hopefully reminding him they worked for the same employer would sober him up. She could see he wanted to respond to that but he stopped himself, instead he shook his head and looked away from her. They sat in silence for an increasingly uncomfortable minute. The whole time he kept his gaze away from her but she kept her eyes on him. She could see his eyes welling up. He must have known what was coming and he was hurting from it. Amy felt love for him in that moment, not romantic love, but simply love for another human being who is hurting.

"Todd," she said gently. "Can you look at me? I want you to look at me, so you really hear this." When he looked at her the cynical attitude dropped. He was vulnerable, she could see that, so she treaded lightly. "This is over. We're no longer seeing each other. We're no longer communicating with each other. I, thank you, for the moments we had..." She felt a lump in her throat and barely got her last words out. She could feel the tears coming but was able to hold them at bay. Todd pounced on the emotional opening by reaching across the table and putting his hand over hers. The way he made the move was somewhat aggressive and it surprised Amy. It wasn't a gentle consoling gesture which she might have allowed. It was more like a dominant grab and hold, so she quickly pulled her hand back.

"Why are you doing this?" He asked

"We did agree there would be no questions if either one of

us were to end it."

"Yeah that was like four years ago. I think a lot changed since then."

"You're right, a lot has changed."

"Well, I'd just like to know why."

"You even have to ask me that?"

"Yeah, I do. Did something happen that I wasn't aware of?"

"My husband dying, for starters. Kind of makes a person think, you know. But you were aware of that, so. . ." she said looking at him in disbelief, "I can't believe you don't get it."

"And we agreed to cool it. Which I got. Totally."

"Goodbye, Todd," Amy gathered her purse and was about to stand.

"Wait. Please. Just, let me just say something first. Please… please," in Todd's soft plea there was that vulnerability again and when Amy hesitated, he continued, "I think with your husband dying that you actually need this, us, more than ever. This can be a place for you to escape to. Don't you agree?"

"Did you really believe this would go on forever, Todd? Us up in some room?"

"When he's gone this will be your primary relationship. We can, you know-"

"Move it out of room 304?"

"Well, I don't know, you know, just, I. . ." he bumbled for something to say, moving his hands in the air, as if they might form the words he couldn't come up with.

"Todd, I've thanked you. I've given this it's due. Now really listen to me. It's over. Not just over for now but it's over even if Elliot passes away."

"Okaaay, we have a spicy buffalo sauce burger and onion rings with a side of ranch," the waitress said as she rolled out of the kitchen, plate in hand. Amy set some cash on the table and walked away. As she put her hand on the door to leave, she stopped and looked back at Todd. He had craned himself around in his seat and was looking at her. Their eyes locked for a moment, and then she left.

***

After returning from their getaway Elliot woke up and was faced with the increasingly complicated conundrum his lie had created. There were certain realities coalescing which he would have to deal with but he was still determined he could somehow do otherwise. Generally work was his way to escape from any personal problems but having given notice they had granted him permission to work from home where he was finding it difficult to distract himself from personal problems. Nonetheless he tried to get his mind onto something other than his problems. During the pandemic he'd settled for an ad hoc work space in the spare bedroom but never really made it look official, so he finally began putting his home office in order. Throwing himself into the task he mounted a white board to the wall, he hung photos and art and he organized all the boxes and books that had been stacked in the corner. Somehow he even managed to slide an old couch all the way from the garage to his office. With the job done he collapsed on the couch. Drifting off to sleep his mind relented and he began ruminating over his predicament.

It was no longer possible to see the lie as some sort of magical mojo elixir making everything better for everyone. Nor could he allow himself to believe he was actually dying. Reality had sunk in, and yet there was a juvenile desire to pretend the lie was somehow separate from real life, or that it would just go away, or that it would just take care of itself. But it wouldn't take care of itself and it wasn't separate from real life. The lie was an inescapable truth which seemed to be connected to everything, and everybody in his life, and he had absolutely no idea what to do about it. The love he felt for Amy was greater than it had ever been and that love expanded on a daily basis but the more love he felt, the more guilt he felt. Extrapolating the effects that daily expansion of love would have on his conscience Elliot calculated that his future pain from the guilt would be unbearable unless something soon changed.

Mercifully he fell asleep and when he awoke from his nap it was dark and he was momentarily disoriented. As the physical surroundings began to make sense, the situation of his life returned to his consciousness and he groaned. Waking from naps had always brought him a dose of depression and certainly today was no exception. Despite his melancholy, a sore neck and even sorer lower back he managed to swing his legs onto the ground and stand up. Although it felt like it was midnight, his phone told him it was only seven o'clock. A strange hissing noise came from somewhere in the house. After shuffling down the dark hallway he saw light coming from the kitchen. He peered in. The hissing noise had been the sound of the kettle. The one faint light in the kitchen cast a shadow over Amy as she removed the kettle from the stove and poured herself tea. To Elliot's eye this was a hauntingly beautiful image. It began to lift him from depression and into a lucid dreamy state of mind. Just as he was about to say something she convulsed with a sob. Then another sob wracked her and the flood gates opened into one of those choking, short of breath, snot bursting cries. He wasn't sure what to do. It felt like emotional voyeurism to keep standing there doing nothing but he didn't want to cut off the emotional outpouring she clearly she needed to get out. So, he waited and when the torrent subsided he entered the kitchen. She let herself sink into his embrace. He didn't have to ask her what was wrong because he knew. At least he thought he knew.

Elliot dying was not the only reason Amy was crying. It was the cumulation of everything that had transpired that day. The break up with Todd. Stuffing her emotions and going to work. Returning home to a dark house that appeared to be empty inside and which made her imagine what a life without Elliot would be like. Then she found Elliot asleep on his office couch, in an office he had spent the day decorating, the sight of which brought to her a flood of warmth, and somehow that warmth was what broke the dam. The crying convulsions that followed were accompanied by brief intervals of serenity found in Elliot's arms, where she also found a love so full it was indescribable.

Sad old songs played from their sound system and as they held each other they swayed a bit. A slow-slow dance. They looked like the last couple on the dance floor, hanging on each after the music had stopped, long after closing time had come for them.

"I'm sorry," Elliot said.

"It's not your fault."

"No, it is."

"Actually, no. It's not. It's me," there was a tone in her voice, she was annoyed. The sensitivity which had allowed in so much love and sadness was turning towards anger, "can I just have that? Can I just be sorry for something and it not be yours to take on?"

"How could it be you? It's definitely my fault you're sad," his voice rising.

"Stop saying dying is your fault. Just don't. You sound like a martyr."

"Okay. Fine. But if it's not my fault, explain to me how it's your fault?"

Naturally they both felt responsible for Amy's sadness

because they were both responsible but for reasons they couldn't share with each other. Because to share it all, they would risk losing it all. So, hitting a sort of stalemate, they just held each other awhile longer without talking.

If Amy had believed ending the affair would allow herself to feel clean she was wrong. It would be harder than that to remove the dirt. There was also an aspect of her situation she had not foreseen. Something that added even more weight to her burden of guilt and shame. On one hand not confessing to Elliot her affair was the compassionate thing to do. Why break his heart when there was a strong possibility he would die? On the other hand his death was a convenient get out of jail free card, a way out from ever having to tell Elliot the truth and that is what made her feel so guilty and shameful. That his death would benefit her sin. Of course, he could beat this thing and live, and then what? It was what she wanted more than anything but if he lived did that mean she had to confess to him? And did that mean, to avoid confession, somewhere in her mind she wanted him to die? Of course not, but just having to address that thought was sickening to her.

"I don't want to fight," Amy whispered gently.

"Me neither."

"You know what's nice?"

"We're still holding each other."

"Yeah, we're still holding each other. That's what I was going to say."

"Really?"

"Can we try something?" Amy asked with a hint of excitement.

Meditation was a suggestion given to Amy by her therapist, Elaine. A suggestion Elaine gave to all of her clients at one time or another. The percentage of her clients that actually gave meditation a try was less than half. The percentage of those who made meditation a part of their lives was less that half of that. Given Amy's conscientious nature it shouldn't have been a surprise that she gave meditation a whole-hearted effort, but it was a surprise that she had enthusiastically made meditation part of her life. Not only that but she went all in. Singing bowls. Crystals. A gong. A meditation playlist. Cushions to sit on. All of this was arranged outside around their fountain. An inner voice wisely advised her that meditation did not come with a grading system, and this helped her remain light about the whole thing. Normally her inclination leaned towards compulsion and obsession until she mastered something. That, she was learning, was not the point of meditation, and so for the first time in her life she was doing something without self-imposed goalposts. The whole set up she created would have seemed silly to her a month ago and, to be honest, it still was but the difference was her perspective on feeling silly had changed. Meditation usually left her grinning, the same kind of grin Elliot had as they sat down on the cushions and she began serenading him with her singing bowl.

"Who are you?" He asked with a laugh. Despite it being his first time to try meditation, Elliot took to it surprisingly quickly, and much to Amy's delight he was soon sitting there with a placid expression on his face. She set the singing bowl down and joined him.

"Perhaps we don't have to go away in order to have sex." These were the first words spoken in almost twenty minutes. Elliot's eyes opened and they were gleaming. Then he smiled, big.

"That sounds great," he chuckled, " technically, we've had sex at home before. Not often, nor, how should I put it. . ."

"I'll rephrase that," Amy jumped in, "We don't have to go

away in order to have really great sex."

"Really?"

"Your office."

"Okay. Now?"

"Just go in there and start working on something. Then I'll come in after."

He was curious why he needed to work on something but he knew enough not to question a moment like that. There were times in life when you just have to ride the wave. This was one of those times, so he simply smiled and sauntered off to his office.

While they had been meditating Amy had a random thought about Elliot's home office and it had aroused her sexually. Initially this didn't make sense to Amy but she knew enough to follow through on her instinct, knowing there were times not to question, that the answers sometimes reveal themselves intellectually only when they want to and often that can come after the fact. So, while Elliot went to his office, she busied herself with menial tasks around the house. Then it came to her, why she had this idea. The answer was obvious and made her feel a bit silly in good way. The reason she felt sexually aroused was because his office felt separate from their home. It was different. His work was so abstract to her that it held an aesthetic quality. The numbers and symbols were like graphic art. The equations like poems in a foreign language. And stepping into it was like stepping into his work and fucking at his work would be taboo and taboo excited her because you could be caught. Of course, actually fucking at work and actually being caught would be too much for her, but this wasn't. This was thrilling yet safe. All the excitement with none of the shame.

Amy waited as long as she could, busying herself with mundane tasks like cleaning the kitchen counters. Feeling a sufficient amount of task completion she left one world and entered another when she quietly stepped into his office and quietly shut the door. He casually swiveled his desk chair to face her. As she moved closer he pulled her in and began to undress her in a slow and deliberate way. They were completely naked and he explored her body while she stood over him. They were completely present with each other, making frequent eye contact, and they spoke to each other, but not in a way to remove themselves emotionally, but as a way to indicate pleasure and desire.

"Take your clothes off. I want to straddle you right here on the chair," she directed him and so he gently guided her down onto his lap while she guided him inside of her. They began right there on the chair, then moved around the room, to different locations and into different positions. What began gently and quietly built to a passionate finale full of ecstatic howling and moaning. Finally their entangled bodies collapsed on the couch. And once again they promised, "to do that a lot more."

***

After making love in Elliot's office they ate dinner, went to their bedroom, and got in bed together. It was a cold night so they snuggled up to stay warm. On the edge of sleep their conversation felt like stream of consciousness moving freely and deeply from one place to another. For years things had been very different from this. They had slept together but apart, as if there had been an invisible line dividing their mattress in half, a line one didn't cross. Often one of them would be asleep before the other got into bed. Other times they would both lay in bed, looking at their phone or reading something. With a perfunctory goodnight they would turn off the lights and that was that. But that had changed, and they now said "I love you" before going to sleep, often accompanied by a kiss. Occasionally they held each other till they fell asleep. On a rare night, like this particular night, they would talk into the early hours of the morning.

"I feel like there's something you've held inside," Amy said.

"What do you mean?" Elliot wasn't sure he liked where this was going.

"There are just details that you withhold about certain things."

"What things?"

"Well, a lot actually but right now I'm just talking about your childhood."

"Oh," he seemed a bit too relieved.

"What did you think I was going to ask about?"

"Nothing. I don't know. It's just kind of a random thing to bring up. I feel like we've talked about my childhood before."

"Only bullet points really. The truth is, I don't know what it was really like for you."

"The truth is, I don't either, really. Bullet points are easier for me," he was surprised by his own candor and suddenly he had an eagerness to share with her and so he said, "ask me anything."

"I've always wondered what was it like knowing you were adopted and your brother and sister weren't."

"God," Elliot said searching for a place to start, "I did say 'ask me anything.' That's a big question."

"Maybe the biggest."

"No, that's not the biggest."

"What's the biggest question?"

"It's not a big deal."

"It's not? You just said it's not the biggest question, so what is it?"

It was a big deal, actually, and Amy sensed this so she held Elliot just a bit tighter. He took a big breath, trying to release the tension in his body, "oh boy, we're really going there."

"I think we're already there, Elliot."

"I've never told anyone this."

"Told anyone what?"

"It's nothing dark. It's just… complicated."

"I know Brian and Karen have alluded to certain things, about your parents being a bit erratic. But no one has ever spelled it out."

"Because it's one of those situations that's not easily spelled out. It's not like they abused us in some really demonstrative way. That wasn't it. And saying something like, 'they were crazy at times,' isn't really accurate and doesn't quite do it justice."

"Did your parents love each other?"

"Did they loved each other?. . .Yes. I think. I don't know, actually."

"Did they fight?"

"They did fight. Oh, yeah. Usually on the weekends when they had some drinks. And in between the fights there was this low grade tension, kind of like the fight was waiting to happen. And then they had these moments where it was fine. Only moments, though. I didn't understand why they had this dynamic. Until later. At times Mom could be stoic to the point of not caring and then she would love you like no other. She might lay into you, in this really surgical way but then she would blanket you with affection. Dad was actually pretty consistent in how he treated us but his moods weren't consistent. He was pretty checked out at times and that would be hard, but generally he was kind. He could be really sweet when he was present, but he was also manic at times. Yeah, they were both bipolar, in their own ways," he said with an almost forced chuckle, "highs and lows, you know. But they were both mostly caring. They expressed love for us at times.

It was a loving household in some ways but not easy."

"So, when you said there was something you've never told anyone, what was it?"

"It's something that would be good to finally tell someone."

"About?"

"My adoption."

"And am I that someone you want to tell?" She asked sweetly.

"Yeah. You are," he gave her gentle kiss before continuing, "so, this was basically a good family. I was loved. I was lucky I was adopted by them, and God knows, I could have ended up in a horrific situation. Mine was not horrific, so who am I to complain?"

"You're not complaining. There's a difference. I won't let you complain but I will encourage you to share honestly with me."

"I was treated fairly in the sense that all of us kids were given equal amounts of good and bad. My parents had their issues but I didn't feel singled out. . . Not until later."

***

Not knowing their origins is difficult for some adoptees and the question of who their birth parents are is a natural curiosity. The other question adoptees have, perhaps the most powerful of all, is why were they adopted, and many will never know that answer even after finding out who their birth parents are. Somewhere around kindergarten Elliot's parents, Bruce and Gayle, told him he was adopted. So, he asked, "the people that had me, what are their names?" he was told "their names were Taylor and Shauna." At that age Elliot didn't catch the distinction between "are" and "were" when he was told his birth parent's names.

"Did you know them?" Elliot asked his adopted parents.

"Yes," his Mom said, she gave his Dad a furtive look. In

fact, they knew Elliot's birth parents very well but they didn't tell him about that. Not yet.

"Why didn't they keep me?"

"Well," his Dad started but then hesitated.

"Where are they now?"

"They passed away," his Mom said.

"What does passed away mean?" Elliot asked.

"Well, that means they are no longer alive," she clarified.

"You mean they're dead?"

"Yes," his Mom said with a nod.

Little Elliot looked to his Dad, as if for confirmation, and his Dad gave a solemn nod of his head

"Was I a baby when they died?"

"Yes, a beautiful little baby. Almost a year old," his Dad said affectionately, trying to fight back tears. Gayle noticed Bruce was on the verge of crying and it seemed to make her uncomfortable, and she was about to invent a reason to wrap up the conversation when they noticed Elliot's focus was now on his toys. The magnitude of what he had just learned was beginning to sink in and perhaps he needed to focus on something else as a way of coping with everything. His parents, who were sitting on either side of him, waited a few minutes, and then quietly both left the room. When Elliot was all alone the crying came like a geyser and when it did, he was racked with sobs. Both of his parents returned to the room and hugged him. Usually three way hugs were a goofy sort of thing for Elliot but this was different. It was protective. Elliot was experiencing a primal pain. It was the most painful experience of his life but also, in a strange way, one of the best because it was the most loving experience he had ever had. And it would remain the most loving experience he would ever have with his parents.

That day he had asked many questions, as a child will, but

for some inexplicable reason he didn't ask how his birth parents died. Maybe that was too much for him at the time. Several years later when he was taking out the trash, out of nowhere, the question popped into his head, and so he went into his parents bedroom and asked them.

"It was a car accident," his Dad said.

"Was I with them?"

"No, thank god," his Mom said.

"Where was I?"

"With us," his parents both said.

Elliot stared at his parents in confusion. How was he already with his parents? Hadn't he been adopted after they died? His mind was trying to fit all the pieces together but they kept floating away. He tried to reach for the floating pieces but he began to feel weightless, like being in zero gravity, which was something he had recently learned about in school. But zero gravity only happened on the moon, as far as he knew, so why was it happening to him right there on earth? His parents exchanged a look, they could see Elliot's confusion, and when they both put their hands on him, it seemed to pull him safely back down to earth.

"Your parents were friends of ours," his Dad said with warmth in his eyes, "good friends."

The four of them, his birth parents and adopted parents, had grown up together. They had all remained in contact and when Taylor and Shauna had Elliot they all reconnected because they were all parents. Brian was seven and Karen was five when Elliot was born. When Elliot's birth parents wanted to have a date night they would drop him off with Bruce and Gayle and that's what they did the night they died in car accident. It was a drunk driver. She hit them head on. The drunk driver and his parents all died. Since Elliot didn't have any extended family capable of caring for him, the adoption was granted to Bruce and Gayle. And that was how they became his parents.

It was tragic but also heartwarming. His parents had died but their good friends were able step in. It was very conflicting for Elliot over the years, to be grateful for something that came from the death of his parents. Despite his parents imperfections, it was a decent upbringing, the kind that would have brought comfort and relief to his birth parents.

There were, however, certain things about his parents that were not easy, and those things grew worse with time. Elliot's Dad died when Elliot was a senior in high school which felt like an exaggerated version of his Dad's worst quality, he was now literally not present. Dad was only fifty eight when he passed away. When Elliot was in his first year of college, years before meeting Amy, his Mom had a stroke. This seemed to exaggerate one of her worst qualities, a verbal mean streak. Whether it was from the stroke or not, the doctors didn't know, but his Mom had developed early dementia. At the time they did not realize it was early dementia, they had just assumed, that along with the stroke, she was becoming a bit more moody and unpredictable. They also factored in the emotional transitions in her life as influencing her moods, after all her husband had just died rather young and her kids had all grown up. They optimistically wrote it off as a phase.

Before her children agreed to moving her into a full time care facility Gayle was brought home to recover from her stroke because they believed, at the time, she would recover. Initially Elliot tried to visit at least once week. He was living in the dorm at his college which was a two hour drive. The kids had divided up the different responsibilities related to helping their mom.

Karen had moved home to help during the week which

was slowly beginning to overwhelm her. Naively she had thought she would balance work and caring for her Mom, while saving some rent money. It would take a year of this and her first nervous breakdown to convince her the arrangement was untenable. Brian was less reliable for the in-person things. He was already making a decent living so he opted for dropping by a few times a week to have a quick conversation with his mom and charm her into temporary happiness. He was also able to hire a maid to come twice a week who would clean and make meals for the week. Karen complained about this but Elliot didn't see the problem. Everyone did what they could. Often Karen would take Elliot's visits as a chance to take a day or two off and that is what she did on this particular day. Until that day Elliot had been considering moving home for the summer to help with her. After the events of that day he decided to stay in the dorm for the summer.

Before leaving, Karen had given Elliot the usual update on their Mom. Which was that Mom seemed to be getting around the house better but she still was weak and would seem to become stymied both physically and mentally after brief moments of exertion. Karen went over the routine which Elliot knew by heart at this point. He didn't take this personally because he knew Karen was the type of person who treated herself this way. She had to anxiously go over and over lists and she had to practice and rehearse almost everything to the point of ad nauseam. Generally this behavior came off as overly conscientious but occasionally it would veer into what a psychologist would later diagnose as a neurosis. To prevent Karen from going over the routine a second time he gently put his hand on her shoulder and clearly said, "thank you, I've got it." If you did this sympathetically and with eye contact Karen would generally catch herself with a breath. Then she was off, to spend the weekend with her new boyfriend Doug, who she would later marry.

The mood of the house had changed over the last several years and seemed to reflect its primary inhabitant's mood, their Mom, which wasn't a particularly pleasant mood most of the time. And there was the smell of course. It wasn't necessarily a bad smell, just a depressing smell. A combination of mildew, walls imbued with oil from years of cooking, and some unidentifiable slightly rank human scent that seemed to have mysteriously come after the stroke. Opening the doors and windows helped only a little and not much at all on hot days, as the heat seemed to bake the scent. Along with the smell was the sensation that everything felt heavy when you were inside the house. The air felt heavy. Movement felt heavy. The light felt heavy. The light seemed darker than it had when they were growing up. Even with the blinds open it was dark and heavy inside. They had switched everything to the brightest lightbulbs and this finally made a difference.

Elliot generally used his weekends to study and had always preferred a quiet space to study but the quiet there was different. It bore into him. The soundtrack of the house came from the old refrigerator's loud humming and occasional gargling sounds, occasionally accompanied by soap operas and entertainment news coming from his Mom's bedroom. So, Elliot learned to study to music.

That day Elliot checked in on his Mom and she was napping. Elliot prepared his bedroom to study for his upcoming calculus final. He put on his John Coltrane CD, turned on all the lights, cracked a window, and lit some incense. Just as he sat down he heard the bell. It was one of those large old-fashioned school teacher bells, brass with a wood handle. This meant she was awake and needed help. Her speech was slow and had a slurry quality to it but it was much improved over the last few months. Physically she could move, just not very well. Sometimes she needed help getting out of bed and on her feet, like she did that day. With shaky cold hands she tightly clutched onto Elliot's arm while her feet reached the ground. Once her feet were safely planted, she stood up and steadied herself. She had been a youthful beauty most of her life, and technically she was not an old woman but she looked like one. How had this happened in two years? Elliot could list the reasons why but it still didn't make sense to him.

"Got it," she said with a nod and let go of his hands. She shuffled slowly to the adjacent bathroom and shut the door. Around the toilet, bath and shower they had installed rails for her to hold. The bathtub now had a textured floor to help prevent slipping. He could hear the tinkle of her peeing, then the flush of the toilet. She cleared her throat several times and then ran the faucet. She came back into the room and with Elliot's help got back in bed. At her request Elliot added pillows to help prop her up. He was about to turn on the TV for her afternoon shows and get her afternoon snack when she motioned for him to sit on the edge of her bed. She set her eyes on him with a furrowed brow in a look that seemed to convey a mixture of sadness, sympathy and irritability. Elliot felt a strange uncomfortable tingle in his chest. The look was familiar and typically preceded unpleasant words

"I want to tell you something," she said almost conspiratorially. Elliot gave a nod, maintained eye contact and waited. "I never resented you," she said bluntly, letting it hang there.

"Um, well, I never felt like you resented me. I always felt love from you," he was deeply confused by the way she began the conversation. Was she talking about the fact that he was adopted? Was she simply reassuring him? If that was her intention, it actually didn't reassure him, it actually made him wonder if she did resent him, so he asked, "did you resent me?"

"I just said otherwise," she said with a huff, "that's why I'm saying it."

"Well, I'm glad," he believed her but could also sense there was more, "so, why would you need to tell me that?"

Until this point she had maintained eye contact in that head hanging, unblinking way a drunk might level their gaze. Now she took a clear breath, raised her head and looked out her window. The light washing over her face brought out her beauty. In this moment Elliot saw her as the mom he had grown up with. Her poise and youth. He hoped she might rally from this phase and find another chapter in her life.

"You know how much I loved your Dad? How very much we were in love?"

"Yes, I know."

"It didn't always seem that way though did it?"

"Ah, no. That's true."

"Oh, Bruce, too much fighting, " she said wistfully as her eyes raised upwards.

Then her expression darkened and it seemed like the light in the room did too. Her head sagged and slowly she swiveled it back towards him and she leveled that gaze again. The one that made him uncomfortable and this time he knew that look was for him. From experience over the past couple of years he knew she was about to say something mean, or strange, or both. He reminded himself that she was sick and not herself since both the stroke and Dad's death. But nothing could have prepared him for what she was about to say.

"Well, you should know Bruce is your father."

"I know that Bruce is my dad."

"And your birth father."

"Taylor's my birth father."

"No. Bruce is."

"What?" Elliot's mind was beginning to scramble, "so, then, you're really my birth mother?"

"No," his Mom said quietly, "Shauna is."

Elliot's mind lost focus. The pieces didn't fit. They were all up in the air again. It was like the time he was told his birth parents died in a car accident. Was his Mom telling him that Bruce was actually his dad? And that meant Bruce had an affair with Shauna.

His Mom's soft sniffling snapped him out of his thoughts and brought him back to earth. Tears trickled down her stoic face.

"So...?" he trailed off and she softly nodded, then leaned her head back and closed her eyes. When her hand reached out towards the side of her bed he understood what she wanted. He grabbed a tissue for her and himself. After a few minutes of sitting at the side of her bed, while she lay quietly with eyes closed, he went into the kitchen to get her applesauce. When he returned he set the applesauce down next to her, he turned on her shows, and then walked to his room, shut the door and began to study.

They never spoke of it again, and Elliot kept it to himself, telling no one.

***

"There's a way to find out if it's true," Amy said.

"I know."

"All you need is one hair from everyone. There's probably one on your pillow right now. And then get one from Brian, one from Karen."

"Don't."

"Are you sure?"

"I'm sure."

"So, you don't plan on telling Brian and Karen?"

"No. And I hope you won't."

"Of course not. That's up to you. And I won't secretly collect a hair from everyone and take them to some lab. As tempting as that may be."

"I know, I trust you, Amy."

"Thank you, but maybe you should consider telling them."

Elliot closed his eyes and pulled her closer. Before they fell asleep in each other's arms Amy asked Elliot one more question, "don't you want to find out?"

"No."

"Why not?"

12

Over the next several days the reality that Elliot must somehow deal with his lie had begun to set in. This realization had sent Elliot's emotional pendulum swinging from hope to despair. Back and forth it went until it suddenly he was stuck, on despair. Unable to move, trapped in the midst of a mental breakdown. It was as if he were a cemented version of himself, a statue in the center of his small home office posed ridiculously to represent the most anxious man in the world. With slumping posture, knees about to buckle, a bowed head with both hands clutching his hair in a death grip, he was the embodiment of emotional distress. A memory descended upon Elliot in that moment, it carried the necessary wisdom to release him from the emotional and physical paralysis in which he'd become trapped.

When Elliot was a little boy, perhaps seven or eight, his Dad told him a story. A very old parable from the book of Huainanzi written in the Kingdom of Huainan over 2000 years ago.

From what Elliot could remember the parable began in the countryside where a farmer's only horse had run off to the land of barbarians. The farmer's neighbor said, "that is most unfortunate." The farmer replied, "maybe." The horse returned and brought seven wild barbarian horses with it. The neighbor said, "that is most fortunate." The farmer replied, "maybe." The farmer's son tried to break one of the seven wild horses but it threw him and badly broke his leg. The neighbor said, "that is most unfortunate." The farmer replied, "maybe." Soon a war broke out with the barbarians and all the young men were sent out to fight. Almost every young man who had been sent to fight died in battle, but the farmer's son was not sent to the war because of his broken leg. The neighbor said, "that is most fortunate." The farmer replied, "maybe." And so it goes.

Brought down to his knees, Elliot pleaded aloud, "why can't I be like the farmer?" Suddenly, upon seeing himself, he began to laugh.

***

Following the breakdown in his office, the pendulum swung from despair and back towards hope. But something felt different about this, it felt settled. Less like hope and more like faith. That afternoon Elliot continued plowing his way through a pile of work he had to complete before he was officially resigned from his job. As soon as it was done, he was done. With the wind in his sails, he went at it vigorously, until the winds died out. Calmly, he set his work aside and while eating a late lunch made the decision to set aside official work and devote the rest of the day to his theory.

As he rinsed off his dishes his mind once again believed he was dying. This was the first time in many days that his mind played this trick. A terrible sadness filled him because he didn't want to leave this life he loved so much. Then he remembered that he wasn't dying. He was alive. *Alive!* Suddenly he was filled with a warm swell of gratitude unlike any he had ever felt. Gratitude for simply being alive. And considering the extraordinary amounts of gratitude he had been feeling recently that was saying a lot. And when he meant grateful for being alive, he meant all of it. Not just the beautiful part of being alive, not just the wonderful, and the joyful but the challenging, the difficult, and the painful as well. *All of it.*

"All of it, all of it, all of it," he chanted in goofy, bouncy sort of way as he finished wiping off the counters and got himself a glass of water. That's when he noticed his sister-in-law Mona walking up to the house. The mantra stopped. There was a knock on the front door. Fear and cowardice stabbed into gut! He could hide from her. Pretend he wasn't there. Then he caught himself. *Why? What the fuck? Fear?* An almost maniacal smile spread across his face and that great feeling swelled up inside of him again, and he began chanting, "all of it, all of it, all of it," all the way to the door.

"Mona! Come on in," Elliot said with a warm smile and stepped aside. Mona walked in and he closed the door behind her. They stood in the kitchen, both holding a glass of water. It was slightly awkward at first. This was the first time Mona had visited Elliot alone and Elliot wasn't sure what to make of it, given the circumstances with her and his brother. It broke Elliot's heart to see her the way she was looking. She was an attractive woman, the kind of beauty that people sense entering the room even before they see her but even her beauty couldn't hide the toll the divorce was taking.

Looking at Elliot, Mona was having the opposite experience. There had been no toll taken from him. What she expected to see was a weak, tired, and frightened man. A broken man. But, not only did he not look sick, he looked better than ever. His energy and his confidence were attractive. His eyes emanated a type of light that was drawing her to him. This was not a dying man, this was a man alive.

"So, you were saying, you were in the neighborhood to pick up Dulce from a friends. . ."

Mona had lost her concentration thinking about how good Elliot looked and how terrible she looked. What was he doing that she wasn't?

"Ah, yeah, I just thought you might be home because, ah, you know."

"I do know."

"You've been on my mind."

"Thank you. Likewise."

"And in my prayers."

"Likewise, again."

They both chuckled. In the pause that followed they both looked at their glasses and when they both noticed they had done the same "awkward moment" thing, they both chuckled again.

"You seem fantastic, if you don't mind my saying," she said.

"I don't."

"May I ask you something?"

"Please ask."

"What's your secret?"

"My secret?"

"Yeah, you look so happy and so good. Considering your situation, you know, is there some secret?"

There were several ways to answer this question. There was the truth, the big truth, the one that would have rocked Mona, but he wasn't going to do that. There was also another truth, one he would gladly share with her, or anyone, which he was about to share when she began to cry.

"It's just, you look so good, and, I don't know," she was getting her words out between restrained sobs, "and I want that. I feel terrible and I can't. . . not even Dulce's smile makes me happy," it was as if he watched her heart break as she said that about Dulce's smile. Reflexively Elliot wrapped his arms around her and her body collapsed into his. She sobbed for a minute and then held on to him for another before she separated herself and grabbed a paper towel off the counter to clear her nose.

"Thank you. I needed that," she put her hand on his arm, "you still haven't told me your secret to looking great when life sucks."

"I'm no guru."

"Neither are most gurus."

"When I think I'm dying, I'm happy to be alive," he said truthfully and then added, "Mona, good things can come from bad things. This is your life. Live it. All of it."

Perhaps it was the words he said, perhaps it was the timing of the words, or perhaps the words gave Mona the permission she needed, but whatever it was, she began to radiate. He could see electricity within her come to the surface and then he could feel it.

"Yeah," Mona nodded her head, "Yeah. Fuck yeah. That's it." Her brow furrowed and her eyes bore into his with this intense knowing look that almost knocked Elliot over. A glowing light seemed to wash over her, she smiled, and just like that she was back. The Mona he remembered was back. She threw her arms around him, gave him a kiss on the lips, told him she loved him, said goodbye and left.

Watching Mona walk away from the house a lot of thoughts crossed Elliot's mind. Mona could be effusive and spontaneous with her emotions, still the kiss took him by surprise. Partially because it felt forceful enough to go just beyond a peck, and there was a wetness to her lips, that consciously or subconsciously, seemed to intimate an exchange of fluids. Of course, it all happened so fast and was probably just collateral from the extreme swings of her own emotional pendulum. Probably it was just any number of overly personal reactions she was having. She was probably over-tipping waiters and crying to strangers that asked how her day was. And to add to it, he had inspired her, greatly, and she reacted to that with a passionate outburst of pure love. Nothing untoward about that. Yes, there was a certain power to the energy he had. This he knew. He had seen its effects on Amy, on his siblings, and on is friends. *Dying*, Elliot thought, *has given me a platform to inspire people.*

With the goodness of his lie reaffirmed, Elliot determined right then and there he would make a clean, albeit dishonest, break from his lie, not just for his own benefit but for that of others. In revealing the lie, everything would crumble, including what he had inspired in others.

***

The next day Elliot woke up thinking about Mona's visit and about his brother and when he checked his phone, he happily saw he had received a text message from Brian. However, the text Brian had sent, and the ensuing text exchange, felt ominous to Elliot.

We need to talk, Brian had texted at 12:30 am.

Yeah, okay. Let's grab a late breakfast/early lunch somewhere? Elliot replied at 8:30 am.

It wasn't until noon when Brian responded and his text said he wasn't good to drive, didn't really want to go anywhere but asked Elliot if he would drop by. Brian not being 'good to drive' did not sound promising and Elliot had a gut-feeling that by going to Brian's he would be entering turbulent waters. That ominous gut-feeling increased as he approached the half open front door at Brian's. For an instant he feared he might find Brian dead inside. Elliot shook off the intrusive thought, knocked on the door and called out Brian's name as he entered. The place smelled and sounded like a frat house on a Sunday morning. The odor of stale beer and weed wafted up into Elliot's nose. Hip-hop blasted from the house speakers and the sounds of a football game blared from the television. Stepping further into the house Elliot found Brian sprawled out on the couch, feet on the coffee table, one hand behind his head, the other holding the remote. Along with remnants of take out food, there was a bong on the table, a few beer cans and a half drank bottle of whiskey. Brian was definitely not good to drive.

"Hey. Brian."

"Whoa, hey," Brian was mildly startled, "didn't hear you come in." Elliot noticed his brother's demeanor darkly shift as he sat up and began packing a bong load. Elliot remained standing.

"Bachelor living, huh?"

"Yeah, Dulce's with Mona. She's already rented a furnished place. Can you believe that shit?"

"Yeah, you guys are sort of sharing it, right? The co-parent thing?"

Brian ignored Elliot. He took his rip from the bong and set it aside but he didn't sit back in the couch. Instead he remained as he was, sitting on the edge of the couch, hunched forward. Brian's eyes were on the game but Elliot could tell his mind was somewhere else. When Elliot asked him if everything was alright, Brian flashed him a hostile look, and then looked back at the game. Standing there, Elliot began to feel exposed, vulnerable, and cold, so he sat down in one of the large chairs that were on either side of the couch but it didn't help him feel comfortable.

"What happened yesterday with Mona?" The way Brian said it made Elliot's stomach drop. It was not so much a question as it was an accusation. Elliot's mind flashed to the kiss. It really wasn't anything other than an innocent expression of familial love. But maybe that was only how Elliot perceived it and not how Mona intended it. No, no, it couldn't be that. But, what? And then Brian finally turned to look at Elliot, and shook his head, "all I know is we were talking, I happened to mention you weren't working anymore, she said she was near your house and was going to stop by. The next thing I know. . ." Brian drifted off but his eyes remained on Elliot.

"The next thing you know?"

"Alexa everything off." The music shut off. The television shut off. Rather than bringing peace and quiet, the absence of all the noise actually made the situation even more uncomfortable. Finally Brian looked away from Elliot and stared down into the floor, not saying a word, just slowly shaking his head.

"Thanks for coming over," surprisingly Brian's tone had shifted. It veered away from anger and was now heading toward self-pity, "I've worn everyone out with my complaining. Friends get tired of this drama shit after awhile. I really didn't want to bother you, you know, with everything you're going through," Brian took a deep breath in and let out an even more exaggerated exhale, and then the edge came into his voice, he looked at Elliot once again, "what'd you say to her?"

"I'm really confused, Brian. What did I say to her? What did she say I said to her?"

"She said you inspired her to move Dulce across the country."

"She said I told her to move Dulce across the country?"

"Well, no, she didn't say that. Just that you inspired her."

"I did inspire her, but we didn't talk about your divorce or Dulce. Just that she was feeling hopeless and she noticed I wasn't hopeless. She asked me my secret and I told her. And I inspired her. A general inspiration for living."

"Alight. Sorry, I'm not pissed at you. I'm just pissed because they're moving. Mona's moving away with Dulce. A five hour flight. Another city. I'll never see my daughter," Brian began to look to Elliot with fear and uncertainty, "it's a complete disaster. . . right? And I have to fight it. . . right? She can't just unilaterally decide that. She can't just take our daughter and go away. . . right?""

At various points Brian clearly wanted agreement from Elliot, or reassurance, or something, but Elliot didn't want to dive into the fire. His brother was hot and Elliot didn't want to get burned. So he waited and they shared the silence. Elliot could see his vulnerability. He was lost and in pain. The tears welled up. Elliot felt terrible, he felt as though his hubris had somehow caused this situation, this pain. All because he had "inspired" Mona. As if he had given Mona this fire of the God's, but it wasn't his to give, it was irresponsible and Mona had used the fire he gave her to burn Brian. And now in this Promethean unraveling within Elliot's mind, it was Brian who the God's had chained to a rock, and it was Brian whose liver was being eaten by an eagle. But it was Elliot who should be punished.

"I'm sorry, I'm sorry," Elliot blurted out, "you shouldn't be punished for what I said."

"Look, it's not your fault, okay. I didn't mean to blame you. So, she was inspired by whatever you said, but you know what, and no offense, she's giving you too much credit. She was going to do this anyway."

"Really?"

"Probably. Anyways, I need your help."

"Okay,"

"So, so what do I do? Do I have any rights? I mean. . ." Brian threw his hands out and shrugged.

"Brian, you need a lawyer."

"I know."

"These are legal questions."

"I know. I just. . . it becomes official then."

"Does she have a lawyer?"

"Yeah."

"Then it's official."

"You know how fucking rich her dad is, right? Well, her

lawyer, I looked him up, he's some kind of divorce lawyer celebrity. I mean, I can afford a decent one but I can't afford a battle with some legal dream team. The guy's on the fucking news all the time as some kind of legal expert."

"It'll be okay."

"I'm so fucking overwhelmed."

"Take it one step at a time. First get the lawyer."

"That's funny."

"What?"

"One step at a time. She's saying I should get sober."

"Maybe you should."

"It's a fucking divorce tactic."

"Maybe you should take her advice on that one."

"And then there's her fucking PR tour," Brian sat back up, he was hot again, "over to your house. And then to Karen's! She's all buddied up with Karen. Yeah! On top of everything, now she makes up with Karen. Now she does. The irony. And I'm the scapegoat for all their problems. You know, I feel bad for Karen but I've had to fucking feel bad for her all my life. Walk on eggshells. She said I was a bully. Was I bully?"

"Not really."

"Not really? Was I or wasn't I?"

"You can be rough, not in a mean way, but Karen's sensitive. I just think you guys need to forgive each other. I mean, you guys basically got along, until Mom's health troubles."

"That was a not an easy stretch," Brian sank back in the couch again. All the hot air was gone, "Not easy at all. What the fuck with our parents? Talk about early exits."

While they sat in silence Elliot took a better look around. It was dismaying. Brian had regressed. The worst of his college-aged persona. The slob, the partier, the emotionally confused kid. All that combined with the real grown up problems of a divorce from his wife and having a daughter to show up and be a father for. This lost man-child breaking his own heart wasn't his brother and Elliot knew that but he worried Brian didn't. He wanted to find the magic words for Brian but he couldn't find them so he asked, "how are you, Brian, really?" And for the next fifteen minutes Brian poured his lonely, sad, hopeless heart out. Some of it was heartbreaking to hear. Some of it was pathetic. Some of it was frustrating. But Elliot just listened nonetheless. Eventually Brian began drifting further and further away and he wasn't even looking at Elliot anymore, he was just talking to himself. At that point Elliot worried about Brian's mental health. Finally, when it became clear he wouldn't stop swimming against the currents of his own negativity, Elliot pulled him out.

"Brian. It's time to stop talking," this wasn't said harshly, just as a simple matter of fact, "I love you. You need to start listening. To everything," Elliot said.

"I love you, yeah, sorry. Here I am, whining, and ranting, and you're facing death. Like a fucking champion I might add. I'm so proud of you."

As they walked towards the front door, when Elliot was about to say goodbye, he turned to his brother and said, "I'm not going to die," the words walked right out of Elliot's mouth.

Brian shook his head, "Exactly. You are inspiring. Mona was right. What did you tell her. Honestly, she was happy. You made her happy." But Elliot hesitated, had his words been fire in Mona's hands? Or was that fire just part of life and Elliot simply made her feel better about that life? "Hey Elliot, you didn't cause any of this shit but maybe you made her feel better and I want that for myself. You have no idea the thoughts I've had about my life while sitting here on my ass. They haven't been about living life, I'll tell you that much. So, tell me, what's your secret?"

"When I think I'm dying, I'm happy to be alive," he put his hands on Brian's shoulder, "Brian, good things can come from bad things. This is your life. Live it. All of it."

"Even this?"

"Even this."

Brian pulled him in for a solid hug and then gave Elliot a kiss on the forehead. It was strange but it did make him feel better about Mona's kiss. Clearly Elliot was eliciting some sort of instinctual, primal benediction via the lips.

***

First it was his sister-in-law Mona's visit, then Brian, now it was his brother-in-law Doug's text message asking if Elliot didn't mind stopping by to visit Karen.

But please don't tell her I asked you, Doug added. None of it boded well for Karen. It gave Elliot pause. When you have to invite the dying guy over to cheer up your wife, and when that request has to be kept secret to protect her feelings, that's not a good sign.

The door opened and seeing Karen reminded Elliot of the dramatic turn his mother took near the end of her life, how she aged overnight. And in case Elliot doubted his observation, Karen immediately made the same observation of herself.

"But you, Elliot, you look great," she added, staring at him with awe, "you'd think I was the one who was dying," she gasped and put her hand to her mouth, "oh my god, I'm sorry. Oh, my god. I shouldn't talk like that. That's wrong, right?" Standing just inside the front door Karen continued talking. A stream of words which Elliot found too difficult to follow. With both speed and sense she had lost him. As she gesticulated Elliot noticed two dirty gardening gloves in her hand. There was dirt on her jeans, her knees had brown patches. There was even a smudge of dirt on her face. The word string kept unspooling from Karen's mouth and Elliot was looking for the right time to cut her off when she did something surprising. She stopped herself. Gently, she put her hand on his shoulder and put her other hand palm up, facing him, as if she were swearing an oath.

"Take a breath, Karen," she said to herself, "Nice and slow." Then she actually did take a deep breath. Nice and slow. "You're probably asking yourself, can she give me a nervous breakdown? Are they contagious? Right?" She was all easy chuckles now, "come on out back. I've got a new hobby that's really grounding me. Pun intended."

There in the backyard, among the scattering of plants, shrubs and small trees were three separate eight by twelve patches of tilled soil cut into the grass. Two of them had small seedling planted. The third had yet to be planted and this is where Karen knelt down in the dirt and indicated for Elliot to sit on the ground nearby. Watching as she put her gloves back on and began scooping up dirt with her hands to make room for the seedlings, Elliot noticed a change in her energy. Once she put the seedlings in the ground Karen gently tamped down the soil around them. While she was doing this she was much calmer than she'd been at the door. Elliot began to question Doug's clandestine invitation. Maybe Karen was alright.

"So, you know I lost my job?" Karen asked.

"No, I didn't know that. What happened?"

"Well, those SOB's at work happened." She went on to detail how and why she lost her job and as she did her mood quickly plummeted. It was like a tidal wave of depression hit her. The words once again became a non-stop stream, but unlike earlier, there was no emotion behind these. It was a dull monotone. Which was odd to Elliot because she was telling him how "upset and devastated" she was about losing her job, and yet it seemed like she wanted to yawn after every word. There were lots of big heavy breaths and defeated exhales between sentences. Elliot found himself missing manic Karen. The mania brought a certain conversational flourish. Frankly, Karen still had a sense of humor when she was manic. He felt terrible for these thoughts and reminded himself that she was in pain, that she didn't want to feel this low and that listening to her was the least he could do for his sister. "They say it's just part of the cutbacks. Ever since Covid they've begun the paring. If you have a high salary but aren't top management then you're gone. But keep the big dicks and their huge salaries. Oh, and keep the kids. They pay them pennies. Well, not really, but still, you know. And anyway, I know it wasn't the cutbacks. I'm good at what I do but I'm not the best politically. I rub people the wrong way sometimes. Shocker. Truth be told I was surprised I'd made it as far as I had there. Anyway, I had lost any love for that job long ago and had been considering leaving, so, blessing in disguise I thought up here," she pointed to her head, "but in here it set me off for some reason," she pointed to her chest, "another panic attack. Followed by the crash of all crashes. And here I am. Garden therapy. Doctor's orders."

They didn't talk much for the next half hour. At one point Karen looked up and smiled. She told Elliot about her reconciliation with Mona. It turned out it was all Brian's fault. Elliot thought about objecting to such a one-sided view of the conflict but decided to let it lie for the time being. With the last seedling planted she staked the small hand shovel in the soil and stood up.

"You know, I'm sitting here thinking about you. The way you have just accepted your situation and found peace. You're radiant. You are. And I'll tell you what keeps eating me up about the whole job thing. It's not even what happened, which sucks, of course, but, it's the fact that I can't accept that it happened. I cannot move on. I cannot accept it. That's what bothers me. I want, you know," she mimed a flat surface with her hands, "peace."

"And I too wish peace for you."

"How do you do it? What's your secret?"

His secret. It made him chuckle. Once again, someone was asking what his secret was and so he told her the same thing he had told Mona and Brian, "When I think I'm dying, I'm happy to be alive. Karen, good things can come from bad things. This is your life. Live it. All of it."

It was as if she hadn't even heard him. She just stood there, stock-still, her eyes didn't leave Elliot's eyes. Then she began nodding her head slowly. The moment was reaching the point of awkwardness and Elliot was about to say something to break it up. But then he stopped himself. This wasn't an awkward moment, he realized, this was a powerful moment, and he wondered if she would kiss him too.

The words came out of her mouth in a strained whisper, one holding back emotion, "but you tell me how I'm supposed to accept my little brother dying." There was a deep sadness in her eyes from which tears rolled. When she reached out and held his hand, she transmuted her pain to Elliot. The pain was like a jolt inside his chest and he felt tears fall from his eyes. Karen gave him a big hug and for a moment they cried on each other's shoulders. Their crying subsided, she kissed him on the cheek and they stood there. Karen still held his hand.

"All of it, Karen, even this," he said, the words surprising him.

"Well, I guess we cheered each other up," she said and this made them both laugh.

"We did!"

"Really?"

"I'm happy Karen."

Trying to transmit that happiness back to Karen he gave her hand a squeeze before walking away. As he left her he began, once again, to question the notion that he was indulging in hubris, that he was giving to others something that was not his to give because it came through false pretenses. Had he really caused everyone's pain, anymore than he caused the good in their life? Yet, to see his sister's pain when she said, "you tell me how I'm supposed to accept my little brother dying," was to see something that he had caused. One hundred percent. And to her he had actually said, "I'm happy Karen." And Elliot had found himself happy at that moment. But just seconds later he was struggling to reconcile all of this and wrestling with the moral dilemma he'd created for himself when he noticed Doug pulling into the driveway. There was a certain captain of a sinking ship quality about Doug. Beaten yet resolute.

"I know you're going through something that I cannot even imagine how scary and painful and difficult it must be but I also know you always make her happy, or at least less miserable. So thank you. You're selfless. To step up when you're suffering, but actually you don't seem like you're suffering. How do you do that? How are you happy and she's not. You're the one that's dying, she's not?" Doug had no idea but he was taking the knife Elliot had in his soul and was twisting it, and he wasn't done, "well, its been a perfect storm for her. A shit storm really. One step forward, three steps back. She was just saying she wanted to make you some food and bring it over to you, great. Step forward. But then thinking of you dying, well, she starts feeling sad again. And, ah, no food and can't get out of bed. Three steps back. And that's how it's been ever since she found out what you're going through."

"At least the whole thing brought the ulcers to attention. They could have killed her."

"Oh, well, that. Sure, a good catch. Of course. But they weren't going to kill her. She's saying that because she was trying to create some kind of positive."

"Oh. Well. What about the reconciliation with Mona?"

"What about it?"

"It's a good thing to come from all this."

"Come from all what?"

"Maybe it's all been blessing in disguise?"

Doug just stared at Elliot like he was crazy and Elliot could feel his face burning with embarrassment. What was he doing? Trying to make Doug say that good things had come from his lie? Elliot was badgering him towards a positive spin when the poor guy simply wanted to say that his life, at that moment, was shit. And maybe for Doug, that's what he needed, maybe he didn't want silver linings. Not yet. Not when he had a wife that was on the verge of a potentially irreversible mental collapse. But then Doug began to darkly snicker about something.

"What?"

"Oh, Elliot. They really pinned it all on old Brian. They both just beat up on him. Everything's his fault. Actually seems like the Brian and Karen thing got worse from all this. But yeah, the women buried the hatchet. In Brian!"

They laughed but then Doug cut it short. His face furrowed again with worry and he took hold of the knife once again, and begin to twist.

"But this thing with you. It really threw Karen for a loop." Doug actually seemed to be accusing Elliot. As if he were demanding an apology.

"Well, I'm sorry."

"Oh, Jesus! No, no, no. Not your fault. Please, no, Elliot," Doug said empathetically, "I'm just saying even though you caused it, in a way, it's not your fault."

It was clear to Elliot the conversation with Doug, all though well intentioned, was simply destined to be a downer. To continue was like pouring water on a grease fire. So he threw in the towel and said his goodbyes. Happiness had slipped away, it was on a distant shore, and he was swimming though wet cement to get back to it. By the time he got home he was on the verge of another mental breakdown. Trying to make sense of it, to explain it, to quantify it, or to simply clarify what was happening, theories flashed through his mind like flip book animation. Normative decision theory, optimal decision theory, heuristics, probability theory, etc. etc. etc. All his intellectual knowledge flickered across the screen of his consciousness but the notion that he could "figure out" what was happening using some textbook formula was futile given his emotional state and he was beginning to suspect as much but he couldn't seem to turn off his brain which continued to scramble around like a meth tweeker in a house full of broken appliances, screaming "I can fix it!"

***

Elliot walked into his office, images of his brother and sister, their emotional torment playing on a loop in his mind. Once again he physically seized up, unable to move, but this felt different. All of his muscles, right down to his fascia, tensed to the point of pain, his hair follicles even hurt. His teeth were gritting so hard he thought he could feel them cracking. Then the memory of Amy weeping flashed over and over in his mind. In the middle of this unstoppable carousel of guilt came his own words, "when I think I'm dying, I'm happy to be alive. Good things can come from bad things. This is your life. Live it. All of it." He could not even follow his own advice. Hypocrite! That is when he remembered his father and the farmer parable. And then the storm stopped. It was quiet again. He looked around his home office and it all felt ridiculous. Especially the idea that he had quit his job and was sitting at home pretending to be like Paul Dirac, or Einstein, or some other genius with their new theory about how life really worked. A theory he hadn't even had the courage to share with anyone. In almost twenty years! The whiplash in his attitude towards his theory did not go unnoticed. Just a week ago he was inspired, he was daring, and if someone had told him this theory was ridiculous he would have laughed. Back then fear simply passed over him like water off a duck's back. Didn't stick. He had faith. Courage. It didn't matter whether he was going to succeed or fail, that was not his concern. His concern was doing it! That was all that mattered. Now it was like nothing mattered, it all seemed so pointless because he'd fucked his own life up and everyone else's. He had created this narrative which had given him false powers. And false powers usually leave people broken. On their knees. Worse off than they were before.

Over the past few days the realization that he would need to deal with his lie had come to pass. Now, finally, he allowed into full consciousness the most difficult question which had been lurking in the recesses of his mind, *how will I get out of this lie?* For the life of him he couldn't think beyond the question. There was a wall between the question and any possible solution. But at least the question was there, at last, out in the open. That was a start, wasn't it? He could see it, the question, in his mind, all alone, floating in an empty white void. Now the question didn't feel like a start, it felt like a taunt. A rhetorical question meant to thrust itself violently up into his rectum and yank out his guts. A cold blade of fear cut right down the center of Elliot's body, from head to tail. Suddenly his bowels begin to expel as if the question was a morsel of rancid maggot infested meat. He scurried to the bathroom, clenching. As he reached the toilet he barely got his pants down in time. When it was over he remained seated on the toilet. Having rid himself of the intestinal tumult, his mental torment moved into his bones, which began to ache. Mustering all the strength he had Elliot wiped his ass, pulled his pants up, and shuffled to the bedroom where he quickly collapsed.

The first solution that came to him was a terrible one, *I could kill myself.* Immediately he tried to retract the thought. But the fact remained, it had crossed his mind and in doing so it left a stain. This is what it had come to after being life's loudest cheerleader just hours ago. The guru now wanted to throw a rope over his own neck. But the epiphany which had inspired him was real, and even in his miserable state, he was determined to hold onto that. It was real.

"Elliot," Amy whispered, "you don't look well."

It was as if she had materialized, like an apparition. Gently she laid down next to him and began to lovingly stroke her hands through his hair. She gave him a soft kiss before settling in next to him.

"Do you think it's your liver?"

"I doubt it."

"Have you called Terry Algren and set an appointment?"

He hesitated, "not yet."

"Elliot, that's not acceptable," it was a delicate admonishment but he could feel the teeth in it, "you'll call today. Promise."

"I promise." What else could he say.

"You fucking better," she said sweetly. "Can I tell you some good news?"

"Please."

The idea had been percolating for awhile and crystalized during their recent getaway while perusing old books. The inspiration to act on her idea had come from Elliot, a fact which made his body convulse in more pain. Since their getaway Amy and several woman she worked with had begun developing her idea into a proposal. That morning, by chance, Amy found herself talking to her "boss's boss's boss," the district superintendent. Amy gave her an impromptu elevator pitch of her idea. The superintendent, it turned out, was of a like mind on this and wanted to hear a more detailed pitch with the appropriate people in the room.

"Congratulations! What's the idea?" Elliot asked.

In her very clear and organized way Amy began explaining the idea. The proposal was to reintroduce a robust social sciences curriculum from middle school through high school. The idea was a reintroduction of traditional social sciences like ethics, philosophy and merging psychology, spirituality, and theology into the curriculum. As Amy was methodically going over an outline of the idea she stopped herself.

"Hold on. Okay, that's all the 'what' of the pitch but that's not the 'why?' The why is that when I grew up and when things got complicated and things hurt, I realized I didn't know fuck all about how to deal with any of that in a healthy way. The things that were going to bring me to my knees, regardless of my income status, those things weren't included on my SAT. Therefore those things didn't matter. I got straight A's. I excelled at my activities. But I didn't know who I was and I didn't even know that mattered. And maybe I could have skated through like life that but that's not what happened. And that isn't what happens to most people. Look, the world has never been better and it's never been worse. But more than ever it seems like we are simply working to solve the very problems we are creating. Why?" Amy was on a roll and it enthralled Elliot. He'd never seen her like this. Her passion was so intoxicating it took away his pain. No longer did his body ache but it was surging with libido, in fact, she was turning him on. As her flow continued to build Elliot's hold on her grew tighter. "Are we telling kids that the most important thing they can learn is how to take a test? What about how to be a good person? How to make the world a better place? What about how to overcome trauma? What about how to have compassion for another human being? How to maintain your own happiness in the face of unhappiness? What about how to coexist with the planet and not see it as something to rape and pillage? What about how to deal with painful feelings or simply how to deal with the emotions that come with everyday challenges? And we need to do more than a flyer, or a few minutes in an assembly. I mean, who are these kids that we're giving these immense tools too? Really, who are they going to be? I mean, what the fuck?! We're making them smarter, that's good, but if we are not making them better people, then that knowledge is dangerous. Because some really fucking smart people built bombs that can destroy the planet. And there are some kids we aren't even giving anything to. Just sent out into the world feeling angry, left behind, useless and lost. And I was so inspired when I saw our mental health initiative, but then I thought, it's an awareness campaign, terrific, and now it's time for the manifestation of that awareness. Tools, experience, realization. The kids are more than test scores to justify our fucking jobs. They are humans." When she was finished she collapsed onto her back, out of breath.

"Wow. That's your pitch?

"No. I'm just venting with you. That's the subtext. "

"No f-bombs in the official pitch?"

"Here is what I have. . .There was a remarkably popular class in middle school called 'decisions.' It was like a philosophy, ethics and human psychology class wrapped in one. But I never got to take it because it was cut from the curriculum. I'm sure we can all guess why. Because philosophy, ethics, and human psychology were no longer deemed important enough. Perhaps other classes could fill the void in some way? There was one young, idealistic language arts teacher who talked about exploring the human condition in the stories we read. She would take what we were reading and ask us what we learned about ourselves and the world around us. Sometimes she would simply ask us to write about our life or the life of another person. That was the only class that got me thinking about what it meant to be a human being. I ran into that teacher when I started working for the district. She was retiring early. Exhausted from all the newly required learning and standardized test prep we had piled onto her department. 'We have stripped art from language arts' she said. Ever since then it bothered me that I was part of a system that had cut, restructured or downplayed the importance of classes like hers. Why? As grateful as I am for the education I received, and I am, I can't help but wonder where are the classes that will help the children deal with the big stuff in life. My husband recently told me he was dying and I am struggling to think of a single test I took that prepared me for something like that. And it's not just those big things, it can be a million little things. It can even be the very pressure we're putting on them. You know, when we take away the classes that deal with the human condition, we are no longer conditioning our kids to be human."

"If I ever need a reason to live. I'll think about you," Elliot said before kissing her.

"You are my inspiration," and she meant it but what she couldn't tell him is that he wasn't her only inspiration. The other inspiration grew out of the affair she'd had because it had revealed the worst in her and when she pulled herself out of her worst, it revealed her best. Strangely she found herself wanting to share this with Elliot, but instead she said, "the hardest thing in life brought out the best in us, Elliot. I didn't know that my greatest happiness would somehow be tied to my greatest sorrow. I love you and I am so grateful for everything you have taught me about facing challenges and living life."

If she only knew, he ruefully thought to himself.

13

Minus tides bring a particularly briny smell as they expose tide pools to the open air and reveal a world of sea life normally covered by water. Just beyond the tide pools Elliot, Davey and Gordo sat on their surfboards making the most of the small waves by enjoying each other's company. Occasionally there was a little bit of conversation, occasionally one of them caught a little wave and occasionally they sat quietly. With all the drama his siblings were living through, Elliot feared his friends would report similar catastrophes in their lives, but to his relief Davey and Gordo were doing fine.

The water time was providing a nice respite from his worries. It offered Elliot the opportunity to soberly face the lie and begin accepting the situation. Actually it was not "the" lie as he had been saying to himself, it was "his" lie as he was now admitting to himself in a small private demonstration of accountability.

Perhaps the most sobering realization he was beginning to accept was that his lie had an expiration date. Not only was it impossible for him to fake liver disease indefinitely, there was now a doctor eager to examine him. The time for action had arrived, it was unavoidable, but he needed a plan. It was true Elliot wasn't a liar by nature. The lie about dying was an anomaly for him and he very much wanted to get out of it as cleanly as possible, without ruining his life and most of all without lying again, but it seemed impossible to have both. While bobbing around in the surf a solution came to him. The solution enabled him to get out of the lie without ruining his life but he would have to lie again.

"How's everything going with your health?" Davey quietly asked, so as not to be heard by the handful of surfers scattered nearby in the water. The question penetrated Elliot's skin, eliciting the uncomfortable tingling in his center. Up until that point the subject of Elliot's health had not been broached which had been just fine for Elliot. The less he talked about it, the less he had to lie, and the less he lied the better he felt. But, his friends did what friends do, they ask questions and with the conversation veering towards his "health issues" Elliot prepared for another self-created emotional ass kicking, but instead he found the solution. The way out of his lie.

"There's really nothing they can do for you? Maybe there's some miracle cure you could go for," the sincerity of Gordo's suggestion signaled his willingness to believe in miracles, and from the hopeful look on Davey's face, he too was willing to believe in miracles. It was deeply touching for Elliot and it also sparked an idea. *The* idea.

A miracle cure, that's it!

Their surf was over and the guys were carefully making their way in through the tide pools when a small rush of whitewater caused Elliot to lose his footing. Fortunately the rubber booties he wore protected his feet from getting cut up by the rocks but they couldn't protect his feet from everything. The sea urchin's sharp quill poked right through the rubber sole of his booty and right into the soft flesh of his foot. When he lifted his foot out of the water he saw a tennis ball sized sea urchin stuck to the bottom of his foot. Its hundreds of needle like quills gave it the look of a medieval weapon while its shades of purple gave it the beauty of a flower. Reaching out with his free hand, he carefully grabbed hold of the urchin and pulled it from his foot. With its release came an acute pain that hurt like hell.

"Gotta piss on it," Gordo advised as they stood on the sand, "could wait till later but the sooner you do it, the better it works."

"Yeah, just gotta piss in your wetsuit. Let it trickle down into your bootie where your foot can soak it up," Davey added encouragingly.

A solemn look came over Elliot's face as he concentrated on relaxing his bladder. Soon the pain was gone.

***

To pull off his final lie Elliot couldn't simply invent a miracle cure, that wouldn't suffice. What he needed was an existing story. Something he could use as a template for his "recovery" and something which bolstered his credibility should anyone look into his claim. It didn't take long after he got home from the beach to find an article online about a man who had, using various plant medicines, miraculously survived the same type of liver disease Elliot had lied about having. The article had been written several years earlier and was vague on details. In fact, it was more accurate to say the article wasn't exactly an article. Rather it was a dubious and slightly bizarre blog post by a woman who was a self-proclaimed "medical industrial complex truth teller." Since Elliot wasn't necessarily after truth, just plausible believability, he looked past the numerous red flags in the blog post and began his search for the man who had supposedly cured himself. The man's name was Duc Nguyen and he happened to live just a few hours north of Elliot. Then it took Elliot only a few minutes to find what appeared to be Duc's social media account. Elliot messaged Duc and included a short summary of his situation and his phone number. With the message sent Elliot decided to take a quick break and eat lunch. While eating some leftovers it occurred to Elliot that everything was easily falling into place, maybe too easily, so he decided to look for more miracle survivors in case Duc didn't get back to him.

After an hour of searching online he couldn't find any more miracles. There was an herbalist treatment center that indicated something about liver disease but when he called he discovered their number had been disconnected. Then he checked the blog site again where he had found the article about Duc. There he found an email contact for the blogger, Claire Murphy. So, he copy and pasted his message to Duc and put it in the email to Claire.

From there Elliot kept researching. If he was not able to get a hold of either Duc or Claire, and if he couldn't find another person who had miracle cured themselves, he would have to come up with his own alternative cure. And it would have to be based on as good of science as he could find. Fortunately Elliot found some scholarly research about herbal medicine for Wilson's disease. After doing a quick scan of the articles he was fairly confident they contained enough information to help him create a believable treatment. Just as he was about to dig into the research and begin writing up his own miracle cure, his phone rang. It was Claire Murphy, the medical conspiracy blogger.

The first thing Claire wanted to do was make sure Elliot wasn't an agent of the medical industrial complex.

"I'm dangerous to them," she said matter of factly, "and I'm pretty sure they recently tried to take me out. Physically. So, it's not too hard to imagine them sending someone to gain my trust and gather information." From there Claire began asking detailed questions to verify Elliot was a "real person."

Perhaps it was her paranoia rubbing off on him but Elliot began to question who Claire really was and what she would do with his information. She was, after all, asking him a lot of personal questions. He began to hesitate when she asked a question, and became evasive, but this only seemed to pique her interest. To entice him she dangled a carrot, saying there was information about Duc that wasn't in her article. It worked. Elliot finally answered all of her questions. Satisfied, Claire proceeded.

"Before calling you I tried to find the notes from my interview with Duc but lo and behold I couldn't find them. Go figure."

"They're lost?"

"No, stolen. They stole them."

"Who?"

"Who do you think?" She practically scoffed at him.

"Okay, so what was the additional information you had about Duc that wasn't in your article?"

"Well, I don't have it."

"But you just mentioned there was some information about Duc that wasn't in your article?"

"Well, yes."

"Which is?"

"Gone."

"Sorry, Claire, I'm not understanding, you indicated there is information that wasn't in the article."

"Exactly. That information is in the information they stole."

"So, you're saying the additional information you have, you actually don't have."

"Bingo. Now what does that tell you?"

As Claire continued on about the persecution she was facing, Elliot began to glance over her blog site. The stated mission of her blog was, "*THE* global medical industry is actively trying to reduce the world's population through a variety of ways." Early posts on her site were about mainstream medical and pharmaceutical conspiracies, several he also suspected were true. Then there was a progression into the very deep end of conspiracy theories. There were posts with titles like, "Optometrists Are Really Trying to Impair Eyesight in Effort to Cause Auto Deaths" or "Pacemakers Are Being Laced with Slow Release Cyanide. True." By far her most written about conspiracy was how the government was secretly implanting tracking devices into babies. It seemed as though she was simply believing things she imagined. It made him feel sad for her. What was going on in Claire's mind that had taken her so far from any sense of reality? And if Claire ever did stumble upon a true conspiracy, Elliot thought, who the hell would ever believe her. And if no one believes her, isn't she inadvertently helping the real conspirators in the world?

Elliot was embarrassed his own lie had led him into this sad world of delusion. He began to question himself. Was he really thinking clear enough to pull off an elaborate lie about a miracle cure? Was it even a realistic strategy? Or would he come off as transparently delusional as Claire was? So, while Claire thundered on passionately, revealing to Elliot a global network of euthanizing dentists, Elliot went back to the blog about Duc. It wasn't a terribly bizarre headline, "Defying the Establishment Man Saves His Liver and His Life," but the word establishment was a clue he'd missed. Now knowing what he knew about Claire even the first sentence to the post read differently. She had begun by writing, "if he continued on the so-called course of treatment his so-called doctor's had prescribed Duc Nguyen was as good as dead." Still, as crazy as it all was, as silly as he felt for going this far with it, he held out hope the whole thing with Duc was real. Just because she was nuts, didn't mean he was.

"Now if all of that doesn't illustrate to you what you're up against here, well, I don't know what will. You may wish it weren't all true. I wish it weren't all true. I do. But it is. So.

There." And with that she finally stopped talking and waited for Elliot's response.

"Okay. Um, would you happen to have a phone number for Duc?"

"It was in the notes."

"The ones that are missing."

"Yep."

Claire was eager to continue milking the rare opportunity of a somewhat captive audience but Elliot eventually managed to get off the phone. Talking to Claire had left him dejected, so he took a moment to consider things as they stood. Even if he could cobble together some fake treatment for himself from the few bits of research he had dug up, it just felt like the whole lie about the miracle cure was flimsy. It was all beginning to feel shaky. In an effort to stop his doubt spiral he stood up and literally shook himself to shake off Claire's creepy sad vibe while making a strange vocalization, like someone talking in tongues. His mantra from earlier, "all of it," came to mind and he smiled.

Sitting back down at his desk Elliot began a fresh, more optimistic assessment of things as they stood. He had one major thing going for him, he wasn't actually dying, which meant he would continue living, and therefore people would have to believe him. To help them believe he really didn't need much, just throw out a few herbs and tinctures and people would go right along with it. People wanted to believe in miracles and people wanted him to live. Normally Amy was a somewhat skeptical person with these types of things, as was he, but she was showing a greater inclination towards an open mind lately, what with all the meditation and singing bowl stuff. Of course that was a long way from trusting Elliot to go on a treatment plan that had never been undertaken. However, he could tell her that he'd been doing the "miracle cure" all along and had not told about it her because he thought she might think he was crazy. While he sat there at his desk ramping up his confidence his phone rang. It was Duc's daughter, Sarah.

Right out of the gate Sarah bluntly told Elliot she wasn't going to call him because she was worried he might be another "lunatic" but then she decided to call because it would have been negligent not to if he sincerely needed help.

"Are you really in need of help?" Sarah asked.

The question hung in the air for a beat, "yes, I am in need of help," he said, feeling as though he had technically told the truth, even though he ignored the true context of her question. Elliot went on to assure her that he was not insane and was grateful she called.

"First of all my Dad passed away a few months ago. So, it's difficult. But I have been monitoring his social media in case any old friends reached out."

"My condolences for your loss."

"Thank you. Anyway, after beating the odds with his liver disease he accidentally stepped in front of a bus."

"He didn't die from anything related to his liver?"

"No."

"May I ask why you suspected I was a lunatic and why not calling me would be negligent?"

"Because that blog, or whatever it is, was not accurate. My dad was at the store where he got his herbal medicine from when he met that woman. They spoke for a half hour and my dad told her his story. Then the next thing we knew there was this blog about him. He tried to get her to remove it or at least to add a corrections but she refused. Actually it got a bit strange," Sarah snickered, "she accused him of being one of the lizard people."

"Really?"

"Yeah, so he dropped it. Who knows what someone like that is capable of. Besides, no one actually reads her blog. Well, I guess some people do."

"Me?"

"Yeah. But I guess you were desperate."

"The whole plant medicine, herbal remedy thing was all fake?"

"Not entirely, that's the frustrating part. There is some truth, even his doctors would tell you that. He was taking treatment from his doctors, and as you know, it's simply a disease you have and usually it doesn't get too bad. Well, for some reason it began to progress to the point where he could have died. The doctors began to treat it and my Dad also started to take different herbal remedies. But I can tell you my Dad would never advocate taking only the herbal remedies, but that's what her blog claimed he said."

From there Sarah began to rattle off a list of medical terms associated with liver disease and she began to differentiate where the herbal remedy helped and where the doctors helped. None of the medical jargon around the disease made sense to him but the herbs she listed did. Everything she said he wrote down and he also wrote down the name and number of her father's doctors. The herbs she mentioned matched the ones in the research articles he had found. Hanging up the phone after his conversation with Sarah, Elliot felt very confident a successful plan was taking form.

***

It was getting dark outside when Elliot finished typing his blueprint for the miracle cure. The time to actualize the plan was nearly at hand. With his head cluttered and tired from everything he had accomplished today he knew unveiling the miracle cure tonight would be unwise. At the moment no one had any reason to suspect he was lying. Any blunders moving forward might expose him and tip his hand. He would get a good night's rest and begin implementation in the morning. A clear head for a clear plan.

With the sound of Amy arriving home came the now familiar feeling of overwhelming gratitude which fortified his resolve. This was the life he wanted. A life which had just begun for them and he knew right then and there he would do whatever it took to protect it. And if that meant telling one more lie, then so be it. The radiance she brought into his office nearly moved him to blurt out something about a miracle cure. Given his mental acuity at that moment it would have been a strategically stupid move. If he just played his next lie right the threat posed by his first lie would be removed. And then they could live happily ever after. He smiled as she sank into his lap and he held her tight while breathing in her smell. He just needed a little more time and then they would have all the time in the world.

"Just saw Terry and Norah walking their dogs," she said excitedly. The mention of the Algren's alarmed him but he kept a smile on his face. But maintaining that smile became impossible as she continued talking. Dr. Terry Algren had, "insisted" Elliot come in Monday next week. It was Thursday night. That was three days away! Elliot's heart jumped into his throat. His mind was too exhausted to deal with this new information and how it factored into his plan. The optimistic feeling he had just moments earlier was gone and his spirits were once again sinking. Amy rattled on about taking the day off to go with him while Elliot's brain completely shut off.

"Elliot!" Amy nearly shouted, her hands cupping his face, and her eyes right up to his.

"Huh?"

"I said your name three times."

"Sorry."

"Can you get everything from your doctor over to Terry ASAP."

At this point he was flying by the seat of his pants. No time for a plan. He blinked, and sputtered another lie, "I lost everything."

"Then call your doctor. Have them email Terry your records."

Of course he couldn't have his doctors email Terry the records. There weren't any records. He almost shouted out, "the doctor's lost their records too!" Which would have been one lie too far. And a clumsy one at that. Instead he nodded his head and said, "yes." If he wasn't careful she would discover the truth. Unwittingly she was already circling around it. Now that she was hyper-focused there would be no more diverting, distracting, or delaying her.

"Let Terry give me a full round of tests when I get there," these words came out of his mouth without a single thought before them. It sounded crazy as he heard himself say it but then he realized something. It was so incredible he almost began to laugh. A new plan had just dropped into his lap like manna from heaven. This idea was bold, perhaps even brazen, but at this stage boldness was his only way out. The new plan was simple. He would arrive at Terry's office on Monday and make up some excuse as to why his doctors didn't have his results, or maybe he would just say he forgot to call them. Of course, Terry would predictably run his own tests anyway and those tests would reveal, lo and behold, that Elliot was actually healthy! And the conclusion would be that it had all been a misdiagnosis! End of story. Or perhaps before seeing Algren he would unveil to Amy the secret miracle cure he has been taking, then Algren's tests would prove the cure worked! Now he had two plans. Tomorrow he would have to think it over and choose one of the plans. It was either the miracle cure or the misdiagnoses discovery, but whichever plan he chose, the good news is that everyone would live happily ever after.

"I'm going to call Norah," Amy said at last.

"What? Why?" Elliot almost shrieked. Norah wasn't part of his spontaneous plan. A well known legal bulldog who specialized in medical malpractice, Norah was relentless when something smelt fishy, and this certainly would smell fishy to her. If anyone could get to the bottom of it, Norah Algren would.

"Why?" Amy was almost incredulous, "I want to see what she knows about this doctor you went to."

"Why?"

"Because I'm a little suspicious here."

"With what? Why? Who?" The words fell all over each other on the way out of his mouth. The fact that Amy was still on his lap wasn't helping him. It wasn't cuddly, loving, or sexy anymore. It now felt like she was pinning him down.

"This doctor of yours. It doesn't make sense, it's like, he went, 'oh, well, this disease is fatal, nothing to do about it, you're dying. Too bad. Move along.' Where is the advice? Where is the second, third opinion. It just, I don't know, something about it feels a bit negligent."

"No."

"No, what?"

"No," Elliot was stumbling. In an effort to buy his brain time he twirled his hands in the air, "just, just, no. No, Norah. No lawyers. No stress. No stress. Okay. The stress of a legal battle, on top of it all. It's my fault. The doctor did do all those things. The advice. The recommendation for another opinion. I just sort of shut it out, I guess. Really. It's on me. Please don't make this some legal battle."

"Okay. Okay, I hear you."

For a moment it seemed like she was done, her body relaxed and he was able to wrap his arms around her. While they quietly held each other he thought about the two new plans. Either could work. Letting Terry discover that he was healthy was rather elegant. He could imagine Terry saying, "Wouldn't you know it, Elliot, you're in the clear." Depending on which plan he chose, it would either go down as being one of those strange things that happen to people or the power of plant medicine.

"Oh! I can't believe I almost forgot!" Amy practically shot up from his lap, "you'll never believe this. The disease you have is genetic," her tone was gossipy, her eyes had widened and were fixed on Elliot, waiting for his reaction. The implications were obvious to her, so when a look of confusion came over Elliot face, she became annoyed, "your brother and sister?"

"What?"

"Your brother and sister may carry it. And their children."

Gently he nudged her off of him, stood up and walked to the window. He felt claustrophobic. Ever since she had come home and walked into his office it had been one thing after another. But it wasn't her fault. It was his fault. While she went about eating the fruits of his lie, he forgot from what tree those fruits had fallen. A poisonous tree. And she knew something was sick, even if she was wrong about what the sickness actually was. But she knew there was sickness nonetheless, and in her knowingness she was doing what any caring and loving wife would do, she was trying to make it better.

"You know what, this whole thing makes absolutely no sense to me," her voice coming from behind him, gentle and soft, but her words landing like blows from a sledgehammer, "can you explain it to me? This thing you've been keeping secret."

How had this suddenly turned? How had she suddenly figured it out? Not knowing what to say he simply stood quietly, his back to her, and continued to look out from the window at the world outside. In the fading twilight Elliot could see the buds on their big jacaranda tree were beginning to flower early.

"Actually, I'm rather impressed by your persistence. That's a long time to keep something like this going," there was a hint of a chuckle as she said this. There was something about her demeanor that didn't feel right to Elliot. If she had just begun to suspect he'd been lying, or had somehow just figured out he'd been lying, why was she snickering.

"Elliot, at some point you're gonna have to talk about it."

Finally, he turned around to face her but instead of standing behind him with accusing eyes, she was reclined in his chair, gazing curiously at the whiteboard where he had been working on his theory. She playfully extended her leg to reach him.

"Can you just try and explain it to me? In layman's terms. Because to me all these numbers and letters and equations might as well be written in some Martian language."

"It'll sound crazy," he said as relief swept over him once he realized what she was actually talking about.

"As any great new idea often does."

"Okay, I suppose I would start by asking, do you know for certain that you and I will be together, in this room, thirty seconds from now? The truth is we don't know because it hasn't happened. Nothing is certain about the future. And this applies to everything because everything is in a constant state of unfolding. So we are constantly faced with not knowing. Even that sliver of time that is always right in front of us is unknown. Is this making sense?"

"A continuous horizon of unknowingness," Amy said.

"Yes! Well said."

"The theory of unknowingness."

"Yes! Again, well said. Can I use that?"

"So, you're trying to extrapolate this idea into that Martian language?" she gestured to the whiteboard.

It seems to be a uniquely human desire, to know and control one's future, and for obvious reasons. Yet, no matter how smart, or clever, or intuitive one is, that power remains allusive. One can, however, be certain that how they approach the present moment will certainly effect how they will feel in the future, as Elliot and Amy would soon learn.

14

The shower's warm water gently rolled down Amy's body, she closed her eyes, and began to visualize her pitch. Later that morning she would be presenting her social science curriculum to the district superintendent. But the presentation didn't hold the most prominent place in her mind. By far the most significant event on the horizon was Elliot's appointment with Dr. Algren on Monday, which she believed would mark a turning point for his health. There was so much positive energy within and around her that she felt assured everything would work out for best. At some point she became aware she standing in a pool of warm water because the shower drain was backing up. After stepping out of the shower and getting herself ready she noticed the water in the shower basin had still not drained and a thin film of grayish soapy water had settled on the surface.

Sailing through the kitchen Amy grabbed a quick bite of the breakfast Elliot had cooked for her, "in honor of your big day," he said, handing her a fresh cup of coffee and then ushering her to sit at the table.

"You inspired me. Our second honeymoon has forever been a cherished gift. Let's keep it going." When she was finished with breakfast they walked to the front door where they shared one last kiss and he wished her luck. He was just about to close the front door when she turned and called out to him, "please call a plumber today and have the shower drain snaked. Thanks, love you."

Before calling the plumber to unclog the shower drain Elliot decided he would give it a shot. Finding some stiff wire which he straightened out and fashioned a little hook on the end of, he hunkered down over the shower basin and jammed the wire in. Almost right away it snagged something so he tried to pull it back up but it wouldn't move. He pulled so hard it began to feel like the wire was cutting into his hand. He was reminded of a time when he was beach fishing as a child and his fishing line became stuck on a large rock just under the surface of the water. And like his beach fishing experience he was groaning with effort to pull the wire free. But unlike fishing line, wire does not break free or snap. Getting down to serious business he took his shoes and socks off, he rolled up his pants and he stepped into the water. Power squatting, he took hold of the wire again and he gave it one last powerful tug. Trying to thrust upward he lost traction and his feet slide out causing him to fall on his ass in the pool of dirty water. Sitting there in a puddle of defeat he was absentmindedly working the wire around in circles. And without trying the wire came loose but the drain remained clogged. The thought of calling the plumber came across his mind but he couldn't resist one more try. This time with a different approach. Instead of jamming the wire down, he delicately slide it in. The wire went much further down than the first time and when he felt it come up against something mushy he slowly pulled the wire back up. What emerged, with a slurping sound from its suction release, was what looked like a dead rat but what was in fact years of hair and soap grime. The water quickly began to drain until the last bit formed a tight whirlpool.

The sound of the ambulance drew Elliot's attention. Hopping up from the shower basin Elliot peeked outside from the bathroom window. The ambulance was parked outside of the Algren's house. Another siren cut through the air as a fire truck turned onto the street and pulled up behind the ambulance. Several people had stepped out of their homes to see what was happening.

As Elliot neared the Algren's driveway the front door to the Algren's house opened. A stretcher with Terry on it was wheeled outside and Norah was right behind it. There was a quick exchange between the paramedics and Norah before they closed the ambulance doors and the sirens once again blared. The ambulance and firetruck sped off leaving Norah standing there alone. Her face was red and swollen from crying. When she reached into her purse to retrieve her car keys, she noticed Elliot, and so he said to her, "Norah, is there anything I can do?"

"Thank you, no, not right now."

"Will Terry be alright?"

She hesitated before saying, "I honestly don't know," and then she hurried towards her car which was parked in the driveway. As she drove away and passed by Elliot, he gave a gentle wave.

The implications of how Terry's sudden and unexpected rush to the hospital would effect his own life were unavoidable - it looked more and more likely he would be able to get out of his lie and get on with his life. Surprisingly, something about this didn't feel right to him.

Maybe it was seeing Terry Algren carted off, a person who was actually facing imminent death, but a profound insight emerged which completely changed Elliot's plan regarding the lie. Suddenly, nothing was more important than the peace and freedom the lie had given him, not even his relationship with Amy was more important. It all became clear to him. He now realized what he had to do. It was simple.

***

The pitch was a success. Amy and her team were given the green light to continue developing the idea further and they were all headed to lunch together for a celebration when Lisa said, "oh, look it's that guy Todd." They had just stepped out of the building and were headed to the parking lot. Looking in the direction Lisa indicated Amy saw Todd standing in the middle of the parking lot by his car. He was clearly looking in their direction. The other women kept walking but Amy had stopped. She felt like she was in one of those falling dreams where the falling never seems to end, no matter how badly you wish to wake up from it.

"Who?" Amy could hear Maria asking.

"You know, that guy, he used to work here. In accounting or something. Remember the one who. . . ?" Lisa's voice faded out of earshot. When her friends noticed Amy wasn't in step with them anymore they stopped to look back.

"Gotta do one more thing. Meet you all there. I'll have to drive myself," the words sounding hollow and rushed as she somehow managed to push them out before turning around and going back inside the building.

Peering out from the floor-to-ceiling tinted windows Amy could observe Todd without being seen. He was still standing by his car. He pulled his cellphone from his pocket. Her phone rang. It was Todd, or Talia as the phone read. She didn't answer. The idea of hiding from him never crossed her mind. She knew she would have to deal with him but there was no denying the fear she felt. Not only had Todd completely surprised her by coming out of nowhere but by doing so Todd had recklessly stepped out of bounds. Suddenly she felt like she didn't know who this man was or what he was capable of. This was either the final last gasp of a dying relationship or it was something worse. The whole situation was uncertain but whatever it was, her instincts told her to act aggressively. So she took a deep breath, held her head high and left the building. Striding directly towards Todd she never once took her eyes off of him but she noticed his eyes had darted away several times.

"In the car," she commanded and without stopping she let herself into the passenger side of his car.

***

The path Elliot had chosen took him over a ridge and down into a meadow full of wildflowers and upon seeing them he immediately thought of Amy. Breathing in their scent, both bitter and sweet, with pollen tickling his nostrils Elliot peddled hard towards the final summit which lay straight ahead. The incredible thing about e-mountain bikes is that they make the nearly impossible rather easy. It felt a bit like cheating but in what would have taken an hour, he was at the final summit in ten minutes. He stopped and took the view in.

The pastoral landscape reflected the inner peace he felt. The peace came from the decision he made that morning after seeing Terry Algren carted away by paramedics. At that moment he made a new plan as to how he would deal with his big lie. There was a tremendous risk involved in this new plan and therefore a great deal of fear should have come with it, yet he felt complete tranquility. Although his life was not at stake, everything worth living for was. The new plan would require the courage that others had been mistakenly projecting onto him. Grabbing hold of the handlebars he swirled the bike around, pointed it towards the final leg of the trail, and headed downhill.

It was almost noon when Elliot finished the ride and he was back in cell coverage. He noticed a message from Amy. Her presentation was over and it went "fantastic." To celebrate Elliot decided he would surprise Amy for lunch. It was absolutely criminal but true, this would be his first visit to her work. The hillside where Elliot's car was parked was filled with wildflowers, so before driving off, to surprise Amy he picked a large bunch to bring to her.

As he drove he thought of his early relationship with Amy and how they would make a point of going on wildflower walks. The bunch of flowers Elliot had picked for Amy rested on the passenger seat of the car. At a red light he took in their beauty, their unique colors and intricate design. They were also so delicate which reminded him how Amy had always brought water for the wildflowers she picked. Elliot pulled into a shopping center that had a home goods store. He moved the flowers off the seat so they wouldn't be in direct sunlight and then he raced into the store where he found a simple white porcelain vase. Once back in the car he used the remaining water from his bottle to fill the vase. With the vase of flowers secured in the car he drove off. Then a thought came to him. Chocolate. He had just passed an organic market she frequently spoke about. She would often buy a certain speciality chocolate from there. One she loved. So, he made a u-turn and headed for the store. Just a small detour. He would still be at her office in five minutes. Plenty of time to catch her before lunch.

***

"Can I just say, the way you, sort of, came out all boss lady, it was kind of hot."

Those were Todd's first words when Amy got into his car and to her they sounded so cheesy and out of place they made her nauseous. Before she had a chance to call him out for his juvenile and alarmingly out of touch behavior he began a rambling monologue so inane she could barely follow. He started off by describing their love in the sort of codependent delusional way a pop song would. His words lacked any depth or connection to reality. As he kept talking he veered away from sappy puppy love towards himself and when it became all about him, it soon became all about his pain. A theme surfaced, how badly she was treating him and how much he had sacrificed for her. It became clear to her Todd was not in a good place mentally or emotionally. This stirred both her compassion and her caution. He was not hers to fix she reminded herself but at the same time she didn't want to see him suffer.

"I mean, I left my wife for you-" she finally cut him off as he bemoaned her about this mistruth for the third time.

"Stop right there. Just stop-"

"But-"

"No. My turn. Take a breath, Todd. Seriously, breath and listen. Please. Okay?" He didn't nod or respond but he did fall silent which was good enough for her, "first of all you did not leave your wife for me. Your wife left you after she discovered an affair you were having with another woman who was not me."

Todd raised his voice and it quickly began to feel like things were escalating towards the type of situation Amy had feared most. He had gone from pathetic, self-centered rambling to barking loud belligerent reduced sentences at her.

"You were there? With my wife? You know what happened?! You have no idea what happened. I waited for you. I've been waiting for you. But you're just done with me. Well, guess what? I'm not done with you. What do you think of that?"

"I think I'm getting out of the car now," Amy said as she reached for the door handle but he locked the doors first.

"No. You to listen to me, you cold bitch."

"Unlock this door."

"No. You will listen to me first."

"Fine, I will listen and then I am going to get out of the car. But first unlock this door."

"Look, I'm sorry. I didn't mean to yell," Todd said in a slightly more measured voice but he didn't unlock the door.

"The door, Todd. Please unlock it first."

"Why?"

"You're scaring me Todd."

Suddenly all the energy he arrived on the scene with slipped out of his body and he crumpled in his seat. Almost as if unconsciously, he unlocked the car doors. Just as she was about to throw open her door the weeping began and Amy hesitated. For so many reasons she wanted a clean end to her relationship with Todd and wasn't sure what move was the most optimal in achieving that goal. The conflict between her anger and compassion was paralyzing. So, she took a deep breath, tried to recenter herself, and when she looked away from Todd she saw a very familiar car.

At that moment all of her attention, one hundred percent of it, was on the car that had just parked within her eyesight. She watched as Elliot stepped out of his car with a vase of wildflowers and bar of her favorite chocolate.

Then Todd made a grotesque sound as he choked down the mucus produced from his crying and she suddenly remembered where she was. *This isn't happening* were the words replaying in Amy's head as she once again experienced the falling feeling she'd had upon seeing Todd in the parking lot earlier. This time she was able to resist the fall and as she did so the world around her slowed down. It was like everything around her was moving in half-speed. She began to separate from her physical body and was able to witness everything from a bird's eye view. This was accompanied by that sense of deja vu, where she knew exactly what was going to happen next. From above she watched Elliot walk towards the entrance and then she saw herself slowly rotate her head, as if it were on an axis, until she was looking at Todd. She saw Todd's body lightly jerk with the occasional hiccuping sob as he watched Elliot. With horror she noticed the sense of recognition in Todd's eyes.

"Elliot's here," Todd mumbled as if to himself.

"How do you know what Elliot looks like?" She saw herself speak the words.

Slack-jawed and with his mouth half-opened, Todd let his head fall down to his right shoulder, and it sort of flopped around, like one of those bobble head dolls. When he lifted his eyes to her she could see they were bloodshot, red-rimmed, and surrounded by puffy flesh. The sight made her shudder. This wasn't the Todd that Amy knew.

"You've been spying on us?"

Todd nodded vacantly.

***

There wasn't anyone at the reception desk so Elliot wandered from the lobby into the office area on the first floor. There he asked a woman if she knew Amy and she directed him to the second floor. On the elevator an energetic young woman gave him a curious look. He realized that he was in shorts and a slightly dusty t-shirt, his hair was a bit matted with dried sweat and there might have been a whiff of body odor. Both he and the young woman stepped off the elevator. She walked ahead with purpose but must have registered he was just floating around so she stopped and turned to him.

"Hi, are you delivering something?"

"I'm looking for Amy."

"Oh, Amy. I think she just left for lunch."

"Can you tell me where her office is? I'll just leave these on her desk. "

"My apologies but I have to ask who you are?"

"I'm Elliot. Her husband."

"Elliot. Oh," her face immediately softened into a concerned look. Clearly she knew he was dying. Allegedly. "Hi, Elliot. I'm Emily. Follow me through these doors and then Amy's office will be on your right. Her name's on the door."

It hadn't occurred to him until then that her whole community at work thought she was about to become a widow. The extent of his lie and its effects were astounding. The ramifications were greater than he had imagined. How far had his lie reached? What other ripples was he not aware of?

On the door to her office was a placard with her name and title on it. Elliot took a moment to appreciate it. He hadn't known exactly what her title was. It was pretty impressive albeit a bit long, *Director of Curriculum Administration and Development.* You know you're working for a bureaucracy when you have a title like that, he thought to himself with a chuckle.

Stepping inside the office Elliot was hit by a wave of warm feeling, which he ascribed to the residual energy left in the room by Amy. The office was predictably clean and organized. Looking around the tight quarters he noticed a bookshelf filled with binders, educational books, textbooks, and the like. There were a lot of diplomas on the wall next to a framed painting of the small seaside village they had visited. There was a large window which looked out over the parking lot area. On her desk were neatly stacked piles of papers, various files, her personal laptop computer and a desktop computer. There was also a small framed photo of the two of them set on the corner of her desk. It was their wedding photo. He wished he would have done the same thing at his work. When he returned home he would immediately put a photo of them on his desk.

Next to the photo on her desk he set down the vase of wildflowers and the chocolate. On a yellow sticky note he wrote, "Amy, I love you, Elliot," and stuck it to the vase.

***

Outside of the office Amy's physical body was sitting in Todd's car but she still felt as if she were separated from herself, hovering, watching. Drifting through the scene, like small wisps of clouds, were her thoughts. She seemed to be only aware of the most important ones. Elliot must not be involved in any way, this was paramount. All the hope in her marriage would vanish if her affair came out. It would destroy Elliot and the stress might hurt his chances of surviving his illness. Amy looked over at Todd, he was sitting there like a lump, staring straight ahead at the building's entrance. What was the actual threat level? She wondered. She opened his glove box and rummaged around inside of it.

"What are you doing?" He said in a trance-like quality without moving anything but his lips.

"Seeing if you have a gun, Todd," she hoped this might serve as a splash of cold water, so she repeated herself, "I'm seeing if you have a gun, Todd. Do you?" Bug-eyed, she held her stare on him but he didn't reply.

Her cellphone rang and she knew who it would be. Turning away from Todd she watched Elliot walk out of the building with his phone to his ear. Amy looked back to Todd and they locked eyes for a moment. A thin smile crossed his face before he shifted his gaze back to Elliot. Now Elliot was standing just outside of the building, texting. Amy's phone pinged with Elliot's texts and Todd chuckled. *This fucking asshole*, she thought looking at Todd. She could have killed him right then and there. The static noise in her head shot up to maximum volume but it somehow helped her to focus on her thoughts which she could actually see in word form. Typed letters, black on white, underneath her, being pulled slowly past her eyes, one thought after another. *Get out of the car and walk away. Take Elliot back into the office. Get in your own car and drive away. With Elliot. No, without Elliot. Just drive away with Todd. Get him the hell away from Elliot. Don't drive away with Todd. Too dangerous. Just remain in Todd's car, hope to God Elliot quickly drives away. Call the cops.*

Something about her line of thinking didn't feel right. Of course every option had considerable risk, but it wasn't that. It was something else that bothered her. She couldn't put her finger on it. In the midst of her panicked thoughts and the imminent calamity a very calm voice was trying to be heard. Somehow she managed, just for an instant, to be very quiet inside and listen. The voice sounded like her own and it said, *your entire premise is wrong*. She actually frowned when she heard this. Then the image of Elliot's chalkboard, with its maze of equations, flashed through her mind. The continual horizon of unknowingness. *I don't know what to do*, she thought to herself. Right on the heels of that thought came a gentle force which pulled her back into her body and time slipped back to normal speed. The entire sensation surrounding her at that moment had a smooth granular and syrupy quality to it. Suddenly she knew what to do. Relief flooded her body and washed out any fear. She laughed out loud, fully and deeply. It was insane but it occurred to her that she felt great.

"Go ahead. Go on. Just do it. Get it over with. Elliot's right there. Tell him. If that's what you are going to do, then do it. Let's face it right now." Suddenly Todd started his car. There was a flash of heat across Amy's body which settled in her face, "okay, then, Todd. Drive." They were locked in a stare off but she quickly felt Todd's energy shrinking and she could feel herself growing larger. Like they had earlier, his eyes began to dart away from her. Without another word Amy got out of his car and walked away.

Elliot was just about to get into his car when he heard Amy call his name. A big smile lit up his face and he was about to say something but before he had a chance, she jogged up to him, and with great feeling kissed him on the lips.

"Thank you. For that," Elliot said as she got into his car. The moment her body sank into the passenger seat she began to tremble. Elliot noticed and gave her a concerned look.

"Don't worry," she said, "let's go."

***

Their drive to lunch took only five minutes. Which was fortunate for Amy because she couldn't shake the fear that Todd might be following them. A fear that was made more palpable by the small confines of a car. Elliot had noted something was off right from the moment they got into his car. Despite her suggestion not to worry, Elliot did worry. So, he asked her, in that earnest way people do when they really want to know, "how are you?"

"Fine. Really."

"You're shaking."

She couldn't blame it on the presentation and claim it was an adrenaline dump because the presentation was over an hour ago.

"I'm not sure what's going on with me."

"Maybe it's residual adrenaline from the presentation. Combined with an empty stomach."

How could she deny the alibi Elliot had just given her feelings. The very same one she had considered and rejected. So, she didn't protest and in doing so Elliot unwittingly lied for her. The guilt made her feel even more sordid. Thankfully for Amy they didn't talk the rest of the drive but Elliot did offer his free hand which she clutched tightly.

On the drive over to the restaurant Amy had kept an eye out for Todd's car and hadn't noticed anything. Stepping into the restaurant Amy looked behind her at the parking lot. Still no sign of Todd. Fairly confident they were in the clear she began to relax just enough to realize she was hungry. They managed to get a table right away. Amy immediately ordered spring rolls to start. They scanned their menus until the waitress returned.

"Feeling better?" Elliot asked after the waitress left with their order. The shaking had stopped. Outwardly she was much calmer. Inside was another story. There was still a lot going on. She was coming to terms with the possibility that a protracted situation with Todd had begun. He had clearly proven himself unpredictable and the entire fiasco had the potential to explode. But the main objective remained. Keep Elliot out of it. While she was trapped in her worried mind there was a void in conversation. Amy could tell Elliot had hoped to hear more about her presentation. His interest was genuine and he naturally assumed she wanted to talk about it. All of this she appreciated, deeply, and more than anything she wanted to be able to share with him. She wanted to fill his ear with all her observations and thoughts about the presentation. But she couldn't. Instead she mustered up a few words here and there.

"I'll take your word for it."

"What?" She asked.

"That it went well. This morning you were buzzing and I would have thought, given that things are moving forward, you would still be buzzing. But," he hesitated, "I don't know."

"What?"

"Are you sad about something?"

To her it felt like he was looking behind her eyes and into her heart. Now she hoped Elliot would, once again, give her another alibi. Fill in the blank for her because sad was a lot harder to write off than tired. But he didn't offer anything. Instead he did something she normally would have appreciated but today wished he wouldn't. He simply waited and made himself available to listen. As they sat there, him waiting for her to say something, her not knowing what to say, she began to wonder if he suspected something. Then she tried to erase the idea. Of course he didn't suspect anything. Why would he? But then again, how could she be so sure? No, she was certain, this was just his genuine interest and not an effort to put her on the spot. The simplest route around this awkwardness would be to say something. To lie. But she didn't want to lie to him. Not anymore. Certainly people have moods for no specific reason, and that, she hoped would be his assumption. But most likely he will assume her sadness relates to his dying and that would break her heart. His death the alibi for the mood created by her infidelities. At last she gave a half-hearted shrug, thanked him for his concern, and hoped that would be the end of it.

"I realize what I've put you through isn't easy and I'm sorry. More sorry than you know."

And with that he made his death the alibi for her sadness. Her stomach turned. "It's not you, Elliot. That's not why I'm like this. So, please, don't ever apologize for what you're going through. It's me and I'm sorry."

The food arrived and thankfully it was so good and they were both so hungry that it took care of the lack of conversation, save for Elliot's comments on the food, which he loved. When he vowed they would make this a regular work-day lunch date, Amy began to forget her worries, and let herself be drawn back into the moment. And when Elliot's childlike insistence on getting dessert made her laugh, she reached out, took his hand and kissed it.

It wasn't until the drive back that her thoughts darkened once again and her vigilance regarding Todd returned. The idea of a restraining order came to her mind. It made sense on a lot of levels. But a bold move like that brought the risk of a war. And a war would undoubtably draw Elliot in. It might also provoke Todd into doing something dangerous.

There was also the issue of Elliot's health and how that would effect any strategy. In the event Elliot beat his disease the risk of Todd blowing everything up greatly increased because the longer Elliot was alive, the more opportunity there was for something to go wrong. Then a thought she had been fighting back, one from the hinterlands of her mind, finally broke in. The sooner Elliot died the more likely it was he would never find out about Todd. Just having this thought filled her with self-hatred. This led her to another unpleasant truth. It wasn't just Elliot she was protecting, she was also protecting herself.

"Oh, something happened earlier today," Elliot said in a tone that immediately caught her attention.

"What?"

"Terry Algren was rushed to the hospital."

"Oh, my God. What happened? Is he going to be alright?"

"I don't know but it seemed serious."

"What does this mean for you?"

"When you get home tonight," Elliot said as he took her hand and held it, "we need to talk about that."

There was something about the way Elliot said the last sentence but Amy couldn't put her finger on it. Rather than investigating this feeling she let it go because they had just pulled up in front of her work and her stomach began to knot up. It seemed absurd that Todd would still be in the parking lot but not inconceivable. For this reason she quickly gave Elliot a kiss and hurried inside the building. Once inside Amy turned to watch Elliot drive away. She also looked out over the parking lot. The coast was clear. No Todd. This brought her temporary relief, but the fact remained, Todd was now like a shark in the water. Just because she didn't see him didn't mean he wasn't there. But Todd wasn't the only shark hiding in the deep dark waters. Stepping into her office she saw the vase of wildflowers, her favorite chocolate bar and the note with the words, *Amy, I love you, Elliot*. That simple note broke broke her heart - while he was writing it, she was outside in a car with Todd.

"I met your husband," it was Emily, the young woman Elliot spoke to earlier, "he seems so sweet."

"He is." Amy took Elliot's note and stuck it to their wedding picture.

15

While he waited for Amy to arrive home from work Elliot stared at the whiteboard in his office. Since he had committed to a course of action regarding his lie a certain peace of mind had come over him and he was able to deeply concentrate on his theory. For several hours he had been thinking over many of the well known equations that might, possibly, even tangentially, relate to his theory and might offer a clue to the path forward. The event horizon theory and its equation were intriguing to him at that moment because what was known about black holes seemed to mirror physical death which was of course the greatest unknown into which time unfolds and that all seemed to point towards his "theory of unknowingness," as Amy had coined it. He decided he would follow his intuition and study black holes believing there was a connection or intersection there. For years he had searched for points in different equations and theories in the hopes he might find that chip into his own equation. Several times he thought he'd found it but, as his theory would have it, that known lead to another unknown.

The sound of Amy's car drew Elliot from his reverie. By the time he stepped out of his office Amy was at the kitchen window looking out towards the street. The drive home for her had felt like a spy movie. She had been constantly checking her rearview mirror to make sure she wasn't being tailed. Of course if she were being followed it wouldn't be a spy movie. It would be a stalker movie. Fortunately, she had not been followed and Todd was not parked on the street.

"What's that?" Elliot's voice surprised her. From the edge of the kitchen he was indicating the small box on the counter. He calmly walked over and picked it up. It was a wireless home security camera.

"Can you set it up this weekend?"

"Over the front door?"

"Yeah, so it gets a view of the street too."

"Sure," Elliot set it back on the counter and gave her a curious look as if he might ask why she suddenly thought a security camera was necessary. His entire tone and manner caught Amy off guard. She had noticed a cool air when he entered the room and now it flashed through her mind that Todd could have stopped by. Todd could have told Elliot everything and rather than coming in hot, Elliot was making a cold surgical strike. If this was it, what would she do? Deny the truth? Accept the truth? Was there a third option? Run out of the door? Blink herself out of the nightmare? It seemed like he was waiting for her to say something. Was he trying to make her nervous?

"Any ideas for dinner?" Amy said trying to shift the conversation away from anything that might even remotely have a Todd subtext, certainly away from security cameras. She felt stupid now for having come home with one.

"Before we talk about that, I need to talk to you about something else."

Again he seemed to wait around for her to say more. Finally she decided to stop avoiding and turned it on him, "are you okay?"

"Actually, I am. I feel great."

"It just seems like, I don't know, something's up."

"I thought we could talk. About my health."

In her own fear and paranoia Amy had forgotten that Elliot wanted to speak with her about his health. After all this time he was finally initiating and she had forgotten.

"Is it about our appointment with Terry?"

"There's no appointment with Terry."

"Why?"

"Well, for one we don't know if he's going to live or die," Elliot reminded her.

"Right, I guess that's true," she said with a shake of her head.

"And the real reason there's not an appointment with Terry, or any other doctor, is because…I'm not dying."

***

There was no discernible reaction from Amy. Not a word, not a movement, not a single indication that she had even heard what Elliot had said, so he repeated himself, "I lied to you. I'm not dying." Saying she was stunned or frozen didn't do it justice. Not even shock came close to describing what was happening. It was more like a standing coma. Just as serious concerns for her physical health began to register in his mind there were signs of life. First she blinked. Then she began to open and close her mouth, like a fish out of water. While she was doing that she put her hands out, palms up, as if to implore him.

"Why?" She finally asked.

Why? It was an obvious question he should have anticipated. But it was beyond his ability to answer because he truly did not know why he told her he was dying. The answer to the question of why he would lie about dying was well hidden in his blindspot and sometimes blindspots are places we cannot see and sometimes blindspots are places we do not want to see.

"I don't know," was his truthful and disappointing answer.

With a frustrated grunt she began pacing with the combustible energy of a caged tiger which frightened Elliot. The situation, he realized, was out of his depth. The idea of seeking professional guidance beforehand was a clear oversight. An oversight for which he was, at that very

217

moment, deeply regretful.

"I wanna. . ." her anger catching the words in her throat, leaving her only with a strangled grunt. She never finished the sentence and he was left to imagine what she wanted. When her eyes returned to him with a burning stare he imagined she wanted to murder him. Without saying another word she packed a bag and left. Elliot watched from the window as she backed out of the driveway and drove away.

***

She missed him. She hated him. She loved him. And it was true she had briefly thought about murdering him. Nothing made sense to her. Elliot had fucked everything up in the most inexplicable and hurtful way. At least his timing was good. Even though it felt like it would take a lifetime to wrap her head and heart around this, Friday was better than a Monday to start the process. At least there was that, she thought, with a bitter laugh. There were so many questions and so many feelings she couldn't possibly have gone into work the next day. Just the thought of work made her mind collapse further. She was helpless to concentrate, unable to order her thinking, and incapable of processing thoughts. And of course her emotions were not helpful, they had run amok, threatening to destroy everything in their path, including her body, mind and soul. Fortunately, a plan popped right into her head and she got the hell out of the house. A day trip she and Elliot had yet to go on. Fine. She took the idea and ran with it. No need to facilitate about things, not able to. A place with no memories together. Perfect. Able to make it to the hot springs before last light? Who knows? Who cares? Food and wine. Grab some on the way.

Practically skidding to a full stop in the dirt lot she sent a cloud of dust and stress wafting into the sky. The hike in was easier than she'd imagined. It was twilight when she got there which afforded her enough light to get a good look around. It was nothing like she imagined. The oasis tucked in the mountains, under the oaks, with hot pools of clear water surrounded by massive boulders was not what she found. Instead she found a barren patch of hillside with three small hot tub sized pools surrounded by hard dirt and shale ground. Yet, the spartan quality actually held a certain appeal to her. It was simple and honest. She also discovered she was not alone.

There was a group of 20-somethings packed into one of the pools so she headed towards the other two pools which were empty except for a handsome guy who looked to be leaving. Amy purposefully went to the pool he wasn't leaving, which was about thirty feet from where he was drying off. This didn't stop him from walking over to her. She had dipped into the hot water and was trying to relax when she noticed he was standing above her. The man reminded her of Todd. Not in looks but in attitude. The last thing Amy wanted was small talk with a man horning in on her. First there was his mention that he hadn't quite spent enough time soaking. The implication being he could join her if she wanted. Then he probed around for something personal he could exploit but she ignored these cues and several others. When he mentioned she was alone she seized the opportunity.

"I'm waiting for my husband." The magic words that repel guys like him.

The noise from the group of 20-somethings laughing it up in the other pool faded out and she hardly noticed when they left. Skipping the snacks she brought, Amy went straight for the wine, drinking straight from the bottle. The numbing helped. There, alone, under the stars, she cried. It was a weeping full of self-pity and she knew it. She didn't give a fuck. She felt pitiful. Of course, she knew she couldn't and wouldn't hold onto this. No matter where things went she was determined this would be her rock bottom. First Todd, then Elliot. All happening on the best day of her professional life. She was trying to understand how life could be so meaningful one minute and so meaningless the next? So generous and then so cruel. Perhaps, she thought, this was something that didn't require understanding. Only acceptance.

I should come here with Elliot before he dies. . . It was a reflexive thought and she groaned when it landed. Now that he was "going to live" she wouldn't be going anywhere with him, ever. *He's better off dead than alive*, she laughed, *Fuck you, Elliot. Fuck.* What was she going to do about Elliot? It would have been great to talk this over with a friend but that wasn't something she was prepared to do. At least not yet. She would be telling her therapist though. That was for damn sure. What were therapists for if not for times like this. Her appointment with Elaine was for Monday but she'd already had a brief call with her on the drive up. Elaine reassured Amy taking time to get away and think about things was both wise and appropriate. She also strongly recommended not doing or saying anything decisive before their appointment. What that all meant to Amy was that she didn't have to figure out what to do about Elliot right then and there. Which was fine with her because it was all too heady at that point. The intellectual back and forth, the what, why, and how of it, was giving her a headache on top of her heartache.

She nibbled on the snacks, took another gulp or two of the wine, and took in the stars above. After giving the feeling of self-pity center stage it shrank from the spotlight and was replaced by a sort of disbelief at the absurdity. She even said, "what the fuck?" out loud, several times. More than once she found herself laughing about it all. The laughter at the absurdity veered into tears. The tears waned and she felt tired. The emotional journey of the day was finally slowing. And what a journey it had been. The presentation at work, Todd, Elliot and then she went into some sort of standing coma. It was the strangest thing ever, even scary, like locked-in syndrome, trapped inside herself, unable to move but able to see and hear. How had she felt nothing the moment Elliot told her he wasn't dying? When the wheels began to slowly turn again, she was flooded with emotion. Every imaginable emotion. Then a near catatonic depression, which was something she had never experienced. It was so intense that, for a moment, she was concerned about her driving. She almost talked herself out of hiking to the hot springs. But she was glad she didn't. She had finally stopped the emotional slide and was able to plant her feet, albeit on a rocky emotional bottom, and she didn't love where her thoughts were going but at least she could think again. She didn't love how she felt but at least she could understand what she was feeling and could feel one emotion at a time. And what she was feeling was overwhelming humiliation. It felt like she had caught him having an affair. That comparison gave her pause, for obvious reasons, considering she actually had been having an affair. She shook it off. Now was not the time to self-reflect on her own lies and misdeeds. Or was it?

Upon arriving at the little roadside motel Amy was seized by the fear she would have insomnia and be stuck thinking about this shit all night. Those fears were dashed when her head hit the pillow and almost immediately she fell into a deep slumber. It was a dreamless sleep from which she awoke to slices of light cutting through the blinds. Immediately she did two things she wished she'd done the night before. She brushed her teeth and took a shower.

The next thing she did was to pray and meditate. Regarding meditation, there were two things she had read about but had yet to experience, until that morning. The first was that although meditation was a powerful tool towards well-being, it wasn't a key to some magic world where all your problems are instantly solved. Because they certainly weren't that morning. In fact she felt like she had even more problems after the meditation than she did before. The second thing she had read was that you might feel bad the entire meditation and that's okay. Well, she felt bad that entire meditation. And yet, somehow, she felt better afterwards. So, maybe it was a key to some magical world where all your problems are magically solved. She didn't know.

***

Both Elliot and Amy had butterflies in their stomachs when she came home late Sunday night. While she was gone there had not been a word of communication between them. The lights in the house were off and there wasn't a sound anywhere when Amy walked through the front door. She set her things down on the dining room table and went to the kitchen for a glass of water. Because it was late and the lights were all off she assumed Elliot was asleep. The idea of getting in bed with Elliot was not a comfortable one. But sleeping on the couch didn't feel good either. That felt too provocative in some way. Perhaps she could slip into bed and go to sleep without a word and then in the morning she could wake up before Elliot and leave without a word. Essentially her main objective for the next twenty four hours was to be as comfortable as possible given the circumstances and to not speak with Elliot. They could talk another time, but when that would be, she had no idea.

In their bedroom Elliot lay awake in bed with the lights off. He had been drifting towards sleep when Amy's arrival woke him up. Listening to her move about the house he began to wonder what he was supposed to do. Should he get out of bed and go downstairs? That felt a bit forced to him. Should he turn the lights on, sit up in bed, and wait for her to come in? That felt a bit parental to him, and she may not even come into the bedroom. She might just sleep on the couch. Of course, she could enter and ask him to sleep on the couch. Realizing he had no idea what he should or shouldn't do, what would or wouldn't happen, he decided to do what felt right to him, so he remained where he was, lying in bed in the darkness.

There were a number of reasons for Amy not to go into their bedroom and there were a number of reasons for her to go into their bedroom. Why exactly she found herself stealthily creeping into the bedroom and crossing to the bathroom, Amy had no idea. But there she was, quietly closing the door to the bathroom and turning the lights on. Elliot was a heavy sleeper so she had no reason to believe brushing her teeth would wake him up. If it did maybe he would do them both a favor and pretend to be asleep. She finished up in the bathroom and turned the light off. Then she opened the door and stepped into the darkness. She could see the shape of their bed and it gave her pause. The sight made something tighten in her chest. A crisp clicking sound cut through the air and a bright light hit her face. Elliot had turned his bedside light on. Startled, she gasped loudly, which startled Elliot, who then gasped, which made them both laugh. When they both realized they were laughing, their laughter quickly, and awkwardly cut out. For all the thought and worry they had both given towards this moment, in the end, they were both clumsy and bungling. Her sneaking around, him catching her in the act.

"Sorry. For the light. Didn't mean to scare you."

"Didn't mean to wake you. You can go back to bed."

Elliot turned the light off and Amy ever so delicately got into bed. It surprised her that Elliot would be the one to initiate contact and that she was the one committed to avoiding it. There was something about that role reversal that bothered her.

If there was ever a situation where she wanted to fall asleep quickly this was the one, but of course she couldn't, it was as if the tension in her body was keeping her from even touching the mattress. As seconds turned to minutes, and minutes approached hours, Amy's self-consciousness grew to the point where her skin began to itch.

"It's not a thing where I'm storming off, okay, it's just I can't relax," she practically shot up from the bed, "I'll sleep in the other room." She had assumed he too was laying there uncomfortably and terminally awake but he hadn't been. He'd fallen right to sleep, "Elliot?"

"Huh?"

"I'm going to sleep in the other room. It's just. . . I can't sleep next to you."

"I get it."

"Until, I don't know."

"What?"

"Until. I can't sleep next to you until I don't know when."

"Oh. . .Okay."

"Because I still don't understand why you did what you did and I'm still upset. And sleeping next to you feels awkward and I don't think I should sleep next to you. . .Maybe ever. Again."

Amy waited for a reaction to the words "maybe ever again." They were the strongest words yet. Elliot remained silent. She couldn't even see him. It was like he wasn't even there. Before things got worse Amy turned to leave, she opened the door and then stopped. Perhaps she wanted some reaction from him before she left the room, perhaps she wanted to say something more to him.

In the doorframe Amy's silhouette looked beautiful to Elliot. He wanted to tell her so. He wanted to tell her to stay. That he loved her. That what they felt for each other that past month wasn't a lie. But he didn't say any of that.

"I'm sorry," he said.

"Why? Not why are you sorry, but why did you lie like that? And then continue lying? I wish I could just laugh at you but you put me, and everyone else, through unmeasurable, and unnecessary pain. Do you realize that? Everyday I thought about you being dead. And I would cry. And I would despair. And I would ask God, why? But it turns out that question was for you but you can't even seem to answer it. Regardless of what happens, we have to have the conversation where you tell me why. Don't you think I at least deserve that?"

Rather than waiting for an answer she knew was not coming that night, or possibly ever, Amy left Elliot alone in the dark to think about it.

Why? He tried to find the answer. She wanted to know the answer to that question so badly but he couldn't find it. There had to be an answer, a reason why he lied. It seemed insane he would have concocted the whole thing for no reason at all and he was pretty sure he was not insane. But given the circumstances he wasn't entirely sure of that. Trying to find the elusive "why" he kept coming back to cause and effect, and he finally settled on the idea that there is no cause and effect because the cause is the effect and the effect is the cause, and so on and so forth. And then he thought of the farmer parable. And he chuckled.

As he finally began drifting back towards sleep his mind

relaxed enough for a clue to slip through the cracks. The clue circled back to the whole cause and effect riddle. Supposing he was not insane and if the lie about dying was the cause, then it was also the effect. . . So, what had caused him to tell Amy he was dying? As that question landed clearly in his consciousness, he began to feel the answer to it, and that feeling was one of deep sorrow. And although he still could not grasp the details, he instinctively knew that the conversation Amy wanted about why he lied, he too wanted, and the doubt Amy had about their marriage, he too had. And most importantly he knew, he just somehow knew, she held the answer to her own question.

16

The next morning the only sign Amy had been there were the neatly folded blankets and comforter on the living room couch. Not expecting but hoping Amy had left a message Elliot checked his phone and noticed that Brian had texted again. Over the past weekend Brian had called and then texted Elliot. There was something he "really needed to talk about," but he wouldn't say exactly what. Although it would be totally out of character for her to do so, Elliot wondered if Amy had told Brian about his lie. Because of how badly she'd been hurt he wouldn't blame her if she did. Listening to Brian's voice message a second time it sounded like he was happy so it was presumable that Amy had not told him about the lie. Regardless Elliot didn't respond right away, there was just too much up in the air that weekend which he needed to sort out before talking to anyone, most of all he hadn't decided what to say to his family about the lie. While eating breakfast Elliot decided he would go visit his brother in person.

Stepping into Brian's house Elliot was greeted by a wave of dust in the air and stack of moving boxes. It might have been his imagination but it seemed as though the house had an echo when he called out his brother's name. After a moment Brian came down the hallway carrying a box which he set down next to the other boxes near the front door.

"Hey Brother!" Brian practically shouted as he gave Elliot a hug.

"You're moving?"

"Yep, in two weeks. Getting a jump on things," Brian had this big grin and was buzzing with excitement, all of which struck Elliot as terribly odd, considering that moving was a painful benchmark of most divorces.

"Do you need help?" Elliot called out to Brian who had just turned around and walked into another room. As far as Elliot was concerned this question was just as much about helping Brian with boxes as it was about Brian's state of mind.

"Nope! Almost done," Brian said from the other room. He retuned with another box, "my CD collection."

"People have CD collections?"

"They have record collections," Brian said as if this explained it.

"Okay, fine, yeah, and I take it the reason you called this weekend was to tell me you're moving and I get that, but I don't get why you're happy about that and I guess I'm wondering if I should be worried about you?"

From somewhere in the house a door closed and Elliot heard a familiar voice. Brain answered the confused look Elliot gave him by coyly raising an eyebrow. Walking further into the house Elliot saw Mona talking on her cellphone and when she saw him she happily waved.

"Hi, Uncle Elliot," Dulce called out from the other room. Elliot turned around to find his brother holding a goofy, over the top pose, as if to say, "who knew?" Not only that but his eyes had a lunatic shine and his broad grin took up half his face. Brian stood frozen like this waiting for Elliot to say something. The longer Brian held the pose the crazier he looked.

"You're waiting for me to say something?"

"I am."

"I want to see how long you'll stand there like that."

"Come on."

"This is fun. I should take a picture of you," Elliot said chuckling.

"They're not getting a divorce," Dulce said in a deadpan

voice. Elliot turned towards her, she was eating a bowl of cereal as she walked towards him from the kitchen. She gave Elliot a slightly amused shake of her head, as if to say *those crazy kids*. When Elliot turned back around Mona was now standing with Brian. They were holding hands with an expectant look on their faces and seeing them like that, Elliot was struck by their vulnerability. Two imperfect humans doing the best they could. In their own way this was romantic. Dysfunctionally romantic but romantic nonetheless.

"Good things do come from bad. That's what you told us," Mona said. She was holding onto Brian's arm, he was nodding as if to second what she said. The way the entire scene had played out was a bit dizzying for Elliot but he was thrilled for them. However, the good news turned out to be bittersweet. Brian and Mona had finally decided to try marriage counseling, not to reconcile but to better handle the divorce, but after their second session they decided to stay together. Not only that, but the move back home that Mona was planning, the one where she took Dulce, now Brian was going to join them. Her father had decided to buy them a house. So, they got to sell this house, keep the profit, and have another house purchased for them. Everything had worked out extremely well. Elliot was happy they were going to work it out but he was sad they were moving away. After chatting about the big news for a few minutes Mona had to take Dulce to school which left Elliot and Brian alone.

"What about you?" Brian asked, "how's, you know, everything?"

"Well, actually I want to talk to you about some things. But not here. Not now. Can you come over later?"

"Yeah, sure, what's going on?"

"I'll tell you everything later. And Karen will be there. I

need you together for this."

Mercifully, without hesitation or protest, Brian said, "anything for my brother," trying not to let his voice betray the tears he was holding back. He assumed Elliot was going to let them know how many days he had left to live.

***

It seemed like all the siblings were in better moods than the last time Elliot saw them. It was a pleasant surprise to find Karen relatively happy and calm.

"Somebody has some big news," Karen announced as she ushered Elliot to her kitchen table. She offered him some coffee which he declined but he did accept her offer of water. Karen brought him water in a colorful ceramic mug imbued with a faint taste of coffee. Karen had at least three cups of coffee a day. Years ago he asked his sister if the amount of coffee she drank might contribute to her anxiety. She answered, "yes, that's why I cut it down from five to three cups a day."

"You seem in better spirits."

"I am. Karma has that effect I suppose," she chuckled in a conspiratorial way, with a snort at the end. The last time Elliot had seen Karen she was deep in the dumps because her employer had let her go. To Karen the way the whole thing went down wasn't fair. Then as she's in the middle of what seemed to be a never-ending downward spiral she got some unexpected help. Out of the blue she received an anonymous email. Attached to that email were copies of emails between her immediate supervisor and the chief operating officer at her former job. The content of the emails clearly showed that there was a strategy in place to set-up and/or force certain employees out. They had to "cut the fat," which included Karen.

"I've tried to put weight on my entire life. But to them I

was fat!" Karen snorted. When she was in a good mood she occasionally snorted when she laughed. "And Elliot, can you believe it, what this jerk said about me, 'I can make her go crazy.' The plan was to overwork me. They believed, correctly, that they could tip me into a manic state because the 'timing was right,' as they put it, and you know what the timing was? Well, somehow they heard you were dying and they heard it was having an effect on me, of course it was, and they knew that I've had my ups and downs, as it were. Anyway, I handed those emails to an employment attorney and abracadabra, I'm on the cusp of a settlement. In fact most of the fat they were cutting are part of the settlement. We're talking low six figures for me and a few others."

"Really?"

"Oh, yeah. A, you have my excellent record at work. I was good at what I did. B, the whole mental health thing is a hot button issue these days. Doesn't look good for them. C, using my brother dying to their advantage. Gross. Would look horrible to a jury. I could take it to trial and get more, but I don't know, this will be enough. I just want it over with. By the way, you're not dying."

"You're right."

"I just know it. I can feel it. Positive thinking," she tapped her head with her index finger.

"Can you come over later today? I have something important to tell you."

"Tell me now."

"I invited Brian too. I need you both together. Is that okay?"

"You know what?" She said with so much sudden energy he thought for a moment she was going to explode in anger about Brian. "Great! Fine. We're family. But you really can't tell me now?"

"Well, I want to tell you both at the same time. And seeing that he's not here, yeah, that means I can't tell you now."

"Smart ass. Is it about your health?"

"Just come over," Elliot began walking himself to the door. Karen followed, the curiosity getting to her.

"Why do we need to be there together?"

"Karen."

"No, I will be there. I will. It's just I have questions. Suspense is hard. Not knowing is hard."

"Are you okay?"

"Yes, yes, nothing like that. Just curiosity. What did you tell Brian?"

The calmness she had when he arrived was now replaced by hyper energy which was ramping up with each question. Despite her assurances Elliot knew something was beginning to upset her. Death was the ultimate unknown and it was this unknown causing Karen's anxiety to build.

**

During the course of her life the compartments Amy had created to protect herself had become traps. When Elliot told her he was dying the doors opened up. There was a sudden shift of perception. A white light experience had occurred. Life had changed almost instantly and over the past month Amy had begun to see the world differently. There were no longer walls between one part of her life and the other. She felt whole. However, recent events with Todd and Elliot had begun to fissure that wholeness. Rather than allowing herself to crack further Amy took the initiative to invest in her well-being and that was why she found herself at a little vegan market learning about essential oils from Pandora, a young goth woman with dreadlocks. Across from where Amy stood talking with Pandora, separated by a partition of plants, was the market's little vegan restaurant.

"Try this one? It helps me see." Pandora said as she put several drops on the back of Amy's hand. When Amy gave her a curious look, Pandora ran her hand up and down the center of her body from her head to her pelvis, "to see from here."

The scent immediately took Amy for a ride back to the moment she and Elliot jumped off the waterfall. The forest, the moss, the cold river. It was all there. Then something she inadvertently gleaned with her eyes brought her back. On the other side of the partition of plants, sitting at a booth in the vegan restaurant, was Todd. Sitting across from him was a young woman, perhaps in her twenties. After Amy purchased several essential oils she considered leaving but she didn't. Instead she remained where she was and watched Todd and the young woman.

Something panged hard in Amy's stomach. The panging continued, like a pulse within her intestines. Whatever Todd was saying made the attractive young woman occasionally laugh. When she laughed she would toss her head back a little and then run her hand through her hair. Instinctively Amy knew the woman was married. It was all too familiar to her, the behavior, the energy. There was a strong chemistry in the way they stared at each other but the woman would break it off first. Todd had left one hand extended on the table and at one point the woman reached out and held it, for a moment, but then she pulled her hand away and reflexively took a quick glance around.

Todd and the woman stood up and began to leave the restaurant. Suddenly Amy froze in panic realizing she stood between them and the exit. She was able to make herself shift just enough to turn her back from them and pretend she was looking at something on the shelf in front of her. What would she do when Todd saw her? What do you say after an incident like she had with him? Do you act like nothing had happened? Just move it right along? Or do you blast him and warn the woman he's with? All of these thoughts were racing around while she waited to hear her name. But nothing happened.

Finally she got the courage up to crane her neck just enough to glance behind her. They were gone. Amy looked towards the front of the market and saw them walk out from another aisle, and out of the market, without incident.

Hurrying to the front of the store Amy expected to see them driving off, instead she watched Todd and the young woman walk across the boulevard and head in the direction of an old-school renovated 50's era two-story motel. As they entered the parking lot, now safe from prying eyes, they held hands, and with a little pep in their step, took the stairs up to the second floor. In one smooth move Todd took the room key from his pocket, quickly had the door open, and with a gentlemanly gesture ushered the young woman inside. Then the door to the motel room shut and they were gone. Less than a week ago he was in her car weeping and cursing and threatening. Today he was charming and sweet and taking another woman, a married woman, into some hotel room to fuck her.

Suddenly Amy was struck by fear and acute waves of nausea which nearly caused her to lose her balance. Had someone seen her do the same thing? She had always thought of herself as careful. Keeping it separated from her real life. Keeping it all in the hotel room. But that was not necessarily true. There were times they walked into the hotel together. Times they took the elevator together. There were times they walked out from the hotel together and walked each other to their cars. More than once they had inadvertently held hands. Once, in the parking lot, Todd had snuck a kiss while saying goodbye. Everything about that kiss came to her mind. His tongue, his stubble, and the particular smell of his breath was inescapable. The day Todd kissed her in the Hyatt parking lot was also the day Elliot had come home and told her he was dying.

The sea of nausea began rising from her stomach and she bolted for the exit. As if to cap the geyser she put the palm of her hand over her mouth. The market's automatic doors slid open and Amy quickly scurried towards her car. The clenching in her gut grew into violent plunging which was sucking the contents of her stomach upward. Jolting spasms brought on by the painful constrictions of her diaphragm and neck brought her to her knees. Planting her hands onto the dusty hot asphalt she was barely able to brace herself before unleashing a screaming torrent of vomit which splattered all over the front wheel of her car.

***

Brian and Karen had always shared a gallows humor and as their audience Elliot provided the laugh track. However, when the sarcasm cut too deep, when the jokes became weaponized, and when his siblings rivaled, Elliot's role changed to either pawn, peacemaker or collateral damage. Although the reason for bringing them together was to right his own wrong, Elliot did hope this gathering might provide an opportunity for their reconciliation.

"We keep getting crazier but we keep landing on our feet!" Brian joked.

"We do keep landing on our feet, well, except you Elliot! I'm sorry! Too far?" Karen said with sincerity but Elliot waved her off with a smile, "but I am sorry, because it's just not an accurate statement, because you are getting crazier!" And they all laughed, although her joke wasn't technically very funny. Elliot wondered if he were actually dying would he be able to laugh at stupid jokes about his death. Yes, he would, at least he hoped so, because he knew that when they were laughing together, they were loving each other. When the deep rifts began in their family, around the time their parent's died, that's when they stopped joking about the sad things, and their humor deformed into sharp tongues used to cut each other, and their hearts began to close off.

While those two continued yukking it up in the living room, Elliot excused himself to get everyone drinks. It was both surprising and not surprising at all that Brian and Karen were getting on so well. They were family after all. But, after fifteen minutes, they had yet to address one of the elephants in the room. While he moved about the kitchen, Elliot kept his ear to the living room to follow their conversation.

"There is a fine line sometimes, with our humor," Karen observed, "and I know there are times I cross the line. Sometimes I don't even realize it. I just say things. And I may have said some things that hurt you."

"You *may* have?"

"I did say things. I'm sorry."

"It's okay. I think it's in our genes. I do the same thing. I certainly did with you. And I'm sorry too."

"It's okay. We just gotta keep the kids out of the line of fire."

"Or just be willing to laugh at them too."

"You know I thought about that coming here today, I said to myself, and I did say it out loud to myself cause I talk to myself all the time. I said, Karen, you lost your sense of humor in that whole thing with Brian!"

"You can't lose what you never had."

There was more laughter and then the laughter did that thing where it slowly winds down to chuckling and then it finally sputters out completely. And for a moment it sounded like they weren't saying anything at all. Then Elliot's ears adjusted and he could hear them again. They were speaking in hushed and whispery tones about the other elephant in the room. Karen's raucous laughter was replaced by a quiet tear filled murmur. She had brought some tissue which she pulled out and blew her nose into. Although they hoped the reason Elliot had invited them over was a ruse to get them in the same room for a reconciliation, they were both certain the real reason related to his dying. Elliot heard them ask, "how many days left do you think he has?"

While he was in the kitchen Elliot took a moment to gather enough courage to see his plan through. So far the plan was working. The first step was to bring his siblings together, which had been accomplished. The second step, which had to happen before the third step, was reconciliation, and that was now accomplished. But those steps seemed much easier than the third and final step. It was time to tell them about the lie. It was Elliot's belief that he needed the reconciliation to happen first because once the lie was out, there would be no chance at reconciliation. He had so often been the glue and with him removed from their lives, which he would surely be after they heard about the lie, there would be no glue to hold them together.

Their laughter carried in from the other room, their excited voices now talking about their children, the joy of them all being together gave Elliot doubts. It brought the same dilemma he'd faced with Amy, he didn't want to lose them. But even if he did continue lying to them, how would he explain his survival to them? The miracle cure?! With a clear head it now seemed unfathomable he had believed that cockamamie idea would work. Like Amy, they weren't stupid people. They were bright and curious and would more than likely smell a rat. The way he saw it, they were going to figure it somehow. Even if he could guarantee they would believe in a miracle cure or misdiagnosis, or whatever bullshit he threw out, he just couldn't bring himself to lie about dying anymore. Maybe it was selfish to tell the truth. Maybe they didn't need to hear it. Maybe Amy hadn't needed to hear it. But at least this way, by telling them through his own admission, he could salvage some measure of personal integrity. Would they surprise him and laugh it off? Forgive him and write it off as some complicated human error? Despite their large hearts he knew that wouldn't happen. They had only just made peace after years of excommunication. A lifelong shunning was certain, and yet, as it was with Amy, he could not live with himself while living this lie. The lie had given him the feeling of aliveness, of wholeness, of vitality, and the only way to retain that was by telling the truth.

"What're you building a well in there to fetch our water?" Brian called out. He could hear them chuckling. Elliot too chuckled when he heard Brian say to Karen, "being a dad has given me an endless supply of stupid dad jokes."

Just as Elliot was about to bring them their water, and the truth, he noticed Amy pull into the driveway. She was home much earlier than normal. This wasn't part of the plan. He had specifically invited his family over knowing she wouldn't be there. Having her there would add tension to tension. Temporarily baffled as to his next move all he could do was stand there in the kitchen, holding the drinks in his hands, and watch Amy walk into the house. Perhaps she would just go into her bedroom and leave them alone. There was a bit of excitement from the other room when they saw Amy.

"Elliot!" Amy called to him, "wait there. I'll help you put some food out."

Her offer to help him, and the genuinely pleasant tone, surprised him. Even though it wasn't in her character he wondered, was she playing at something? Was this a set up to hurt him in front of his family? That was unlikely. Perhaps, as was her character, she was being classy. His family was there and she would rise above their difficulties, for the moment, and treat her guests warmly. Yet, there something to her tone he couldn't place. She came into the kitchen and walked right up to him. It was obvious to him that she didn't look well. There was an acrid scent about her, like puke, masked by the smell of breath mints. There was an urgent expression in her eyes, both of warning and of love.

"Don't," she whispered stepping forward and gently touching his elbow. Her touch sent a pleasant sensation throughout his body causing his muscles to fully relax. The water glasses slipped from his hands and shattered on the ground. Rather than react in alarm they simply stood there looking at each as they had before the glasses dropped. Of course from the other room Brian and Karen asked if everything was okay. Karen in particular had really let out a shriek. "We're okay, everything is okay," Amy called out. Then she said to Elliot, "you've given them something. Let them keep it."

Elliot went into the living room while Amy began to pick up the broken glass and he didn't tell Karen and Brian about his lie. But there was something else he planned on telling them. It was time to tell them the secret their mother had told him, that their birth father might in fact actually be his birth father too. He was shaking when he sat down. His jaw wouldn't stop jittering and he wondered if he wouldn't be able to speak because of it. But when he opened his mouth the trembling stopped and the words poured out. And then he asked if they could all get a DNA test.

"So, I can know if I'm really your brother," he said in a soft voice.

***

The rising winds were blowing leaves throughout the backyard. Elliot was staring at their fountain and didn't hear Amy over the wind's rustling until she sat down in the chair across from him.

"Why?" He asked her. This was the first word spoken between them since Elliot's siblings had left. The context of his question wasn't clear to her and perhaps that's why it sounded so sharp.

"What are you asking me about Elliot?"

"Why did you come home and ask me not to tell them?"

"You didn't have to tell them."

"But I told you."

"Yes. It was a good thing you told me. But with them it's different."

"Why?"

"You had to tell me."

"Why?"

"It gave us back something we lost and it gave us something new. It gave me an opportunity to forgive you, which I do, and it gave me this opportunity to ask for your forgiveness."

Elliot moved from his chair and sat on the edge of the fountain. He dipped his hand into the water and soon it was so numb he couldn't feel the leaves he was scooping out. "Leaves falling in spring," he said more to himself than to her.

"We have a small net for that."

Ignoring her suggestion he instead switched to his other hand. Eventually he stopped altogether and sat on the ground. To warm his hands he crossed his arms and put them in his armpits.

For the past few days Amy had struggled to understand why Elliot had done something so senseless, particularly because he was a logical, sensible, and typically unsurprising person. It hadn't made sense to her until she saw Todd with another woman. Amy sat down on the ground, close to Elliot, their knees were touching, and she said, "you knew."

17

On the day Elliot told Amy he was dying he left work and went to the doctor for his yearly physical examination as required by his employer Target Aster. However, an employer cannot require an employee to do anything medical related unless it relates directly to their job. The companies reasons for the rule seemed to be a stretch. Some employees fought the rule, and as a warning, the least essential of those employees was let go. A failed lawsuit followed, quashed by Target Asters' army of attorneys. All that lingered around the office was a small cadre of conspiracy gossipers who believed the yearly physical was connected to personal data collection. All of it seemed much ado about nothing because the companies various Big Brother-ish rules were rarely followed up and so life eventually went on. As far as the yearly physical requirement, prior to the pandemic, it went unenforced. Then the pandemic happened and HR began sending out the emails. Agitation within the ranks resumed.

Elliot was ticked off because he didn't like to interrupt his work day. Interruptions to his narrow world, which only consisted of work, eat, and sleep, made him irritable and depressed. It wasn't a stretch to say shutting off his work brain, without proper withdrawal guardrails in place, created a potential mental health crises. Regardless of the fact the physical was not actually mandatory, and regardless of the interruption it caused to his train of thought at work, Elliot decided to just get it over with and so he pushed himself away from his desk and headed off to the doctor.

Something strange happened to him as he began driving away from work. The most unexpected thought was followed by a fit of uncontrollable laughter, *the most surprising discovery the doctor could make is that I'm actually not a robot and I'm really a living human being.* It wasn't necessarily the funniest thing in the world but he found himself laughing and laughing about it, to the point of tears. The emotion flipped and the tears signified pain. "I am a robot," he muttered out loud through his tears, "and the most surprising discovery the doctor could make is that I'm actually not a robot and I'm really a living human being." The moment was so powerful he had to pull his car off to the side of the road and take deep breaths.

In that moment of despair he began to feel a wonderful happiness and he thought to himself, *the life I want starts from this feeling.* Pulling back onto the road and continuing on his way that feeling of hope stayed with Elliot.

The drive to the doctor's became relaxing, almost fun, because it felt more like he was on a ride than running an errand. As the day would have it, he found himself driving right by the diner he used to buy pies from. For years it had been his habit to stop by this particular diner, buy a pie and bring it home. But at some point, this too, Elliot had forgotten all about.

Aside from several large pickup trucks and a beat up economy car, the diner's parking lot was empty, which was strange because it was a such popular place to eat. Following two men carrying a sheet of drywall into the diner Elliot poked his head in looking for pie. One of the guys who had carried in the drywall, a toothpick of a man, noticed Elliot and said, "closed."

"Is it going to be a new restaurant or just a remodel?"

The toothpick seemed stumped by this question. He looked to the other guy he carried in the drywall with. This guy was the older of the two and this interruption seemed to annoy him. "Same restaurant. Open soon. Okay?" he said.

Elliot was still thinking about pie when he saw a TGI Fridays. This TGI Fridays was adjacent to a Hyatt hotel.

Assuming they sold pies he parked on the boulevard and went inside. It turned out, technically, they did sell pies, but they weren't really what he considered pies. Elliot was a bit of a pie traditionalist but he rolled the dice anyway.

"Fine, I'll try the one with peanut butter and jelly," Elliot said with resignation.

"It's good. Really," the cashier was trying to sound convincing having correctly read Elliot's skepticism about peanut butter and jelly pie, "just give me a few minutes."

While considering whether or not he should stop at the market for a backup pie, which he rarely found up to his standards, Elliot wandered over to the large window near the entrance. From the window he could observe the parking lot of the adjacent Hyatt hotel. That's when it happened.

The environment of the restaurant faded away. The noise, the smell, the light, had all disappeared leaving Elliot standing alone in the darkness. The scene he watched no longer appeared to exist beyond the window in 3-D, instead it was like watching a movie projected onto a screen.

The first thought he had was the woman walking out of the hotel looked just like Amy. This woman was even dressed like Amy. A real doppelgänger. Right beside her was a somewhat handsome man with that trendy haircut everyone was getting. The man and woman parted company without touching but they looked back at each other in a certain way. There was this crooked smile on her face Elliot recognized. It was the way Amy smiled when she was being playful. Then this woman who looked like Amy shut the man out and focused straight ahead. Like she flipped a switch from fun to serious. There was something precise about her, just like Amy. Elliot looked back to the man who was watching the woman who looked like Amy. The man slowly walked backwards watching her walk towards her car. The car she got into was the same kind of car Amy had. That's when Elliot's brain finally accepted what it had known all along. The woman was Amy.

Suddenly the screen was filled with Amy and this other man. The perspective Elliot had was no longer a wide view of an entire scene but it was an extremely, uncomfortably close up look. Amy began to back her car out from the parking spot. The man jogged up to her car and she stopped. When she lowered her window all Elliot could see was her face. Time stopped for a moment on her beautiful face, and then in slow motion, the man's lips pushed into the frame until they met Amy's lips, and they began to kiss each other. Elliot could hear the rhythmic sucking sounds their undulating mouths made. And he could feel the moisture and taste the salty tang of their saliva. He could smell the merged scent of the man's musky aroma with Amy's faintly floral scented face cream. Cruelest of all Elliot could feel what it was like the first time he kissed Amy.

As if a switch were flipped the world around Elliot returned to normal. The sounds, the smells, and the light of the restaurant returned. The window was once again a window and not a movie screen. The world beyond the window was once again three dimensional. Unceremoniously Amy drove away and the man walked back to his car and he too drove away. There was a physical breaking feeling inside of Elliot's chest, like something had cracked, followed by a deep and lonely ache. The first coherent thought of his since seeing Amy walk out of the hotel was that heartbreak and heartache were not metaphors but were physically real phenomena.

"Sir?" The cashier had been trying to get his attention. She held the pie out for him. Elliot took the pie and turned back to the window one more time. There was something about that parking lot, something he was supposed to know, but he couldn't put his finger on it. Just like that he had blocked out the whole scene of Amy and Todd.

***

For the next ten minutes, after Elliot had picked up the pie, he drove to the doctors without a single introspective thought. He simply watched the road in front of him and listened to his science podcast. Not even the peanut butter pie sliding around on the floor triggered any memory of Amy and another man. Somehow he had forgotten the entire painful incident.

The medical building Elliot arrived at was unremarkable, as was the surrounding area. Elliot took a parking stub and parked his car. Walking towards the building Elliot noticed what seemed to be an elderly woman wearing a headscarf struggling up the stairs. Although there were only eight stairs, she had stopped on the fourth to catch her breath. Without thinking about it Elliot approached her and offered his help. When she looked up he realized she wasn't elderly but was probably in her mid-50's. She was a beautiful woman but she wasn't well physically.

"Do you need help?"

"Yes. Thank you. Can you help me to the third floor?" She asked and Elliot extended his arm which she took a shaky hold of, "you know, I thought about taking the ramp but then I decided to test myself," she said with an easy chuckle that made Elliot feel like he was basking in warm sunlight. Together they managed the rest of the stairs and walked into the building through the sliding doors.

"Do you have someone to help you?" She was one of those people you immediately like and feel like you've always known, and Elliot found himself hoping to spend more time with her.

"My son was supposed to bring me."

"Where is he?"

"He's a drug addict. So he's unreliable, to say the least. But he's on his way now."

"I'm sorry you have to go through that with your son. Hopefully he can get off drugs soon."

"Doesn't bother me all that much anymore. He will or he won't. Of course I hope he does but who knows. I don't know, I sound crazy these days. . . ." She trailed off and once again there was that warm chuckle and then they were quiet for a moment while they waited for the elevator to arrive. She was still holding his arm. Once inside the elevator Alice introduced herself.

"So, I have a couple months to live," Alice said as if she were telling him her favorite ice cream flavor. They stepped out onto the the third floor and she asked if he would wait with her until the doctor called her in. It wasn't until they sat down in the waiting room that Alice let go of Elliot's arm. While they waited she told him about the type of cancer she had and about the course of treatment she went through. She told him about getting all her affairs in order, how her priority now was to make her remaining time as comfortable as possible, and as such she hoped this was her last hospital visit.

"I used to say I was fighting cancer, and I was, and I would again if my body had any chance. Anyway, now that I'm faced with it," and here she leaned in and whispered conspiratorially, "I don't feel like dying is a loss. In fact, it may be just the beginning."

Something was happening and Elliot could feel it. It was like Alice held a special power which he wanted to hold as well. And even stranger was the feeling that she wanted him to ask her about it. So he did.

"Is it weird to say to a dying woman that I want what you have?"

"Cancer?" She said and they both laughed, "well, that would be weird to ask for, to say the least, but I know what you're asking about and no, it's not weird to want that. And I'm glad you asked because I do have something special."

"What is it?"

"I can't describe it."

"You seem to be at peace with dying, are you?"

"Yeah," the way she said it, there was no doubt to her honesty and there was more she wanted to say but she was searching for the words.

"Is that what you have, peace?"

"No, that's just evidence of it."

"Of what?"

It took her considerable time and Elliot waited patiently until she said, "There's no way I can articulate it but I'll tell you this, on some level I do wish I wasn't dying. I want to live. I do. And I can hold those those two things together in peace, my wish to live and my peace with death. But you know what?"

"What?"

It occurred to Elliot that she was about to say something deeply private. The type of thing a person keeps to themselves, not because they care people might think them crazy, but because they had not found an audience that would understand. With a twinkle in her eye she continued, "I like you Elliot. And I trust you with this."

"With what?"

"The best thing about dying is the worst thing about dying." At that moment a nurse opened the door to the waiting room and called for Alice.

"What do you mean?"

Alice took hold of his arm again and he helped her to stand up. She let go off his arm and walked with the nurse towards the door.

"Thank you, Elliot."

"Thank you, Alice," he said but he was still confused by what she had just said and wished he could have spoken to her longer. The nurse opened the door for Alice but she stopped and turned around to look for Elliot. A great big smile crossed her face when she saw he was still there. With a slight wave of her hand she beckoned him over. Without hesitation he walked right up to her and for a moment they stood looking into each other's eyes, hers shone like orbs.

"Can I have a hug?" She asked. Elliot took her fragile body into his arms and was thunderstruck by the strength and power of her spirit. Spirit was something he had never really considered in his life until that moment, and although she was dying on the earth, he was certain she would continue living in some other form. Releasing each other from embrace, Alice grabbed his hand and her grip was surprisingly strong, the way a baby's grip is surprisingly strong.

"Dying made me realize I fucking love my life," she said with a faint, breathless laugh that held a lifetime of joys and sorrows. With a knowing nod and not another word she let go of his hand, turned around, and walked through the open door which gently closed behind her.

***

When the door closed and Alice had left, Elliot remained standing there for quite some time, basking in something he couldn't understand. Left in her place was a mist of golden yellow light, syrupy and granular in texture, and which moved slowly and gracefully upward where it dematerialized into the air. The entire event, from the time he met Alice to the golden yellow mist, left him holding something wonderful but indescribable. Physically, mentally, and emotionally he understood most of what had just transpired and would have been able to articulate those aspects into words. But that wonderful, indescribable thing which left him standing there awestruck, was not physical, mental or emotional, and for this there were no words. Instinctively he knew trying to isolate and capture the experience was futile. He also knew that if he had tried to grab it and hold onto it, then it would disappear. It would only stay with him if he let it be.

Eventually he left the waiting room, walked down the hallway and waited for the elevator to take him to the fourth floor where his doctor was. For some reason the elevator was delayed for an unusually long time but it didn't bother Elliot. Just that morning he was consumed with agitation at the amount of time it took for his coffee to brew. The elevator came and he took it to his doctor's office where he checked in and, once again, waited. Eventually he was called in. How long he had waited, he wasn't aware, it didn't matter to him because he wasn't keeping track of time. For years there had been this clock in his head which he had dedicated his life to. It was always ticking, always moving moving forward, always one step ahead. But he now understood that was not real time.

The doctor informed Elliot he was moderately healthy. That everything looked good with his labs. Blood pressure and cholesterol were a bit high, but nothing some exercise, less stress and a better diet couldn't improve. Essentially Elliot was given a clean bill of health but she wanted to check a few things before she sent him off.

Stress. The word resonated with Elliot because he recognized there was now, within him, an absence of stress for the first time in years. And being free of it gave him the ability to see how much stress he had been carrying. As the doctor checked his breathing an image came into his mind, it was of himself eternally pushing a boulder up a steep hill, just like the myth of Sisyphus. Then he saw himself simply step aside and let the boulder roll down the hill. It was so obvious a solution. Just stop pushing the damn thing! This thought made him chuckle. The doctor caught his eye with an inquisitive look. Sharing a thought like this wasn't something he would normally do but today wasn't a normal day, so Elliot told her how he had managed to side-step the imaginary boulder he was pushing up the hill. The doctor smiled. She too knew the myth of Sisyphus and she even furthered the discussion mentioning Albert Camus and what she believed was his view about the boulder representing the struggle against the absurdity of life.

"That boulder is one of the biggest adverse factors I observe in my patients. I'm happy to see you have let it go," she said in a sort of cheeky sincerity. She then wished him well and added playfully in a stern doctorly voice, "be mindful of that boulder should it reappear." This exchange, any other day, would not have happened. The doctor would have been an abstract functionary he would have hardly registered. But today he saw an interesting, thoughtful, somewhat quirky human being with an entire life. And because that's what he saw, he engaged with her, and because he engaged with her, whatever phenomena he had experienced with Alice had just expanded.

Once again, as he had earlier that day when he'd pulled off the road in a fit of laughter and crying followed by happiness and hope, he thought to himself *the life I want starts from this feeling.*

Driving back to work he remembered his pie which he brought with him to the office kitchen where he cut himself a slice. It was surprisingly terrific. Peanut butter and jelly pie, who knew?

It was late afternoon and he had more than enough work waiting for him on his desk. On average he left the office at eight o'clock at night, this after having arrived, on average, at eight o'clock in the morning. While savoring each delicious bite he made the surprising decision to go home early, simply because he wanted to, and this was something he had never done before. He finished his slice, wiped his mouth with a napkin, drank a cup of water and happily walked out of the office. In the lobby Elliot set the pie down on the security guard's desk.

"I want you to have this." The security guard looked down at the pie then back up at Elliot with a look of confusion. "I just feel like sharing it," Elliot said as way of explanation.

The security guard took a closer look at the pie, his face brightened, and he looked back to Elliot, "peanut butter and jelly pie?" He asked hopefully.

"Yes! You know it?"

"It's one of my favorites," then the security guard said with a knowing look in his eyes, "it's good to be alive."

"Yes. Yes, it is good to be alive."

On Elliot's drive home he stopped and took a walk on a little trail which had a nice view of some rolling hills. The sun had just begun to set. It's gentle orange glow only just beginning its outward expansion. The setting gave him a place to think about his experience with Alice. Inherently Elliot liked to be able to explain, quantify and/or obtain measures of exactitude, yet when it came to his experience with Alice, he knew this was impossible. But he wondered if there was a way to identify the essence and the broader phenomena which might point towards the indescribable. So in his mind he replayed the physical beats as they happened.

Just before Alice walked away, she had squeezed his hand surprisingly hard, looked at him with those orb-like eyes, and the light in the waiting room had completely changed. When Alice walked away and the door shut behind her, there remained a golden yellow mist which slowly dematerialized. Energy transference was the conclusion he arrived at. Energy was something he had studied a great deal of and until that day it had never occurred to him that humans may have a far greater capacity for energy transference than he had ever realized.

Of course he took a moment before he left the waiting room to make a logical appraisal of the situation and environment. Was it a trick of light? That was the first and obvious question. But there was no light bulb above where she had been standing. The nearest light bulb in the ceiling was six feet away. And all the light in the office was a cool blue light. There was not a warm light with anything remotely close to a golden hue. Had the door opening and closing created an effect? As he stood there observing the room a person walked past him and through the door. There was no light effect. That was when he was compelled to ask the question, one he could not believe he was asking, but was it spirit he saw?

However there was something from his day that he couldn't quite remember. There was something he could not quite put his finger on. Strangely he kept thinking about the pie. This loose thread, whatever it was, had something to do with pie. As a mathematician he of course got stuck on the idea it might have to do with pi. When he pulled up to his house he decided to let go of whatever he couldn't remember and just focus on the present environment, on his neighborhood, on his house, on his physical being and on all that his senses took in. And most of all he decided to focus on that feeling he had found and how much he loved his life.

Walking into his home with a big smile he looked into the living room where he saw Amy sitting on the couch. Everything about her was beautiful. The love he felt for her at that moment was stronger than he had ever felt. When she looked up at him and saw his smile, she seemed confused by it. Something about the look she gave him almost triggered his memory and again he had the sensation that he was forgetting something important. Something he couldn't see that was just below the surface. Something from earlier that day. Then the look on her face shifted and seemed to ask of Elliot, "share with me the secret you've been given so I too may smile like that?"

And without knowing why, Elliot opened his mouth and he told Amy he was dying.

18

The wind abruptly died leaving only the sound of the fountain's gentle and continuous cascade of water. When Amy said to Elliot, "you knew," immediately the memory of that day came back to him. It was all there. Not a stone unturned. Leaving work, stopping for pie, seeing Amy and another man, meeting Alice, experiencing a psychic phenomena, walking into his home, seeing how beautiful Amy was, and wanting to spend the rest of his life with her.

"Yes, I knew," he said to her.

"I'm deeply sorry," she said to him.

"I forgive you," he said with true sincerity.

"Can we just continue being happy with each other?" She asked.

"Yes, please."

The most unexpected thing happened then, they were overcome by laughter, and as the laughter faded their watery eyes warily held each other while their hands met. Their fingers interlaced tightly. They began to kiss, slowly at first, until it built into an unexpected expression of anger, then the intensity released and their lips slowly parted. They kept their faces close, their foreheads touching. Their breathing was heavy. Emotionally exhausted from a storm of their own making, they held each other like shipwreck survivors who had just washed ashore. It could have gone the other way, they could have drowned out there. Forgiveness is a strange thing, it saves everyone.

The week that followed was surprisingly wonderful. The only outstanding issue was how to publicly resolve Elliot's lie about dying. They had gone over every possible option and that morning they had finally made a decision on how to handle it but just to be sure they agreed to sleep on it one more night.

***

From the forecast the waves held little promise and Davey and Gordo couldn't join. But that didn't matter to Elliot, he was going to surf alone in unremarkable waves and he couldn't have been happier about it. Before he left the house to go surfing Amy came outside and put her arms around him.

"Looks like you're ready to go," she said.

"I'm ready," he said, smiling.

"Do you want me to go with you?"

"I would love you to go with me, but I think you still have some work to do here."

"I do," she said, "are you okay to go it alone?"

"Sure. Soul session. Besides, you're never really alone out there."

To get to the surf spot Elliot exited the freeway and took an old two lane highway that ran through miles of farmland before reaching the ocean. To his left he noticed a farmer driving a large industrial tractor. Its long plow blades easily turned the soil to prepare the earth for new crops.

The ocean came into view and it was one of those magical moments surfers dream about. Light offshore winds beautifully feathered the ocean's surface causing an incoming set of waves to look like corduroy. The waves were much better than expected, head high on the sets, and peeling perfectly down the line. The tide was on the low side which was good for this particular spot. Soon the sun would bow out and night would close the curtains on day, but before it left, the sun had saved its best for last and was putting on quite a show. Over the western horizon the sun's orange glow overlapped with red cirrus clouds whose wispy pink fingers reached for the crescent moon rising to the indigo sky above. It gave Elliot the chills, that feeling of connection to something so much larger than himself, something he couldn't ever truly comprehend.

Walking towards the shoreline Elliot noticed the rocky tide pools were completely exposed and he could see the infamous large pedestal rock protruding up from the water. At low tide surfers had to pull off the wave before hitting the pedestal rock which marked the end of the ride, a lesson Elliot had learned years ago when he pulled off a wave too late and was nearly thrown into the miniature monolith, his surfboard left with a deep gouge.

After navigating his way over the tide pools he lowered his board into the water and began to paddle towards the line up where two other surfers sat waiting for waves. As fortune would have it he caught a wave right away. It broke flawlessly from the point all the way to the inside where he safely kicked out of the wave. By the time he had paddled back to the point the other two surfers had caught waves and gone in. Elliot watched them walk up the beach and take the trail which disappeared into the brush. His next wave came right away and it was even better than his first.

There was a lull in the action. The wind was easing off and finally it died leaving the ocean's surface glassy. The final ember of sun vanished below the horizon and its afterglow cast pools of orange light on the ocean's oil slick surface. Soon the afterglow faded away and Elliot found himself cold and alone in the waning twilight. The next wave, he decided, would be his last. However, when the next wave came it was another near perfect wave and so, despite the darkness, and Elliot's lack of night surfing experience, he decided to paddle back out for just one more wave. Surfers have a thing about finding it hard to catch *just one more wave* - it can go on and on. But his next wave would be his last.

Out he paddled to the take off zone where he waited. After sitting in the water for a few minutes Elliot realized he wasn't alone. There was another surfer, their black wetsuited figure hard to discern from the dark of night. They sat much further out in the water, beyond where the waves had been breaking. From where they were, Elliot didn't believe they would be able to catch any waves. But when the other surfer began to paddle hard Elliot watched with surprise as they stood up and thrust themselves out onto the face of a moving wall of dark water. It was only a matter of seconds until the wave and the surfer would pass Elliot but suddenly the other surfer dramatically pulled off the wave, as if flying into the darkness. This gave Elliot a split second to catch the wave. He turned and paddled as hard as he could.

Everything happened so quickly, and being in near total darkness, it happened almost entirely by feel. The wave picked him up, pitched him forward, and flung him down its face. Somehow Elliot kept his composure throughout and with his feet solidly planted on his board he shifted his weight back towards the wave drawing a powerful line with his bottom turn and went right into a sweeping turn off the top of the wave, throwing a shower of spray into the air. From there he was in perfect unison with the ocean's energy, beautifully sculpting the surface of the wave. It was the best he had ever surfed.

The end section, and the pedestal rock, were fast approaching. Racing as fast as he could down the line, he was barely skirting by the tide pools when he hit a rock, and his surfboard suddenly stopped. Elliot was released from the wave and delivered into the night.

***

"How are you?" It was a question often asked of Amy in the week following Elliot's death. Most of the time she would simply say, "it's extremely difficult. Thank you for asking."

Elliot's burial had been that morning, followed by a reception at Amy and Elliot's home, and everyone except her immediate family had left. Her parents had just gone into the guest bedroom to lie down. Brian and Karen had stayed to help clean up and they asked Amy, "how are you?"

"I don't know," is all Amy could say to their question, and that was the truth. She felt a lot of things and when you put them all together, she simply didn't know what that feeling was. There was the week long low-grade headache from all the crying. There was the feeling of nothingness she carried around, it was lower than hopelessness. There was the feeling of everything in the world happening at once. Something like a panic attack. She felt sad. Profoundly sad. And she felt love. And gratitude. And even joy at the strangest moments. So, throw all that together and she really didn't know how she felt. But she was glad to have people who cared enough to ask the question.

Today she heard things about Elliot she already knew and she also learned things about him she didn't know. At the reception Brian and Karen gathered everyone together so they could all have a chance to say something about Elliot. His close friends painted a picture of Elliot being the smart one in the group. Sort of a nerd, they lovingly joked. "*Sort-of?*" One friend called out and they all laughed. But they also spoke about how big his heart was. How he was so sincere growing up. One of Elliot's colleagues described a brilliant mind, a hardworking and humble person. Others described him as someone that was extremely shy at times but was at the same time a very easy person to know. It was mentioned by many that Elliot had drifted away from himself at some point but had recently reemerged with a new found energy for life.

Amy heard many people say that Elliot had died doing something he loved, which *was* true and to which Amy agreed. Many people spoke about how Elliot bravely dealt with a terminal illness, which *wasn't* true and to which Amy said nothing.

With the house clean enough Amy thanked Brian and Karen and told them they could go home, that she was going to take a nap, but before they left there was something important she wanted to share with them. They all sat down and Amy handed Karen an unopened envelope. After looking at the return address Karen realized who the letter was from and she handed the envelop to Brian. He took a breath and opened it.

"Well?" Karen asked.

"It's what we always knew. He's really our brother."

***

The thick fog had dissipated but there was still a layer of mist along the highway. Amy took the exit she and Elliot had taken about a month earlier. From there Amy wasn't sure about anything else. The day they found the waterfall had been the first time they drove off somewhere without directions, and it scared her, particularly when they began taking dirt roads off into the wilderness, but then the surrounding beauty enveloped her and she let go of her fear. Eventually they found a waterfall, one which Amy wanted to find again, so she could spread some of Elliot's ashes there. But after driving back and forth she wasn't sure which dirt road they had taken into the wilderness. Of the half dozen dirt roads available to choose from she couldn't decide which was the right one. It occurred to her she could head back to the gas station and general store by the highway and ask if they knew but then she suddenly saw the right road. Or what she thought was the right road.

The road was a narrow strip of dirt through thick forest. Tall trees on either side blocked out most of the sky. Not that it would have mattered because she had driven into an area where the fog had yet to lift. After about ten minutes she was beginning to doubt herself and fear began to creep in. How could she not remember the exact way they went to the waterfall? Then she began to remember there was a turn off from this dirt road onto another. Or was she imagining that?

Another dirt road appeared. She rolled down the windows in the car and took a deep breath. It all came back to her. That day. The memories and the feelings. She decided to turn to the right. She knew that if this got anymore complicated she would simply back track. She had been jotting down her turns. It had been two rights, so heading back would be two lefts.

Somehow the forest grew even denser and the trees even taller. She remembered experiencing that phenomena with Elliot that day and it gave her hope she was on the right path. The one thing she remembered was the spot they had pulled over was on a considerable incline and had a view of a lake. But after driving for a few minutes she was still not coming to an incline. Was she remembering the slope of the incline correctly? In her memory it was fairly steep, noticeably so, but perhaps in reality it wasn't.

Then the road before her began to slowly rise and then there was a steep incline of about a hundred yards. Noticing a small foot trail that led into the forest, just like the one she and Elliot had taken, she parked her car. There was a lake view where they parked before but the fog was still too thick for her to see anything that far away. It was impossible to be certain this was the trail to the waterfall but she grabbed her backpack and headed out anyway.

When the trail began to rise steeply she knew it wasn't the

same way as before. She was on a new trail. The heavy mist was making it difficult to see the path forward but she was curious and so she continued on. At times she could feel Elliot's presence, as though he was with her, then she remembered the urn with his ashes in her backpack and she laughed.

Ascending from the mist she came to a large boulder framed by blue sky. The boulder appeared to block her trail but she easily walked around it, discovering a meadow full of wildflowers.

Printed in Great Britain
by Amazon